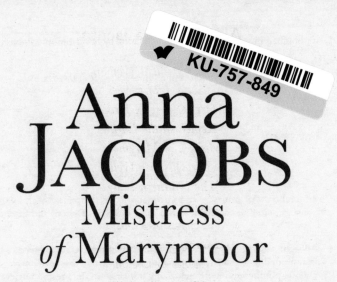

Anna JACOBS

Mistress
of Marymoor

10CANELO

First published in the United Kingdom in 2002 by Severn House Publishers Ltd

This edition published in the United Kingdom in 2024 by

Canelo
Unit 9, 5th Floor
Cargo Works, 1-2 Hatfields
London SE1 9PG
United Kingdom

A CIP catalogue record for this book is available from the British Library.

Print ISBN 978 1 80436 725 4
Ebook ISBN 978 1 911420 98 9

Look for more great books at www.canelo.co

Printed and bound in Great Britain by Clays Ltd, Elcograf S.p.A.

1

Mistress of Marymoor

Anna Jacobs is the author of over eighty novels and is a natural storyteller. She grew up in Lancashire and moved to Australia in the early seventies. She comes back to England every summer to visit her family. Married with two grown-up daughters and a grandson, she lives with her husband in Western Australia.

Also by Anna Jacobs

1

Summer 1759

Uncle Walter turned up while Deborah was arranging the flowers in the little village church. She heard the door slam open then shut with a bang. Her heart sank even before she turned round. No one made quite as much noise with doors as her uncle, or shouted half as loudly. Closing her eyes she prayed for patience and needed it, too, for first he didn't like her arrangement for the altar and pulled the flowers out of the vase, scattering them on the floor and telling her to do them again, then he went on to complain that her hair was too wanton and loose.

After scowling at her and breathing deeply, he announced his intention of crossing the village green and passing on his complaints to his foolish younger sister, who should be here chaperoning her.

Deborah had to wonder yet again at the disapproval she always saw in his eyes. Why did he hate her so? She was neither ill-favoured nor pert – nor was she remiss in any of her duties. In the end, she lowered her eyes and risked a lie. 'My mother is working on your new Sunday shirt, Uncle. If you disturb her, she'll not be able to sew for the rest of the day. You know how easily upset she is.'

She could see from his expression that he didn't like the idea of slowing down progress on his new shirt, for her mother's exquisite needlework was much called for by the folk at the big house. It was, her uncle said, only right that his poor relations pay back his generosity in any way they could. Generosity! Anger boiled up inside Deborah at the mere thought. He grudged them every penny of their keep and had housed his only sister in a damp cottage that had brought her low with a wheezing chest the previous winter.

'I shall visit Isabel tomorrow, then,' he decided. 'I've arranged to go out shooting this afternoon with a neighbour and mustn't keep him waiting. But make sure you keep that hair of yours tied back in a more seemly manner from now on, Deborah. Unlike your father, who was a wastrel and gambler, I have a position to maintain in this county.'

Yes, she thought rebelliously, the position of being the meanest man and the worst master for twenty miles around Newgarth. And she could only suppose he picked on her for her hair because it was truly her crowning glory and showed up his own daughter's limp, mousy locks to disadvantage. Or it would have done if Deborah had been allowed to wear it in a more flattering style. But her uncle dictated even that, as he'd controlled every facet of their lives in the year or more since they'd had to throw themselves on his mercy after her father's death.

When he'd gone she let out her breath in a long, slow sigh. If there were any alternative to her uncle's charity, she'd seize it with both hands, whatever it was. Only there was nowhere else to turn. Her father's sudden death had had left them penniless – worse than penniless, in debt – and her uncle was their only close relative. Her mother hadn't been herself since they'd come here and they could no longer pay their maid the wages she more than earned.

Bessie had been with her mother since they were both girls and was more like a member of the family than a maid. She refused to leave them, but still, it wasn't fair that she worked for nothing.

Deborah sighed and began to pick up the flowers, shoving them into the vase anyhow, no longer caring what they looked like. No one could spoil the day like her uncle.

–

Late that afternoon, a man rode into the village. It was a rare enough event for a stranger to visit Newgarth but someone like him – so tall and darkly handsome – was enough to make heads turn, then turn again for a second look. Two young women nudged one another and giggled, an old woman sighed for the days of her youth and an old man yearned suddenly for the muscles he'd once taken for granted.

The stranger went first to the Bird in Hand to ask for directions and leave his horse, then followed the ostler's pointing finger across the village green to the small cottage. Walking briskly along the stone-flagged path, he rapped on the front door, then rapped again.

When it was opened by an elderly maid, he spoke curtly, with no smile of greeting, 'I'm looking for one Deborah Jannvier.'

'Miss Deborah? Not the mistress?'

He tapped his riding crop impatiently against the side of his leg and repeated, 'As I said, *Miss – Deborah – Jannvier.* Is she in or not?'

Bessie sniffed in disapproval of his brusqueness. 'I'll inquire whether she can see you, sir.'

As she stepped back, he pushed the door open with a growl of annoyance and followed her into the house. 'She'll see me.'

Bessie backed away from him along the small hallway, feeling suddenly nervous, for he was so tall and grimly determined.

He waved one hand to hurry her. 'This is an extremely *urgent* matter, a question of life or death.'

She slipped into the kitchen and closed the door, setting her back against it as if to keep out intruders. 'Miss Deborah, love! There's someone to see you. He looks like a bailiff's man, but we don't owe anyone money, do we? Not now.'

Deborah stopped stirring the large pan hanging over the fire and sighed. Her face was flushed, for they were making strawberry preserve that afternoon, though it had been a mediocre crop this year and they wouldn't have enough of the preserve to last the coming winter. 'No, Bessie, we owe nothing, so he can't be a bailiff's man. What does he want?'

'He didn't say, except that it's urgent, and to tell the truth, miss, I didn't like to insist on knowing. Stern sort of face, he has. Not a gentleman by his manner, yet acts with authority.' She lowered her voice and gestured behind her. 'He walked straight into the hall without I even invited him in and is out there waiting now.'

They stared at one another in dismay, then Deborah swung the jack to move the big pan off the flames and rinsed her sticky hands in the bucket. Pulling off her apron and working mobcap she pinned up the tumbled, shining mass of hair under a prettier, lace-trimmed cap and examined her skirt hastily for stains.

The maid didn't move from the doorway. 'Miss Deborah?'

'Mmm?'

'You shouldn't see him on your own.' For there was something very masculine and forward about him. A good-looking man, the sort to set women dreaming, this, and no one but Bessie to guard Miss Deborah from his like, for her poor mistress never noticed things like that nowadays – or maybe Mrs Isabel just didn't allow herself to notice things any more.

'Very well. Come with me.'

Bessie followed her young mistress back to the hallway, her face rigid with determination.

The man had been leaning against the wall near the front door, but he straightened up and stared at the younger woman without making any apology for his rudeness in pushing into their home. 'Deborah Jannvier?'

'Yes. Won't you come through into the parlour, Mr— er?'

'Pascoe. Matthew Pascoe.' He followed her into the tiny front room but before she could invite him to take a seat, he asked sharply, 'Might I ask your father's full name?'

She looked up at him in puzzlement and not a little apprehension. Other men didn't seem to take up as much space in a room as this one and his broad shoulders spoke of great physical strength.

His voice became sharper. 'Your father's full name, if you please?'

'Paul Edward Jannvier.'

'Born?'

'In Lancashire, near Rochdale, in 1709 – and died eighteen months ago.' Was it only eighteen months? she wondered. It seemed much longer.

He fumbled in the pocket of his coat. 'Then you're definitely the one I'm seeking.'

She exchanged puzzled glances with Bessie before indicating a chair. To her relief he took it, but he was no less disturbing sitting than standing. She put up her chin and gave him back look for look as she waited for him to explain why he was here.

'I've brought a letter for you, Miss Jannvier, from your great-uncle – Ralph Jannvier of Marymoor House, the other side of Rochdale.' He passed her a crumpled missive and got up to stand by the fireplace while she read it, impatience visible in every twitch of his long, lean body.

Bessie, stationed near the door, saw Deborah gasp in shock and stare blankly into space for a moment before re-reading the letter carefully. Trouble, then. Always more trouble. That poor girl had had more than her fair share of it lately. She cast a suspicious glance at the stranger. If he'd come here hoping to get anything from Deborah's Uncle Walter in payment of her late master's debts, he was bound for disappointment, for Mr Walter and that long-nosed wife of his were a pair of mean toads, and you'd not convince Bessie otherwise, not if you talked all night!

But when Miss Deborah looked up and studied the messenger, who was now standing by the window silhou-etted against the sunlight, she didn't look anxious only thoughtful, so Bessie breathed more easily. Not bad news, then. Or at least, not very bad.

'Do you know what this letter contains, sir?'

'Yes. I wrote it for your great-uncle. He was too weak to do so himself.' His voice betrayed nothing of his feel-ings, nor did he volunteer any more information.

Blinking her eyes against the patterns left in them by dazzling sunlight, Deborah looked down again, frowning. 'And if I agree to this offer?'

'We can set off at once, ride cross-country and be at Marymoor House before morning. Your uncle's not got long to live and he urgently wishes to see you. Pray God we arrive in time.'

'I must think. Give me a few minutes to consider the matter, at least.'

Matthew shrugged agreement and continued to watch her as she sat there, head bent, staring at the piece of paper. Wisps of hair were falling out of the cap, drawing attention to the slender white neck. She was pretty and to his relief seemed respectable. Moreover, when he'd asked for her at the inn, people had spoken kindly of her. But even if she hadn't been respectable – which had been a distinct possibility with Edward Jannvier's daughter – Matthew wouldn't have let that stop him from dealing with her. She was, quite simply, the path to his dearest ambition, so he would take that path whatever the cost, because it offered him hope of a better future than he'd ever dreamed of in the hard years of his growing up.

She stayed where she was for a moment or two longer, head bowed, then looked up and asked, 'Do you know exactly what my uncle wants me to do?'

'Yes. Though he forbade me to speak of the details.'

'Will you tell me this, then? Is it anything unlawful or – or harmful to others?'

He shook his head. 'No. Ralph Jannvier wouldn't ask such a thing of anyone. He's stern, harsh in his judgements sometimes, but honest and direct in all his dealings.' And Matthew owed him a great deal, even affection, though that wasn't something either of them ever spoke about.

He watched her nod and guessed her answer before she even spoke.

'Very well, then. I'll come with you, Mr Pascoe, but you'll have to provide a horse for me. I don't have a mount of my own, or even the means to hire one.'

He nodded. He hadn't really expected her to refuse, given the circumstances, but he felt relieved nonetheless not to have to waste time on persuasion – or even force. 'I'll go and get the horses while you change your clothes. Wear something warm, for we'll be riding through the night.'

He left the room without another word, not waiting for the elderly maid to show him out. He was thoughtful as he walked slowly back across the village green. Ralph's great-niece was pretty enough to turn heads, something he hadn't expected. Matthew would have stopped to watch her walk past, that was sure. Her eyes were the most striking part of her, being a vivid blue with a very direct look to them, and her hair, what little he could see of it under the cap, was pretty too, curly and of a light brown colour burnished with red-gold glints. She didn't look like a Jannvier, well, not like Ralph, who had had the dark Jannvier looks until age faded them, nor like the paintings of various ancestors hanging on the walls at Marymoor. Perhaps she favoured her mother's side of the family?

His frown deepened as he continued to think about her. Her face seemed full of contradictions, somehow, and that in itself was intriguing: the nose straight and determined, the lips tender and full, the eyes full of intelligence and the cheeks as rosy as a child's. It didn't give an easy clue to her nature, that face didn't. But she was pleasing and wholesome in appearance and wouldn't be unwelcome in his bed.

As soon as she had heard Mr Pascoe leave the house, Bessie went into the hall and banged the front door shut behind him, then whisked back into the little parlour. 'You *can't* go off on your own with a strange man, Miss Deborah! Who knows what'll happen to you? And how do you know he really does come from your great-uncle? Have you ever seen Ralph Jannvier's handwriting before?'

'Mr Pascoe seems an honest enough man and this— Oh, Bessie, it's a chance of something better for us all – perhaps our only chance of getting away from here.' She clasped the maid's hand for a moment. 'If there are risks involved, so be it.'

'Well, at least ask your Uncle Walter for a groom to go with you.'

'I can't do that. My uncle would either prevent me from going or he'd come with me and interfere. Thank heavens he went out this afternoon and won't hear about this till it's too late to stop me. Come with me to find Mother, Bessie. I don't have time to explain the letter twice.' She hurried out to the back garden, the maid close on her heels, still protesting.

Mrs Jannvier glanced up, smiling. 'Look! Aren't the beans coming along well now?'

'Mother, stop working and listen carefully!'

Something in her daughter's voice made Isabel Jannvier set down her trowel and stand up. 'Is something wrong?' Her voice was wobbly with nervousness, her muddy hands were clasped tightly at her breast, and fear showed in her gentle, faded blue eyes.

Deborah laid one hand on her arm. 'Not wrong, no. A messenger has just brought a letter from my Great-uncle Ralph Jannvier, the one who lives at Marymoor House.'

'Dear me! I thought he'd have died years ago!'

'It seems he's dying now and wishes to see me.' Deborah took a deep breath and added in a tone of wonder, 'Mother, he promises to make me his heir if I will do as he asks, whatever it be.' That phrase had worried her, but she had decided the rewards were too great to quibble. 'The messenger won't say what my great-uncle wants, but he assures me it's nothing unlawful and – and I believe him. So I shall go there and accept the offer, then come back for you. Only I must set off at once.'

Bessie gasped in shock.

Isabel frowned. 'I don't think Great-Uncle Ralph is rich, Deborah dear. Your father always used to say it wasn't worth trying to tap him for a loan because all he had was a rambling old house and some stony moorland acres. Those were your father's exact words.'

'My father knew nothing of farms and land values. Besides, anything is better than nothing, which is what we have now. I'd deal with the devil himself to get an inheritance that would enable us to leave here. Wouldn't you? And we don't need to be rich, just – just have enough to live on quietly.'

Isabel nodded.

'Mother, I can't – I simply can't! – let this opportunity pass!'

She heard her mother sigh longingly and knew she had won her point.

–

Walking round the village green to stretch his legs while the ostler saddled the horses he'd hired, Matthew paused as he heard voices from the other side of the wall. Deborah's voice carried particularly clearly and her words made him scowl. Maybe she was more mercenary than he had thought.

'I can't – I simply can't! – let this opportunity pass!' that determined voice declared.

Matthew gave a snort of bitter laughter. She was little different from other women, it seemed. Most of them would do anything for money. Well, he'd be interested to see if she was still determined to accept the offer when Ralph told her exactly what he wanted. Very interested.

He grimaced at his own scruples. Who was he to judge her? She wasn't the only one unwilling to let this opportunity pass. But at least his motives included love of Marymoor House and a fondness for Ralph, as well as a desire to better himself.

'So we're agreed on one thing, at least, Miss Deborah Jannvier,' he muttered. 'Let's hope it'll be enough.'

–

In the garden there was silence for a few moments, then Isabel's vague blue eyes came suddenly into sharp focus. 'I do understand,' she said quietly and patted her daughter's hand, leaving a smear of rich brown soil across the slender wrist. 'You must do whatever you think right, dear. When do you leave?'

'In half an hour – less. The man who brought the message will escort me to Marymoor. We're to ride there. How far away is it?'

'I don't know exactly. I've never been there. About thirty miles, I suppose. A ride of several hours at night. You will be careful?'

Deborah hugged her again. 'Of course!'

Bessie could stay silent no longer. 'Mrs Isabel, you're never going to let her go!'

'Why should I not?'

'Riding alone – across country – with a strange man! It's not *decent*.'

'I trust my daughter absolutely.'

'But we know nothing about him and—'

Deborah started walking towards the house. 'May I borrow your riding habit, Mother?' she called over her shoulder.

'Yes, of course, dear. You know I have no need of it.'

Indeed she did know, Deborah thought bitterly. Her Uncle Walter had a stable full of horses, but none was ever offered for the occupants of this cottage to use. They had to walk everywhere, except when he sent the carriage to take them up to the Hall to dine, which he only did when he had nothing better to entertain him, and this kept them effectively prisoner in Newgarth village.

The maid stayed behind with her mistress to say urgently, 'You can't let her go off like that, Mrs Isabel! It's too dangerous! He's a stranger. He might even be an impostor. And besides, she has no experience of men like him.'

'What do you mean "men like him"? What was he like?'

'Well,' Bessie sniffed in disapproval, 'he was good-looking, you can't deny that, the sort of man women run after and make fools of themselves over. But you can never tell what's behind a face, can you, not on one short meeting? He's no gentleman, that's for sure, for all his clothes are of good quality.'

Isabel's blue eyes became vague again. 'I shall trust Deborah's judgement in this. Besides, when have I ever been able to stop anyone from doing what they want?'

Bessie sighed, gave her lady a quick hug, sighing for the way life had reduced Isabel to a shadow of her old self, then bustled off to help Miss Deborah.

—

When the voices faded from the other side of the wall, Matthew glanced across at the inn and decided that another pot of ale and something to eat would not go amiss before the journey. As he strolled back, he pondered on what he'd overheard. Was the mother complaining of the daughter's wilfulness – or of her husband's feck-less nature? Was the daughter as mercenary as she had sounded? He shrugged. Only time would tell – and whatever Deborah Jannvier's nature, he would so as his dying friend wished.

Anthony Elkin was not going to profit from Ralph Jannvier's death.

—

Upstairs, Deborah hastily donned her mother's riding habit, a garment which was very old-fashioned, but of good quality dark green cloth and showing little wear. The jacket and waistcoat, which were like men's garments, fitted her perfectly, but would have hung on her mother's thin frame nowadays. The full petticoat was a little short, because she was taller than her mother, but there was no help for that. Under it she put on a pair of the yellowed flannel trousers her mother had always worn when riding to protect her legs. On her head she wore the rather battered three-cornered hat that went with the outfit.

Bessie stopped protesting and started to help pack. Shaking out Deborah's best cloak she folded it carefully, saying, 'It may grow cold later.' She then put a change or two of clothing into Mr Jannvier's old saddlebags, muttering, 'You'll have to sleep in your shift, there isn't room for much more.'

There was a hammering on the front door, then it opened and that deep voice called out, 'Are you ready yet, Miss Jannvier? I've got your horse waiting at the inn.'

'The cheek of it!' huffed Bessie. 'Opening a lady's door and yelling at her like that! A gentleman would know better.'

The listener below scowled as he heard the maid's words echo down the stair well. Who would want to be a fine gentleman if the few he had known were examples of the species?

'Never mind. I'm ready now!' Deborah stole a last glance in the small mirror, not displeased with her appearance.

Bessie's face crumpled and her eyes grew bright with tears, 'You will be careful, won't you, dearie? I shan't rest easy till you're safe home again, that I shan't! Let me carry this down for you.'

Downstairs, Isabel Jannvier had come out of the parlour and was asking Mr Pascoe about Ralph's exact state of health.

'A seizure,' he said, his face betraying sudden sadness. 'Very unexpected. He had seemed hale and hearty for a man of his age until two days ago.'

'He's enjoyed a long life,' she said quietly.

Mr Pascoe's mouth twitched. 'Enjoyed isn't exactly the word I'd use for Ralph Jannvier. He's a stern and determined man.'

''Tis a pity he never had a son.'

Silence, then. 'Aye. I suppose so. Ah, there you are!' With a nod to Mrs Jannvier, he moved towards the door, holding it open impatiently.

—

Not until Deborah and Mr Pascoe had galloped off down the lane did Bessie realise they still didn't know exactly where this great-uncle lived. And all Mrs Isabel would say was, 'Marymoor village lies somewhere to the north-east of Rochdale, I believe. On the edge of the moors. I just hope my brother won't pursue her. You know how he likes to have a finger in every pie.'

'He'll be angry about this.'

'Yes. But then he's always angry about something.'

'Hadn't you better do some more work on his shirt?'

'Not today. I shall enjoy myself outside while the weather is fine.'

As her mistress drifted out to work in the garden again, always her refuge in times of trouble, Bessie tutted to herself and went back to the kitchen to deal with the strawberry conserve with much sighing and rattling of pans and jars. She had one of her feelings about all this. There was trouble brewing. As she worked, phrases like, 'murdered in her bed' and 'never heard of again' floated through her mind and she prayed fervently that Deborah would be all right. And that somehow, she would be able to take her mother away from this dreadfully unhappy life.

Neither of the two older woman was surprised to receive a visit from Walter Lawrence just after nightfall.

'Is it true what Frank tells me?' he demanded, bursting into his sister's cottage.

'What does he tell you?' Isabel tried to quell her fear of him.

'That my niece has ridden off with a stranger.'

'She's gone to visit her Great-Uncle Ralph. There can be nothing wrong in that.'

'*Nothing wrong?* How dare you let her go anywhere without consulting me, Isabel, when I am the head of the family and responsible for you both? And this man she went with wasn't a relative, I'm sure.'

'Only a messenger from Ralph Jannvier,' she said placatingly.

'Who knows what will have happened to your daughter by now? By heavens, I guard mine more carefully. Have you no sense? You told me the old uncle refused to pay your husband's debts, so you owe him nothing. Nothing at all!'

'He's dying. Wants to see her. There was no time to be lost, Walter.'

'It'll be a trick of some sort. You'll see.' His eyes narrowed as the words sank in. 'Is this to do with his will? Is it?'

Isabel lost herself in a morass of phrases, but by the end of it her brother had the information he required, or near enough. 'The less you have to do with the Jannvier family from now on, Isabel, the better – unless there is some profit to be had. You were a fool ever to marry into it.'

He growled in annoyance as that vacant look settled in his sister's eyes again. He was beginning to suspect that she was losing her wits. And if so, he'd have no hesitation in locking her away, because a mad sister could do him no credit. Not that she'd ever been very sensible, running off to marry a feckless fellow like Paul Jannvier, a man with no income but what his wits and the cards brought in.

As he left the house he threw at her, 'And don't come to me for help if your daughter gets herself in trouble and comes back with a swelling belly. I'll condone no immorality.'

Isabel roused herself from her abstraction to say, 'Deborah wouldn't do anything immoral.' She focused on a particularly pretty vase of flowers, which she had just finished arranging, and prepared to endure more homilies and scolding.

But for once Walter cut the diatribe short and left her to her own devices. He wanted to ask the people at the inn about the stranger and where the next change of horses would be. It should be easy enough to trace him. It might even be worth sending Frank after the two of them. His manservant had helped him in many ways over the years, ways other people knew nothing about. He had complete trust in the fellow. If there were any profit in this situation, Frank would find it for his master – and be rewarded for his troubles, as usual.

Well, why should Walter not profit from any inheritance, if that was why Ralph Jannvier had sent for Deborah? His sister and niece owed him something, for hadn't he paid all their debts – well, the tradesmen's debts, anyway? Gambling debts were no concern of his.

And he'd not only housed them since then, but made them an allowance. Yes, they definitely *owed* him repayment for all that. He would start drawing up the accounts the following day. He smiled at the thought.

Yes, Frank should definitely go after them and invest-igate the situation.

—

As she cantered along on the sure-footed mare, Deborah threw back her head and breathed deeply of the warm evening air. She couldn't help wondering what her great-uncle wanted her to do and wishing he'd offered her a hint. She had to be content with the fact that her companion had assured her it was nothing unlawful. Matthew Pascoe had a way of saying things that made you believe him.

She stole another glance sideways at him. He rode well, looking very much at home in the saddle. He was wearing a dark riding coat over a cloth waistcoat, and but there was no pretence to fashion in the garments, no wide cuffs or rich materials. Under the simple three-cornered hat he wore his own hair, rather than a wig, dark hair tied back with a simple leather thong.

She had never met anyone quite like him, but she trusted him instinctively, could not have said why, just did.

One thing was certain in her mind: whatever was asked of her, she would do it. And if she never set eyes on that dreadful cottage, never saw her Uncle Walter again, she would be delighted, for she'd known nothing but unhap-piness and humiliation since going to Newgarth.

'How long will it take us to get to Marymoor?' she asked her taciturn companion a little later.

'If we ride steadily, we'll be there soon after midnight. It's a good thing there's a nearly full moon tonight. We'll take a rest when we change horses.' He eyed her with a dour look that didn't bespeak confidence in her equestrian ability and added, 'Can you keep going for that long?'

'I haven't ridden for a year or two,' she admitted. Her Uncle Walter said frankly that he didn't intend to waste his money on supplying mounts for indigent relatives who had no reason to go anywhere, anyway. 'I think I can manage, though. I used to ride quite a bit before Father died.' When her father was on a winning streak, that was, and could afford to hire horses. She reached forward to pat the mare's neck. 'This one has a nice steady gait.'

His only answer was a grunt, and whether it was of encouragement or disapproval she couldn't tell.

Later she asked more directly, 'What's my Uncle Ralph like?'

'Old. And dying.'

'Could you not tell me more than that?' she exclaimed, disappointed.

'You'll see him for yourself soon enough.'

Which didn't help much. 'Well, what about Marymoor, then? Tell me about the house.' She heard his voice soften as he spoke.

''Tis built of stone, with eight bedrooms and attics for the servants, though parts of it are in sore need of repair. It comes with some decent land, for those parts, though people who don't know the district might say differently. It could be made more productive with an owner who was not set in his ways. I've made a start on mending matters, but it's been slow going.'

'And you are what – the bailiff?'

'I don't have a fancy title. I manage everything for your uncle and have done for a few years.' He shut his mouth firmly, as if he'd said more than he intended, and when she next asked a question, he told her curtly to save her breath for riding.

After another hour they stopped briefly at a tiny wayside inn to change horses and take some refreshment, but were off again within the half hour. This time she was riding a steady chestnut gelding, and she noticed that the ostler didn't try to fob off Mr Pascoe with poor horses.

'Are we going fast enough, do you think?' she asked a little later.

'Who's to say? It's in God's hands.'

She gave up trying to speak to him, enjoying the ride and above all, the feeling of freedom, praying fervently that she need never return to Newgarth.

2

Time passed and gradually the long summer evening wrapped them in shadows so that they rode through a gently blurring landscape. It was lucky the fine weather had held, Deborah thought, for she didn't even feel the need of her cloak.

The sound of hoof beats seemed to echo in her brain and cut out all other noises. As they rode she saw the dark shapes of animals here and there in the fields or the outlines of houses in the distance, but it all felt unreal. She was, she admitted to herself, getting very weary now, her back and legs aching fiercely from the unaccustomed exercise. Only determination kept her upright in the saddle.

Her companion must have noticed that, for he said abruptly, 'We've just skirted Rochdale and a mile away there's an inn where I'd thought to get a meal, for there'll be little to offer you at Marymoor. We can get a change of horses there, too. Can you hold up till then?'

'Yes, of course.' Deborah studied him covertly, wondering why she was so very conscious of his presence beside her, when he barely acknowledged her existence most of the time. She was aware of him not just as a companion, but as a man – and one she found attractive. She had had so few chances to spend time with men of her own age and had resigned herself to spinsterhood, but she could still dream, couldn't she? Dream of a home and family of her own. She sighed and gave a wry smile at her own folly.

Maybe this night's business was folly, too. If so her Uncle Walter would make her pay dearly for her act of rebellion.

Whenever she looked sideways, Matthew Pascoe usually had his eyes on the road ahead. He spoke only when she addressed him. He was *almost* handsome, *almost* a gentleman, and totally unlike anyone she'd ever met before. She wished he'd let her know him better and she'd have liked to hear about those who lived at Marymoor, but he wasn't generous with words.

Just as she thought she could stay upright in the saddle no longer, they came to a small wayside inn, not the sort of place gentry usually patronised. A lantern at the door showed a hanging sign saying *The King's Head* with a crude painting of a man's crowned head on it. Lights showed in the windows, so it couldn't be as late as she'd thought.

As Mr Pascoe helped her down from her horse, Deborah's legs buckled and she sagged against him help-lessly. 'I'm sorry – I'm not used to—' Her voice faded to nothing. She felt strange, breathless and as if she had no bones in her limbs, while he felt strong and warm. She looked apologetically up at the face so close to hers, but he was studying the small inn yard, not her. His firm arms were still supporting her, though, as if he knew she couldn't yet stand on her own.

He looked down at her and gave one of his half-smiles. 'Hold still for a moment and let me support you. You've done well for someone who hasn't ridden for a while.'

So she rested against him, content to be there.

When a lad came out of the stables, Matthew called across Deborah's head, 'We'll need new horses in half an hour, Billy. See to these, will you?'

'Yes, Mr Pascoe.'

Deborah, who had now regained some measure of control over her aching legs, realised suddenly how closely pressed against his body she was and flushed, trying to pull away from him. But he wouldn't let her.

'Keep hold of my arm as we walk. We don't want you falling.'

'I shall be all right.' But her legs gave way at the first step and she stumbled.

He was there again, to catch and support her. She hoped he hadn't seen her blush, hoped he wasn't aware of how her hand was trembling as she clutched him and tried to make her stiff legs move properly.

Matthew was all too aware of the blush and the trembling hand, but it pleased him rather than otherwise that she wasn't forward in her ways. And he had, he decided, come to like her elegant profile, not to mention the determined and intelligent expression on her face. He couldn't abide fussy, complaining women, but he thought he might be able to get used to this one without too much trouble.

As she clung to him, he had a sudden urge to brush those strands of soft, curling hair off her forehead. Which was strange, because he didn't have much time for women nowadays. Ladies usually looked down their noses at him, deeming a man who worked for his bread below their notice, though some of them had signalled an interest in him since he'd gone to live with Ralph. But that hadn't pleased him, either. He wanted nothing more to do with women until he was ready to marry. He'd sown some wild oats as a young man – well, who had not? – and had nearly been snared by one young woman. Luckily she'd lost the baby before he could be forced to wed her.

He'd taken a deal more care after that, not wanting to bring a bastard into the world, not wanting to make any child suffer for its birth as he had.

–

Inside the inn they were ushered straight into a tiny private parlour as if they'd been expected. Deborah stifled a groan as she sank down on a hard settle.

'I'll fetch you a nice glass of mulled ale, shall I miss?' the landlord said. 'And send my wife to tend to your needs? Got a minute, Mr Pascoe?'

Matthew nodded.

The landlady bustled in, with a cheery word and a tray bearing enough food to supply the whole household at Stoneyfell Cottage. She pointed out a room at the back of the inn where her guest could tend to her personal needs and was gone, leaving the tray on a small table near the fire. Deborah went along the passageway to relieve herself and wash her hands, then came back, feeling more than ready to eat.

The smell of the food made her stomach growl with hunger. She wondered whether she should wait for Mr Pascoe, then noticed the tray was only set for one, so made a hearty meal of tender boiled fowl and cabbage, accompanied by a slice of pigeon pie, crusty new bread and a side dish of summer greens. To follow this there was a large piece of apple pie smothered in thick cream and a fresh chunk of crumbly yellow cheese. She ate every crumb, sighing in satisfaction as she finished it.

She'd have liked to linger over the table afterwards, because the food had made her feel sleepy, but she didn't wish to keep Mr Pascoe waiting. Pushing herself up, groaning at the stiffness of her limbs, she went to look for him, impatient now to get this journey over.

In the corridor she bumped into two young men whose eyes lit up at the sight of her. When she tried to pass them, they moved to block the corridor, one in front of her, one behind, and she realised in dismay that both were drunk.

She addressed the nearest and said crisply, 'Please to let me pass, sir.'

He chuckled. 'Not till you've paid a forfeit, fair one.'

'A kiss, a kiss!' cried the other.

'No!' She tried to step back into the small parlour, but the man behind grabbed hold of her. She jerked away from his hands, but his companion had also closed in and before she could prevent them, they had tossed her hat away and tugged her hair loose from its pins. Laughing, they began to push her from one to the other.

'She's a tidy armful!' one cried, trying to fondle her breast.

'Let go!' She jerked her knee into a rather tender part of his anatomy, as her father had taught her to do, and followed it by a kick to his shins. As he yelped in pain and clutched his privates, the amusement faded quickly from his face.

'You'll pay for that!' he threatened.

Even as she opened her mouth to call for help, a voice roared, '*Let go of her!*' and Matthew Pascoe strode out of the shadows at the rear of the passage.

Deborah couldn't hold back a sob of relief.

So quickly that he took them all by surprise, Matthew punched the nearest man in the face, sending him sprawling, and grabbed Deborah's arm, drawing her behind him.

Even as he was squaring up to the other fellow, the landlord came hurrying up to join them, his expression horrified. 'John Redley, whatever's got into you this night?'

The younger of the two men took a step backwards, his face sulky now. 'Just having a bit of fun.'

'That's the last time you drink in this inn, if this is how you treat my lady guests.'

'She's no lady, else she'd not be here.'

The young man's companion, a stranger to the district, scrambled to his feet, glaring at Matthew, but Redley tugged at his arm. 'Not worth it.'

Trying unsuccessfully to keep up a brave front they swaggered out, but both kept a careful watch on Matthew. Deborah sagged against the wall, then realised her clothing was awry and began to set it straight.

Matthew put his arm round her and guided her back into the small parlour, asking urgently, 'Are you all right? They didn't hurt you?'

She gulped back the tears that threatened. Only because she was so tired, she told herself. She didn't normally *allow* herself to weep. 'No. They just – annoyed me. I don't know why they thought I…'

He continued to hold her, patting her back and giving her a moment or two to recover.

Once again she was grateful for his support, trusting him to hold her and not try to take advantage, unlike *them*. In the silence she could hear his slow, deep breaths against the shallow sound of her own gasping. She tried desperately to pull herself together, but the feeling of utter helplessness as the men pushed her to and fro had terrified her. 'I'm s-sorry.'

His voice was a soothing rumble above her ear. 'What for? 'Tis them as should be sorry, and will be if I catch them here again.'

She must have shown her puzzlement at that remark.

'I own this place.' He gestured round with his head. 'Not the grandest of inns, the King's Head, but 'tis mine and does an honest trade.' He gave a bitter laugh. ''Tis all my damned step-father ever did for me, pass on this place when he died.' Then he shut his mouth, as if regretting this confidence, and pushed her away. 'I'm sorry to rush you, but we need to set off again if you're all right.'

'I must set my hair to rights first and find my hat.'

'I'll get it.' He fetched it, then stood back and watched, seeing how her fingers trembled as she pinned up that wonderful mass of shining hair under a small cap, then set the hat squarely over it. She had clearly been shaken by the assault, and must be weary and uncomfortable after all their riding, but hadn't complained once or asked to delay their journey.

Against his will something stirred within him. It was respect for her courage, he decided. He didn't need telling that she'd done nothing to invite such attentions from those two young roisterers. She didn't have a wanton look to her, thank goodness, even if she had a mercenary attitude to this possible inheritance. Well, only those with money could afford to despise it and she had none, that was clear!

He couldn't get the memory of her hair out of his mind as they set out on the last leg of their journey. Soft and shining, it had flowed down her back like a waterfall when released from its bonds. His body also kept remembering how soft and womanly hers had felt pressed against his, remembering and reminding him of its need. She was a luscious armful for a man to hold.

He dismissed such thoughts from his mind with an irritated click of his tongue and concentrated on making the best possible speed. Pray heaven they'd reach Marymoor in time. If they didn't, then Elkin would win everything and Matthew's own future would be far from rosy, because Elkin wouldn't want him living nearby.

Her future would be bleak, too.

–

Deborah's head jerked as she nearly fell asleep and she forced herself to sit more upright, though her whole lower body felt to be a mass of bruises now. She didn't know how much longer she could manage to stay on the horse and was wondering whether to tell him that.

Matthew's voice cut across the darkness. 'We're almost there now, just a few minutes longer. Can you manage?'

'Yes.' She hadn't the energy to say more. At that moment, the moon sailed from behind a cloud, illuminating the dark, square outline of a house in the distance.

'That's Marymoor,' he said softly.

She could hear love for it in his voice and wished she could see it more clearly.

It seemed a long time until they came to some half-open gates and clopped slowly through them, to stop in front of the house.

This time she waited for his help to dismount, dismayed at how stiff her body felt, how weak her legs. A fitful breeze tugged at her cloak and blew strands of hair across her face as she clutched him, unable to take a single step. 'I'm sorry. I can't seem to move my legs.'

With a muttered exclamation, he swung her into his arms and carried her towards the front door.

She was too weary to protest, but laid her face against his chest and let him do with her what he would. She could feel his heart beating against her, its steady thump in great contrast to her own, which seemed to be skittering round like a frightened foal.

The front door was opened by a man holding a single flickering candle. He gaped at them, then stood back to let them in.

'How is he, Simley?' Matthew asked even before he had stepped across the threshold.

'Still alive, sir. The doctor's with him.'

As Matthew carried her inside, Deborah gazed round the dark hallway, which rose for two stories, with railed landings along each side above them. The only light came from one candelabrum on a side table and a single flickering candle in a tin holder carried by the grey-haired servant. Even in the dimness she could see that the wooden floor was scuffed and in sore need of a polish, while the square of carpet in the centre was badly frayed. The hall itself was, however, of good proportions and the staircase was cut neatly at an angle across the back wall, with the lower three steps turned forward as if to invite you to climb up them.

A tall clock standing watch near the foot of the stairs chimed softly.

'Look at that! Two o' the clock,' Simley announced gloomily, 'and I ain't been to bed yet! Be good for nothin' tomorrow, I won't.'

Matthew ignored him and strode forward, carrying Deborah into a dark room on the right, where no candles were lit, even though there was light coming from underneath a nearby door. He set her down beside a sofa, keeping hold of her until she had sunk down on it with a sigh of relief. She missed the warmth of his body and couldn't help shivering slightly.

'Are you all right?' he asked.

'Yes. Just – very stiff and a little chilled.'

'I must go up and see Ralph, let him know we've arrived.'

'Yes. Yes, of course.'

'I'll send for a dish of tea – unless you'd prefer a glass of wine?'

'Tea would be very welcome, thank you.'

'Simley!' he shouted. 'Fetch some tea. Our visitor is tired.'

The man scowled at her. 'There's no one in the kitchen and the fire there's damped down.'

'Then build it up again. And if you can't see to things, wake your wife, man! I need to check on Mr Jannvier.'

Muttering something under his breath, the man went out without another look in Deborah's direction.

Matthew came back holding a lighted candle and used it to set light to the kindling set neatly in the fireplace before lighting another candle in a tarnished silver holder on the mantelpiece. 'You'll be all right for a few moments?'

'Yes, of course I will. And I can see to the fire now.'

He nodded and went out again without a word. She heard his footsteps running lightly up the stairs, a door opened somewhere above them and closed with a sharp clap of sound, then there was silence. Although she wasn't of a fanciful nature, she couldn't help looking round nervously, for the room seemed full of threatening shadows and heavy pieces of old-fashioned furniture behind which anything – or anyone – might be concealed.

She got up to tend the fire, still moving slowly and stiffly, building it up with bigger pieces of wood and then holding her hands out to the flames. It wasn't a cold night, but she was grateful for the warmth and for the brightness of the fire to dispel some of the shadows.

The manservant returned with a candle. 'Oh. You've lit the fire. 'Twas set for morning, that was.'

'Mr Pascoe did it.'

He stared at her as if trying to work out who she was. 'Come far?'

She didn't like his surly expression and saw no need to explain herself to him. 'Far enough.'

He gestured towards the fire. 'It'll burn all right now, so I'll leave you to it.'

'And the cup of tea?' she reminded him.

'Mrs Simley is in bed and no one but me to tend to things. I usually work outdoors, not in the kitchen.'

She wondered if he would have been as rude had Matthew Pascoe stayed with them. 'Then I'll come and make it myself. No doubt Mr Pascoe would also be grateful for a warm drink.'

He scowled at her. 'No need. I'll see to it. But it won't be set out fancy. We're short-staffed here. And Mr Pascoe don't curdle his innards with tea. 'Tis a woman's drink, that.'

It seemed to take him long enough to bring anything and the fire was blazing cheerfully by the time he returned. She'd drunk only half the dish of weak tea when Matthew

31

came into the room, closing the door carefully behind him.

'I forgot to tell you to say nothing about yourself to Simley,' he said abruptly.

'I didn't.'

'Not even your name?'

'No. I disliked his manner.' She drained the dish and set it down. 'How is my great-uncle?'

'Failing. We – the doctor and I – feel you should come and listen to his offer immediately. It's unlikely he'll last more than a few hours, I'm afraid.'

'Very well.' She'd never attended a death bed before and the prospect made her feel shaky inside. Her father had been dead for over an hour by the time they carried him home, and it was Bessie who had laid out the corpse.

As she and Matthew mounted the stairs, it became obvious that the rest of the house was as shabby as the entrance hall and equally ill cared for, though it was a commodious enough place, the sort you'd call a small manor house. From the landing two wings led away, one passageway dark, the other lighted by a candlestick on a small table. Portraits decorated the walls, but they were so dark in tone and the light so bad she couldn't make out who they showed.

Beyond the table another manservant was standing outside a door, as if on guard, but this man had an alert expression on his face and bobbed his head to her respectfully. As he opened the door for them, Matthew ushered her into a room lit by such a blaze of candles that she stopped for a moment to blink and allow her eyes to grow accustomed to the glare.

A gentleman rose from beside the bed and bowed to her.

Matthew made the introductions. 'Dr Lethbury, Miss Jannvier.'

'Is that her?' rasped a voice from the bed.

'Yes. This is your great-niece.'

'Bring her closer! 'Tis plaguey dark in here. Why don't they light more candles?' The voice was slurred, the mouth twisted.

Urged on by a firm hand under her elbow, Deborah moved forward to stand beside the bed. The dying man stretched his hand out to her and she reached out automatically to grasp it. With a strength surprising in one so near to death, he tightened his fingers round her wrist and pulled her down to sit on the edge of the bed.

Her great-uncle was gaunt-featured with a great beak of a nose exactly like her father's, and sparse, frizzy white hair. The slight resemblance comforted her as did the fact that the old man's eyes were still lit by a sharp intelligence, even though one side of his face was drawn down and a line of dribble trickled from that corner of his mouth. She found herself thinking that this was a man of whom she might have grown fond had circumstances permitted – unlike her maternal uncle, whom she had quickly learned to hate.

'Hmm. You're prettier than I'd expected.' He fluttered his fingers towards her head. 'My mother had hair like that.' Another scrutiny and he added, 'You've got an honest face, too. Don't you think so, Matt?'

'Yes.'

'Good thing you didn't inherit the Jannvier nose. Looks even worse on a woman.' Ralph chuckled breathily, then grasped her hand again. 'Got my letter, did you? Couldn't write it myself so Matt here did it for me.' He paused, panting a little with the effort of speaking.

'Yes, I got your letter,' she said quietly.

'Your mother wrote – when was it, last year? – to say your father had died and left you both badly off.'

She contented herself with a simple, 'Yes.' She didn't want to go into details in front of strangers.

'Paul was a stupid fool! Gambling never pays unless you cheat. He was a daredevil as a lad, always into mischief, but there was no real harm in him. I never thought a Jannvier would end up dying in a tavern brawl, though.'

She shrugged and remained silent. No doubt the old man would tell her what he wanted in his own good time.

'What d'ye think, then, Matt?' he asked, still holding her hand tightly but looking beyond her. 'Will she do?'

Deborah turned and flushed under her guide's renewed scrutiny and the dying man noticed. 'Well, she can blush,' he wheezed, 'and that's not a bad thing in a young woman.' He looked her straight in the eyes again. 'I ain't got time to be tactful, niece.'

It was near enough to an apology for her to nod and the words made her feel better, somehow, as did the acknowledgement of their relationship. She continued to wait patiently for him to explain the conditions under which she would inherit.

'I'm content enough with the bargain,' said Matthew. 'She has an open face, at least. If she agrees, I believe we can trust her to keep an honest bargain. Let's ask the doctor to leave us in private for a few minutes and put the proposition to her.'

The doctor stepped up to the foot of the bed. 'I suppose it's no use my asking you to be brief, Mr Pascoe? Mr Jannvier really should rest now.'

'What's the use of rest to a dying man?' grumbled that slurred voice from the bed.

The doctor sighed, but left the room with a courteous nod to Deborah.

After a minute Ralph asked querulously. 'Has he gone, Matt? Are they all gone except her?'

Matthew returned from the door. 'We're alone, as you wanted, and my groom's stationed outside. Jem will make sure no one can overhear what we say. Parson is waiting in the library but the Simleys won't think anything of that – given the circumstances.'

'That's all right, then.' Two fever-bright eyes looked up at Deborah from the bed. 'You ain't saying much, niece.'

'I'm waiting for you to tell me what you want of me,' she countered.

'I think we can help each other,' he said. 'You need money, don't you?'

'Yes. At present we are dependent upon my Uncle Walter's charity – and he isn't a generous man. My mother has had a hard life and deserves better than his many unkindnesses. I should like to give her a few comforts. She's been a good mother to me.'

'What about yourself? Don't you want some money? Pretty clothes, jewels, servants to look after you, comfortable home? Most young women would.' His voice had a jeering tone, as if he was trying to make her angry.

'Of course I want money!' she said fiercely. 'But only because it'll buy our independence. I have no hankering for jewels.'

He cackled in his dry old voice. 'Well, there won't be enough to make you rich, so that's a good thing.'

'Is there enough to make us independent of my Uncle Walter? That's all I care about. Having enough to live on. Not – not grandly, but in quiet comfort, at least.'

35

'Oh, there's more than enough for that. This is a decent enough estate, though the house is in a sad state. I always cared more for my horses than my furniture. But you'll have Matthew to help you, and he's got some sense in his head.'

He sighed and closed his eyes for a moment, then stared at her again. 'She ain't got a greedy face, Matt,' he murmured. 'I think I'd like her. Pity I didn't know her sooner. I was wrong to deal with Elkin.'

He let go of her wrist and stroked her hand, murmuring, 'Soft and warm. Young flesh.' Raising one shaking hand he glared at it. 'Mine's old and withered. You never think you'll get to look like this, girl, but you do. We all come to it in the end, if we live long enough.'

His eyes closed for a moment and Matthew drew nearer, looking a little anxious.

Ralph sighed and looked up again. 'It's all right, lad. I ain't quittin' this world yet. Not till I've seen my plan through.' He turned towards Deborah. 'Well, niece, this is my proposition. I'll leave you this house and the estate. There's some land left. If you let Matt farm it carefully for you there'll be enough to live on decently and there are one or two cottages and farms that bring in rents and…' His voice faded for a moment and he sighed as if it were a great effort to concentrate. 'Where was I? Oh, yes, I'll leave you everything I've got on condition that you marry Matt here and share it with him.'

She cast an astonished glance at the tall man standing beside the bed as she exclaimed. 'Marry a complete stranger! But why?'

'Because I owe him a lot and anyway, he's a relative too, from the wrong side of the blanket. My son, actually. Estates should pass to the legitimate line, but you and

36

Elkin are the only ones left – and *he* was never one to hold his purse. Bad blood in the Elkins. I didn't realise how bad till he – but that's neither here nor there. If *you* marry Matt, he'll look after Marymoor properly and look after you as well. And you *are* a Jannvier legally, born and bred, not an Elkin. There should be a member of the family inheriting. Well, what do you say?'

She did not know what to say and continued to stare blindly at three candles until they blurred into one bright smear of light. She couldn't possibly marry a stranger – could she? But if she didn't, she'd have to return to Newgarth and her uncle's harsh ways.

She turned to stare at Matthew Pascoe. 'Why do *you* want to marry me?'

'I love Marymoor,' he said simply.

'And he's got a right to it. He ain't got the Jannvier name, but he's got the looks. No doubting who fathered him. That counts for a lot with me.' The breathing from the bed was growing shallower, but the old man's voice was still harshly mocking. 'He's a good man, though he don't show his feelings to the world. Good farmer, too.'

There was a pause while Deborah struggled to come to terms with this strange offer. Should she accept? Could she do it? It was hard to think when she was so very tired, when it seemed as though every bone in her body was aching. She stared from Matthew Pascoe to the figure in the bed, then suddenly she remembered her Uncle Walter's grudging charity, the gratuitous insults, the darned stockings and frayed gowns, and her spine stiffened.

She turned to the man she would have to marry. 'I presume, sir, that you would not object to my mother coming here to live with me – with us?'

37

'Would she not be better staying at Newgarth near her brother?'

'No sir, she would not! She is – we are both – living a life of purgatory!'

He shrugged. 'Very well. She can live with us if you wish.'

'And – and our maid, Bessie.'

He smiled suddenly as he agreed, 'Her too.' He saw her puzzlement at his smile and added, 'I value loyalty, especially in the woman I'm about to marry.'

She took a deep breath. 'Then I'll do it. I'll marry you.'

The grasp on her hand slackened and she turned to look down at her great-uncle in alarm, afraid he'd died. But he was smiling too.

'Good girl! Matt, go and fetch that damned parson and lawyer. Let's have you wed as quick, as we can. I ain't gettin' any stronger.'

'Do you mean we are to marry now?' gasped Deborah as Matthew left the room.

Her uncle nodded. 'You must, girl. I'll be dead in a day or two and I won't sign anything over to you until the knot's been tied.' His voice grew fainter. 'What difference does it make *when* you marry?'

Useless to tell him that she'd dreamed, as every girl did, of a joyful wedding day. Useless to talk to this stern-faced man of church bells, a pretty dress, sunshine and flowers – and above all her mother standing beside her, smiling in a carefree way, as she used to when Deborah was younger.

She took a deep breath. 'Very well.'

'Good. And always remember you can trust Matt with your life. Trust him whatever seems to be happening. Elkin's a tricky devil. But Matt won't let you down.'

She swallowed hard. 'I'll remember that, Uncle.'

His eyes closed again but he still held on to her hand as if, through it, he held on to life. She didn't try to pull away.

The doctor came back to hover over his patient and shake his head in disapproval. Matthew ushered in two more black-clad gentlemen shortly afterwards. One's clothing proclaimed him to be a clergyman and the other was, presumably, the lawyer.

Ralph Jannvier opened his eyes again. 'Get on with it!' he commanded. 'Marry them as quick as you can, Norwood! Marry them so that no man can put them asunder. Downie, you'll make sure it's all watertight?'

The lawyer stepped forward to grasp the hand that was waving at him in an equally age-spotted one. 'Did I not promise you I would, old friend?'

'Aye. And you've never broken a promise to me yet.'

Mr Downie turned to Deborah, studying her face. 'I must ask you first: do you enter into this marriage willingly, Miss Jannvier?'

'Yes. Very willingly, sir.'

He turned to the bed. 'And how are you feeling, Ralph?'

The old man glared up at him. 'I'm dying. How do you think I'm feeling? Angry. Regretful. Too much left undone! How would you be feeling?'

A smile flickered over the lawyer's countenance. 'In other words, you are yourself! And do you approve of this marriage, Mr Jannvier?'

'Approve of it! I arranged it, damme! Matt's my bastard son and Deborah's the only real kin I've got left. After what happened on that last visit, Elkin won't do. In fact, I disown him. I could never trust him to look after Marymoor. The place needs a mistress, a decent woman, not the sort of trollop he associates with. So get on with this marriage, man, before I drop dead on you!'

Matthew looked at the lawyer. 'You will be able to bear witness that he is of sound mind, Mr Downie?'

Again that brief smile. 'Oh, yes. His mind is unimpaired and his intellect is as sharp as ever. And no one is coercing the young woman. I will bear witness to all that, if it should be necessary.'

Matthew turned to the clergyman. 'You, too, are satisfied, I hope, Mr Norwood?'

The clergyman nodded. 'Yes. Ralph's as cantankerous as ever, but he knows what he's doing.'

'*Will* you get on with it, then!' demanded the invalid.

The clergyman tut-tutted and stepped forward. 'Please to stand here, Miss Jannvier. And Mr Pascoe, here. Thank you. Now — we are gathered here today to witness the giving and taking in marriage of...'

Deborah looked up at Matthew in near panic. He took her hand and pressed it briefly, as if he understood how she was feeling, and she felt comforted. She made her responses in a low voice and was mildly surprised when the ceremony ended and they were declared husband and wife. Matthew planted a chaste kiss upon her cheek. She couldn't stop her hand from trembling in his or frame a sensible remark, could only stand there and force herself to breathe slowly and smoothly, so that panic was held at bay.

'Come here, girl!' said the rusty old voice.

She moved nearer to the bed.

'Lean closer,' he commanded and as she bent over him, he pulled her head towards him and planted a kiss on her cheek. 'Look after him,' he whispered. 'He'll make you a good husband, if you treat him right. He ain't had an easy life.'

'I'll do my best,' she promised.

He nodded and she moved away.

'Matt!' he commanded. 'Come here.' He drew the younger man close and whispered a few words in his ear, then fell back. 'Tell that damned lawyer to hurry with the will,' he rasped.

The lawyer approached the bed. 'I have it here. Do you wish me to read it to you?'

'Aye.'

The will was so short, Deborah blinked in surprise.

'And that's all it needs?' asked Ralph.

'It's not a complicated estate.'

'Then let me sign it. I'll feel better once it's all settled. I can go in peace, then.' Ralph took the quill pen and painstakingly traced his signature at the foot of the large sheet of parchment, then lay back and watched through half-open eyes as the clergyman and doctor both witnessed it.

'Ahh!' he said softly, when it was done. 'Elkin won't get anything now, will he?'

'Did I not promise you that, Ralph?' The lawyer blew sand across the signatures to dry the ink. 'I may be old, but know my trade.'

Matthew moved across to Deborah. 'You must be exhausted. Let me show you to our bedroom.'

'My uncle...?'

'I'll stay with him.'

'You'll call me if... if I'm needed?'

'I will.'

She let him guide her to a large comfortable bedchamber where another fire was burning. 'What time is it?' she asked, seeing the faint lightening of the sky outside.

'Just past four. Nearly dawn. You should try to get some sleep.'

'I doubt I can. It's all so strange.' She looked up at him and felt herself blushing as she blurted out, 'I don't really feel married yet.'

'You will gradually get used to it.'

She thought for a moment he was about to kiss her, but he merely set his hands her shoulders, pressed them in a friendly manner then walked from the room.

She stood motionless in front of the fire for several minutes after he'd left, trying to come to terms with her new status. Less than a day ago she had been making strawberry jam, had had to endure in silence a scolding from her uncle, had been in despair about what the future held for her and her mother.

And now she was Matthew Pascoe's wife and heir to this estate. Soon she would be mistress of Marymoor. And it wasn't the money, but the thought of having a home truly her own that pleased her most, for that was something her father had never given them.

Only time would show whether she'd done the right thing or not, but she didn't think life here could be any worse than it had been at Newgarth. And her new husband had an honest, if stern face. In fact, he was a good-looking man if he would only smile more. Very good-looking. She blushed at that thought and admitted to herself that she was not unmoved by him.

Then exhaustion descended on her like a leaden weight and she had to summon all her remaining energy just to force her tired body to move across to the bed. She would, she decided, rest her aching head on the pillow, just for a moment or two before she got undressed.

She was asleep within seconds.

3

An hour later Ralph Jannvier's breathing faltered then stopped completely. As Matthew bowed his head in a quick prayer, the doctor stepped forward to examine his patient, then closed the staring eyes and drew the sheet over the dead man's face. 'He's gone.'

'Yes.'

'He was a good friend,' the doctor went on. 'And a good neighbour, too. I shall miss him.' He looked at the young man, wanting to say, *And at least he found the son he needed*, because his patient had confided in him that 'the lad will do', which from Ralph Jannvier was high praise. But the stern face on the other side of the bed had its usual closed expression, not inviting confidences or sympathy. So like his father's face!

Feeling the old doctor's eyes on him, Matthew took a deep breath and squared his shoulders. 'Well, at least Ralph had time to put his last plan into operation. That meant a lot to him.'

'Yes. And you can rely on me to support you there. After what Elkin did last time he came to visit, I'm surprised Ralph waited so long to change his will.'

'He believed that a legitimate family member ought to inherit and you know how he hated to change his mind once he'd made a decision.' Matthew hesitated. 'I wonder – would you mind making a deposition before a magistrate about his state of mind and competency to make a will, just to – to tidy things up.'

The doctor looked surprised. 'Well – if you think so.'

'And will you do it today?'

'Is there really need for such haste? Elkin won't contest the will, surely?'

'The man is desperate and will stop at nothing. And yes, there is need for haste. Quite frankly, *you* will be safer, Dr Lethbury, if it's known that you've already made the deposition. You can blame it all on me, tell people I demanded it.'

'You think *I* might be in danger?'

'Yes. I believe Elkin is that desperate and that ruthless.'

The doctor couldn't hide his astonishment but shrugged and said, 'Very well. I'll do it this morning. I have to travel into Rochdale and the magistrate there will see to it for me.' He cast one more glance in the direction of the bed. 'I'll send Mrs Gurrey to lay him out.'

'Thank you.'

Matthew watched the doctor leave, then turned back towards the bed. 'I won't let Elkin take Marymoor and waste all we've built here, Ralph,' he promised. He had never been invited to call the old man father and would not start now, but he was fiercely proud of being this man's son, and of the trust Ralph had placed in him.

This was a father to be proud of and Marymoor was an inheritance to be cherished.

He had a wife, too, he thought in faint surprise. He hoped… He didn't know what he hoped for from that.

–

Back in his own chamber Matthew stood for a moment staring down at the figure on the bed. Deborah was so sound asleep she hadn't stirred when he came in. She looked pretty and wholesome with that glorious hair tumbled across the pillow and her cheeks softly flushed like a child's. She must have simply have fallen on to bed, for her saddle bag was lying on the floor nearby, still fastened, and she'd made no attempt to undress. She'd be sore today, poor lass, but her courage in persevering during that long, hard ride had made all the difference to the outcome. And had taught him to respect her.

He hated to wake her after such a short time, but there was a lot to do and plans to be made between them, as well as explanations furnished. He didn't want her taken unawares by Elkin. He reached out to touch her shoulder, but she didn't stir and he had to give her a shake to rouse her. When she stared up at him in bewilderment, her eyes still fogged with sleep, he said gently, 'Ralph died half an hour ago.'

She sat up then, wincing as she moved her body. 'Is it morning already? I just lay down for a moment and...' She stared down at her dishevelled clothes and blushed, reaching up automatically to push her hair back. 'You must think me very—'

'You were exhausted.' So was he, after two nights without sleep. He rotated his shoulders, weariness overtaking him for a minute and tricking a yawn out of him.

She reached out to touch his hand fleetingly. 'I'm sorry he's dead. You were fond of him, weren't you?'

Matthew nodded. 'You must have guessed he was my father. My mother knew he'd never marry her, so married someone else. I didn't know about him when I was younger and after I found out I was angry with him, because my mother was unhappy with my stepfather. But when I grew up and me Ralph, I grew to respect him, even if I didn't always agree with his views of the world. I shall miss him.'

Silence hung between them for a moment, not awkward so much as filled with their mutual tiredness. Like her, he was still wearing the clothes in which he had ridden across the moonlit countryside, but he had obviously not been to bed.

'You must be exhausted,' she said at last as he sat slumped beside her.

'Yes. But we need to talk before I snatch some sleep. Elkin will no doubt be over here as soon as he finds out Ralph's dead. His home, what's left of it, is less than an hour's ride away, though he spends little time there these days. He'll expect to be the heir to Marymoor. *Was* the heir before Ralph changed his will. So I need to tell you about Elkin, prepare you.'

'Oh?'

'Elkin's mother is a cousin of Ralph's on the maternal side, which means they're not really blood relatives of yours. You have a far closer relationship to Ralph, and I suppose to me, though not too close to prevent our marrying. Anthony Elkin is about my age, a little older, perhaps.' He hesitated, frowning as he chose his words carefully. 'He has turned into something of a dandy lately and dresses more finely than I would have thought he could afford. He wasted his own inheritance, which didn't amount to much, and then tried to recoup that by gambling. Which lost him most of the remainder.'

'Gambling rarely brings you a fortune, as my mother and I can bear witness,' she said bitterly, remembering some of the bad times.

Matthew nodded. 'So how Elkin has come into money is anyone's guess. Not by any honest means, I'd wager. I'd not trust him an inch and nor should you. Last time he was here he stole some of the silver. He must have been desperate to do that. Ralph refused to have him accused of theft, but vowed never to receive him under this roof again. I'll keep a better eye on the silver this time.' And on everything else about his home, including his wife.

After a pause he went on thoughtfully, 'The mother may come with him. Mrs Elkin is a feather-brained fool who dotes on her son and never used to see wrong in anything he did as a lad. I don't think she'll pose any danger to you, but everything you tell her will go straight back to her son, I'm sure.'

'So Elkin will assume he's the heir?'

'Yes.'

'Shall you tell him that's changed?'

'Not until the will is read, I think. It'll be easier and – safer for you.'

She looked at him in shock.

After another hesitation he added, 'I think, if you don't mind, we should pretend we've known one another for some time. It would be better for your reputation than what really happened. It'll help if we display some sort of mutual affection – in public, that is. I can assure you that I shall not inflict my attentions upon you in private until you feel,' he hesitated, seeking a tactful way to phrase it, 'more comfortable with me.' As he watched her consider this for a moment, head on one side, then nod, he couldn't help wondering if her skin was as soft as it looked. And he knew it would be hard to delay making her his wife.

'I agree,' she said with one of the firm nods he was coming to recognise. 'If people knew I'd married in order to inherit, they'd think me mercenary and—' her voice faded and she looked at him pleadingly, '—wouldn't understand how desperate I was to get us all away from my Uncle Walter. But Matthew, I sincerely hope we can make a good marriage, in spite of how we came to meet and – and I do appreciate your forbearance.'

He nodded. 'We should exchange some personal information, then, or we'll betray ourselves.'

A sound outside made her turn her head suddenly.

'It's all right. I've set Jem outside the chamber door so that no one will be able to eavesdrop on this conversation. The Simleys often seem to linger near doors these days. I don't trust them, but like your Bessie, Jem's been with me for a long time and you can trust him absolutely.' He smiled. 'Though he may not have the most winning manners.' Another yawn took him by surprise.

He looked so drawn and weary, she couldn't help asking, 'Have you had any sleep at all since we got back?'

'A little, dozing in a chair. I didn't want to leave Ralph to die alone, you see. He's been kind to me – in his own way. Once he found out that I existed, that is. The relationship was a shock to him, but he never doubted the truth of my mother's tale once he saw me. We looked too much alike.'

She began to pleat the material of her riding habit, not looking him in the eyes. 'I don't think Elkin will be our only problem. My Uncle Walter will probably try to take things over here if he can. He's greedy for money and ruthless. I'm a little concerned about him.'

'Your uncle has no power over you now that you have a husband. Is he so very bad?'

'Yes. He's a mean-minded tyrant, who makes my mother's life a misery whenever he can. We haven't even had decent food to eat at times and you can see how badly I'm dressed now.' She glanced down at herself apologetically, then added with a sigh, 'It always surprises me that he can be my mother's brother. He is, apparently, very like his father and if so, I don't wonder she ran away from home to marry.' She smiled reminiscently. 'When my father was in pocket, he could be great fun and he was always kind to us in his own way, never raised a hand to me or to her.'

'I'm not sure it's safe to bring your mother here yet,' Matthew admitted. 'Elkin is a dangerous man. I fear he'll stop at nothing to get his own way.'

'But what can he do now? Surely the new will has—'

'The only thing he can do now is get rid of us. He would then become the legal heir to Marymoor.'

As the implications of this sank in, Deborah stared at Matthew in horror. 'Is he that evil?'

'I believe so. I think perhaps we should leave your mother where she is until we're sure it's safe for her to come here. Though we could send her some money, of course, to make her life easier.'

She thought of how it would be for her mother in Newgarth and shook her head. 'No, I *must* get her away as soon as possible. My uncle will be furious that I've escaped his control and I wouldn't put it past him to turn her out of the cottage.'

'*His own sister?*'

She nodded. 'Yes. Or lock her in a mental asylum. He's threatened that as well. And there's Bessie. She's been our maid for as long as I can remember, often without receiving any wages. She's devoted to my mother and must come here as well. She's a good worker. You don't mind?'

He reached across to grasp her hand for a moment and that seemed to stop the conversation again as they stared at one another. What was there about him that affected her so? she wondered dazedly.

His voice was gentle. 'Of course your Bessie is welcome to come here. We'll be needing new staff anyway before we're through, because I intend to dismiss the Simleys, who've been sending information to Elkin.' He patted the hand he was holding. 'Very well, then. While I'm getting some rest, you can ask Jem to make the arrangements for your mother and Bessie to come here. He can send young George to fetch them. He's the under-groom and a promising lad.'

'Thank you.' Deborah knew there were tears of relief in her eyes, but didn't care if he saw them. Her mother was going to escape from Uncle Walter, they all were, and that was the most important thing of all. If that brought them into other dangers, well, it was a risk well worth taking.

His voice drew her back to the practicalities of their situation. 'Now, let's work out where and how we met.' He watched as she again cocked her head on one side, twirling a stray curl round and round one finger as she listened. He liked watching her graceful movements, but couldn't afford to let her charms distract him, so cleared his throat and said brusquely to break the mood, 'You should know that I'm the bastard son of a farmer's daughter. She was pretty enough to attract old Ralph's attention when he was visiting friends over in Rochdale. He apparently had the ability to attract women even when he was past sixty.'

She remembered the vigour and life in the old man's face, even when he was dying. 'I'm not surprised.'

'As a young man he wed a woman chosen for him by his father, but she bore him no children – I think he believed he couldn't father any.'

He paused and looked at her as if he expected her to scorn him? He kept mentioning his bastardy. Was he testing her reaction? 'That must have been hard for him,' she said gently. 'And you.'

He shrugged an acceptance of that. 'I was brought up by my stepfather, but he grew increasingly bitter when the only child he gave her was still-born and she didn't quicken again. A few years ago he died suddenly of a heart seizure and soon afterwards my mother fell ill. When she realised she was dying she wrote to Ralph, commending me to his care – as if I needed anyone to look after me at five and twenty! His wife was dead by then, so when he summoned me here I came out of sheer curiosity, knowing it could hurt no one.'

He paused, his eyes full of memories. 'I found a man worthy of respect and as for Marymoor – well, who would not love it? Although I came to live here, I still maintained my interest in the King's Head, but when his bailiff died, I gradually took over management of the estate under Ralph's guidance. We had five years together, at least, he and I. He was nearly ninety when he died, you know, and was hale and hearty until almost the end.'

'He was a fortunate man.'

'In some ways. He didn't make life easy for himself, or for those around him. But he was honest and fair in his dealings, everyone would tell you that. And he had no legitimate son. That always rankled with him.'

Another silence fell but neither found it uncomfortable.

'Now, where could we have met?' he wondered. 'Have you ever been to Manchester?'

She nodded. 'Often. My father had friends there.'

'Then that's where we met. I go there occasionally. Now, how shall we explain why we didn't marry sooner?'

'Shall we need to explain?'

'Not *need*, exactly. It'll just look better.'

'My father's death early last year,' she suggested. 'My mother needed me and my uncle swept us away to live on his estate.' At his nod, she added with a smile, 'But we've been writing to one another secretly.'

'Love letters?'

She watched a sudden smile blossom on his lean, dark face, one that made him look years younger and extremely handsome.

'I doubt I'm the sort to write love letters under any circumstances,' he said with a chuckle, 'but who's to know that? Yes, it'll do for a tale. As to our sudden marriage, Ralph knew about our fondness for one another and took a whim to see us wed before he died, because of your being his closest legitimate relative and me his bastard son.'

'It's rather a thin tale.'

'Perhaps if we demonstrate some affection, we can make it seem real enough to serve? And 'tis only for a few days that we'll be the centre of gossip and speculation.' His head dropped forward as if he were falling asleep, then he snapped upright again. 'I'm sorry!'

'You need to rest.'

'Mmm. But be very careful if Elkin turns up. Say nothing to him about our marriage or that you're to inherit. I'll tell Jem to come and wake me as soon as he arrives.'

She watched him go to the door and have a few quiet words with the man he called his servant, but who seemed as much of a friend to him as Bessie was to her. She liked that.

He came back inside. 'I don't think Elkin will arrive until this afternoon, because he won't get my message until mid-morning, so you should be safe enough for the moment. Don't tell the servants anything. There's a maid, Merry Thompson, who's a nice enough lass, but I intend to be rid of the Simleys as soon as Ralph is buried and the will read.'

As he moved towards the bed, he stopped and turned round again. 'When you write to your mother, explain the situation here and ask her to pretend we knew one another before.' His voice trailed away in another huge yawn and he lay down on the bed as if he could stand up no longer. His eyes closed immediately.

She watched him for a moment or two, liking what she saw, hoping the marriage would turn out well for them both, then realised she was still wearing the clothes she had ridden to Marymoor in. She cast a doubtful glance towards the bed. No, he was not feigning sleep. She took some clothes out of the saddle bag and changed into them, then straightened her hair and went downstairs.

Should she wait to bring her mother and Bessie here? No, she didn't doubt they were in a difficult situation because of her absence or that her Uncle Walter was being as disagreeable to them as he could.

Whatever they had to face, they would face it here at Marymoor – together.

–

Walter Lawrence beat a tattoo on the door of his sister's cottage at ten o'clock the morning following Deborah's departure. His man Frank stood outside holding the horses and grinning in a knowing way that always irritated Bessie, who was peering out of the parlour window to see who it was.

When she opened the front door, Walter pushed past her to fling open the door of the parlour and peer inside. It was empty.

'Where is my sister? And more to the point, where is my niece?' he demanded. 'Did Deborah return last night? I heard she rode off with a stranger and hasn't been seen again.'

So he knew, Bessie thought with a sinking heart.

'Well? Answer me?'

Only the knowledge that he would throw her out of the village if she spoke sharply kept her anger under control and her voice even. She didn't even dare try to shield her poor mistress. 'Miss Deborah hasn't returned. And Mrs Isabel is out in the garden. Would you like me to fetch her?'

'I'll go to her.' He strode through the kitchen and out of the back door, leaving it swinging open.

Bessie followed, keeping out of sight but watching what was going on. You'd think a man would treat his own sister more kindly, 'deed you would.

Isabel looked up and saw him, pushing herself to her feet quickly. One hand fluttered up to her throat, a nervous gesture that showed she was afraid. 'Walter!'

'Has Deborah returned?'

'No, of course not.'

'I want the address of this Ralph Jannvier and if I find you've been lying about her, that she's been out whoring with this stranger, then you'll all leave Newgarth on the instant. I'll condone no immorality in my family.'

'I don't have it, not the exact address, anyway. I never went to visit him, only Paul did that.'

'I don't believe you,' he roared. 'Even you could not be so foolish as to let your daughter ride off through the night with a strange man and not know exactly where she was going!'

'Marymoor village is near Rochdale,' she offered.

He turned to Bessie. 'Go and bring me your mistress's papers. There must be some better clue than *near Rochdale*.'

The maid hesitated.

Isabel stepped forward. 'Go back to the kitchen, Bessie. And don't touch my papers.' She stared at Walter, who had tormented her in childhood and was doing the same in her old age, and although her voice wobbled, she said, 'It isn't for you to command my maid, Walter, or to go through my papers.'

'Oh, isn't it.' He stepped forward, one hand upraised.

She stepped hastily backwards, turning her heel on the hand hoe she'd been using and falling to the ground.

Bessie came rushing to help her mistress stand up. 'Shame on you, sir!' The words were out before she could prevent them.

A singularly nasty smile twisted his face. 'I don't tolerate servants who speak to me like that. You're dismissed. Make sure you're out of the village by nightfall.' He turned towards the house. 'If you won't fetch them, I'll find those papers myself.'

Isabel rushed to push him out of the way and stand barring entrance to the back door, her chest heaving and her face pale but set. 'Stay away from us! And Bessie is *my* maid. You don't pay her wages, so it's not for you to dismiss her.'

He debated shoving her out of the way, but that damned maid went to stand beside her and anyway, Frank would be able to trace his niece easily enough. He looked at Bessie again. His sister would be lost without the sturdy maid to do the housework, but he wouldn't miss her impudent face about the village. 'This is my cottage,' he snapped, 'and I say who shall live here.' He pointed his forefinger at Bessie. '*You* may continue to call yourself my sister's maid or anything else you like, but you are to be out of the village by nightfall. Don't ever dare return to Newgarth or I'll have you taken up for vagrancy.'

Left alone the two women looked at one another in consternation.

Bessie sobbed suddenly. 'Oh, Miss Isabel, I'm so sorry. The words just jumped out of my mouth. I'll go and apologise, beg him on my bended knees to change his mind.'

Isabel put her arm round Bessie's shoulders and drew her across to sit by the table. 'No, don't. He'd enjoy watching you grovel, but he wouldn't change his mind. He *wants* to hurt me, has been doing it since I was a child. I never did understand why he hated me so much. And now – heaven knows why, we cost him little enough and I sew for them – he still has to bully us.'

For a moment she sat in silence, then said in a firmer voice than Bessie had heard her use for a long time, 'We shouldn't have stayed here when we found how he was going to treat us. It's more than time for us to leave.'

'*Us? Both of us?*'

'Yes.'

'But where shall we go?' Bessie asked in shock.

'Where else but Marymoor?'

'We've no money to hire a conveyance. You know how little there is left now.'

'Then we'll walk.' Isabel stood up and brushed down her skirt. 'I can still walk as well as you.'

'I can't ask you to do this. Let *me* go and find this Marymoor and you stay here in comfort. I'm sure they'll send for you when I tell them how things stand.'

'No. We've been together for a long time now and we're leaving together. He's not going to separate us. No one is.'

It was she who comforted the weeping Bessie as they started packing, she who led the way out of the cottage carrying a bundle containing clothes and a few other necessities.

4

The man who rode the scrawny old horse from Mary-moor village to Sedge House, a tumble-down place on the edge of the moors, was an undersized and sour-smelling creature, but Seth's eyes brightened at the sight of him. His master had been expecting someone for several days now, ever since Mr Elkin heard the welcome news that Ralph Jannvier was dying at last.

He took the fellow straight to his master and concealed a snort of laughter as the poor sap gaped and was at first speechless. For Seth's master wore clothing more suited to a London dandy than a country gentleman and his bearing these days was distinctly haughty.

With all but Seth.

'Well, fellow?' Anthony Elkin demanded impatiently.

The man jerked and said hastily, 'Mr Simley says to tell you the old man's dead, sir.'

'Do you bring no note from Simley?'

'No, sir. There weren't time to write none. He says you'd best get over there as quick as you can. There's a woman moved in, some friend of Pascoe's, and he's afeared the two of 'em are plotting summat.'

'They can plot away. Ralph won't have changed his will. He was the most stubborn old devil on this earth once he'd taken a decision. I'm his only legitimate heir.' Anthony narrowed his eyes as he thought on this, wondering if stealing the silver could have pushed the old fellow too far. No, surely not? He had left a letter apologising and promising to repay – as he had done. There were no other relatives left to inherit, but on reflection he'd been stupid. But when you're desperate you don't always think clearly.

He turned back to the man, who was still hovering with a hopeful expression on his face. 'Here.' A coin changed hands. 'You go back and tell Simley I'll set off within the hour.'

While Seth ushered the messenger out, Elkin poured himself a glass of brandy and raised it to his image in the tarnished mirror hanging crookedly over the smoke-stained fireplace. 'To the new master of Marymoor! And may I not spend another night in this hovel.' He drained the glass and tossed it into the hearth, laughing as it shattered.

The small parlour was as shabby as the rest of the house, its furnishings threadbare and none too clean. The place was all he had left now, hardly more than a cottage, not worthy of an Elkin. But Marymoor, ah, that house was a proper gentleman's residence, well suited to his new station in life. With it behind him, he would be able to find a rich wife. He grinned, a mere baring of the teeth. He had started to mend his fortune already, with his man's help, but was tired of that game and the risks involved.

Seth returned at that moment. 'He's gone.'

'We'll follow as soon as we can get ready.'

'Is the old lady to come too?'

'She must. For all her faults my mother is a lady of good family and will command the respect of the neighbours over there.'

He went upstairs to tell her the news, taking the steps two at a time, his whole body filled with exultation. He flung open the door of her chamber without knocking to find her still a-bed, with her maid in attendance and fussing over her. Both women squeaked in shock at his sudden appearance.

'The old devil's dead at last!' he announced.

Mrs Elkin's expression brightened and she sat up quickly. 'Did the lawyer send for you?'

'I'm not waiting for the lawyer. I have my own ways of finding out what's going on over there. We need to set off immediately. That clod Pascoe is in charge at the moment and I'm not letting him steal any of my inheritance. He's been living off the fat of the land at Marymoor for long enough now. As soon as the funeral's over, he's out.'

'I'm sure he wouldn't—'

'We can be sure of nothing where he's concerned, except that he's my enemy. Tell your woman to pack. We leave in an hour, sooner if we can.'

Harriet looked at her son in dismay. 'But Anthony, I'm not well enough for a journey. I've not left my bed for a sennight!'

He glared at her. 'If you're not ready to leave when I say, I'll carry you out to the carriage myself, dressed or not! I need you there,' he gave her a sneering smile, 'to mourn with me.'

With a whimper she fell back and when he'd gone, looked at her maid, tears in her eyes. 'We must do as he says, Denise.'

'But you're *not* well.'

'Maybe I shall be better away from this dampness.' She cast a resigned look round the shabby bedroom, where she spent most of her time now.

The maid's mouth set tight in disapproval. In her opinion the only thing that would help her mistress was to get away from her son. He'd brought them to this penury by gambling away what was left of his inheritance, and Denise set the ruin of Mrs Elkin's health squarely at his door. He might have started to mend his fortunes lately, though how he had managed that they couldn't work out, because he'd never been a lucky gambler, but he'd done little to make his mother's life more comfortable with the new money. All of it had been spent on his own clothes and who knew what other depraved pleasures? For he went away regularly, and always with an eager look on his face.

When she thought of how the old carriage would jolt her mistress's poor aching bones on the rough road across the moors, Denise could have wept. And where would she be if her mistress died? In dire trouble, that was sure, because she hadn't been paid her wages for many a month and a reference from *him* would be worth nothing – less than nothing, given his reputation.

But they set off in just over the hour he had specified, knowing better than to upset him.

–

When Deborah went out of the bedroom, she found Jem still lounging in the corridor outside. 'Matthew's going to get some sleep,' she told him.

'Aye. Needs it, too.'

She lowered her voice. 'He suggested you could send a message to my mother and arrange for her to join me – us – here.' She liked the straight way he looked at her, the alertness in his bearing. Like master, like man, she thought.

'He said he was going to wait to bring them here.'

'My mother is in a difficult situation herself. My uncle, Mr Lawrence, is very callous in the way he treats her.'

Jem pursed his lips but made no further protests. 'Well, if Matthew says do it, you'd better write a letter to your mother and I'll send young George across to fetch her. He can ride there and I'll give him the money to hire a carriage to bring her back.' He grinned at her. 'No need for an old lady to gallop across the countryside like you did.'

'We didn't exactly gallop,' she murmured.

''Twas a hard ride, though. Matt said you did well.' Not many women would have managed that. His new mistress had courage, that was sure. 'I think he'll manage all right. He has a bit of sense between his ears, George does, though he's never left the district before. Is there somewhere he can hire a carriage in this Newgarth place?'

She nodded. 'From the inn, the Bird in Hand. It's not a large village, but it's on a fairly busy post road.'

'And is there a carter who can bring your goods and chattels over?'

'Yes. Bessie will know about that. Our maid is very practical.' She couldn't help a wry smile as she added, 'And of an independent turn of mind, too.'

'You write your letter, then, and I'll go and instruct George on what's needed.'

'Is it as easy as that?' she marvelled aloud, not being accustomed to having things done for her.

Jem shrugged. 'Seems straightforward enough to me. How long will it take your mother to pack, do you think?'

'Give her one day's notice and she'll be ready the next. We're used to moving.' Had done it secretly in the middle of the night many a time to avoid her father's creditors.

'Well, then, I'll see young George is ready to leave as soon as your letter is finished. Your mother could be here in two or three days' time.'

As Jem vanished down the narrow back stairs, Deborah turned towards the broader front staircase, finding herself strangely reluctant to face the other servants while her position here was so anomalous. But she couldn't go back into the bedroom and disturb Matthew.

There was no sign of anyone in the hall, so she went into the small parlour she'd used the night before. There was no fire lit, though it was a damp, chilly day, with rain threatening. She shivered involuntarily and looked for a bell pull, then smiled at her own folly. Marymoor was not her uncle Lawrence's well-appointed house, but an old place and wouldn't have such modern conveniences as bell pulls. She found a handbell on the mantelpiece and rang it loudly.

No one came to answer her summons, so after a while she rang again, feeling irritation begin to rise at this slovenly service.

Once Matthew had made her position as mistress of Marymoor known, she would make sure the servants knew their jobs better than this, she thought angrily as the minutes passed and still no one came. The death of a master was no excuse for neglecting one's duties.

Leaving the room, she turned towards the back of the hall where she presumed the domestic quarters would lie. As she opened the door she found herself in a short passage that led to a large kitchen, with the servants' stairs to her left. Simley and an older woman (presumably his wife) were standing by the kitchen window speaking earnestly while they sipped at pots of ale. Dishes lay unwashed on the table, where two rabbits lay waiting to be skinned. The wooden surface was in need of a good scrubbing.

The Simleys turned at her entrance and to her amazement Mr Simley set down his pot and went outside without acknowledging her presence.

The housekeeper stared at her with a hostile expression on her face, then sighed and asked, 'Did you want something, miss? You should have rung and waited for someone to come. I'm Mrs Simley, the housekeeper.' And, her expression said, this was her territory and she didn't want strangers invading it.

Deborah drew herself up and stared right back at the woman. 'I did ring. Twice. I'd like some breakfast and a fire lighting in the parlour. As no one answered my bell, I wondered if something was wrong and came to investigate.'

'It's Merry who attends to the bells. The girl's a lazy piece if ever I saw one. If you'll return to the parlour,' Mrs Simley hesitated for a few seconds before adding, '*miss*, I'll see that she comes and lights your fire. I'll send some food through in a few minutes. You'll understand that things are a bit – upset-like today. With the master dying and all. Mrs Gurrey's laying him out and she does a beautiful job.'

Even though she was ravenous, Deborah decided not to take issue with the woman, but thought it a poor excuse. 'Thank you. I'd appreciate some food.'

'We're waiting for the new master to arrive, you see,' Mrs Simley said as she turned to go. 'We've no one to tell us what to do till he comes.'

Deborah stared at her in surprise. 'But surely Mr Pascoe is in charge and—'

'He *was* the bailiff, in a manner of speaking. For the *old* master. But he won't inherit because he was born on the wrong side of the blanket, so if you came here expecting any profit, I'm afraid he's misled you. It's Mr Elkin as is proper *family* and will inherit the estate.'

Mindful of Matthew's warning, Deborah bit off a sharp response and went back to the parlour.

Shortly afterwards a young maid came through carrying a shovel filled with burning embers and soon had a fire going. 'There,' she said cheerfully. 'Sorry I weren't around when you rang, miss. I was up helping Mrs Gurrey. It burns well, this fire. Soon have the place warm. Proper chilly today, isn't it? Wouldn't think it was summer.'

Well, at least one person wasn't hostile, Deborah thought. 'What's your name?'

'Merry, miss. I'll just go and fetch you something to eat now, shall I?'

'Please. Anything will do.'

But all the girl brought was some rather stale bread and cheese, with a wrinkled apple cut in four quarters. Poor fare to set before a guest, but Deborah ate it hungrily. It would hold her until Matthew woke and took charge.

As soon as she'd finished, she rang the bell again and it was answered more promptly this time. 'Where can I find some paper and pen? I need to write a letter.'

Merry led her into what she called the library. 'This is where the old master used to write all his letters. He could write fine as King George himself, Mr Jannvier could. There's paper, quills and such-like, and I saw Mr Matthew mixing up some ink only the other day.' She peered into the inkwell. 'Yes, see, it's not dried up yet. Eeh, the poor master won't be needing these things again, will he?'

'No.' Deborah looked round. The room was chill and damp, for although it was late June the weather had turned grey and rainy. 'I think we might light the fire in here as well as in the parlour, don't you?'

Merry looked embarrassed. 'I'll have to ask Mrs Simley, I'm afraid. I should have asked her before I brought you in here, really. I daresay she won't mind, though.'

'Very well. I'll wait here while you do that.'

Deborah looked round, liking the room in spite of its chill. It wasn't large and had only one bookcase, for all its grand title of 'library', but it had a cosy feel to it as if people had been happy here. Through the leaded window there was a delightful outlook over the rather bare garden and rising beyond it the moors. She would have loved to explore the whole house and grounds, for she still couldn't believe they were hers, but knew she mustn't betray that yet. Besides, she needed to write the letter to her mother as quickly as possible. Who knew what further cruelties her uncle Lawrence would be inflicting on his sister?

She was just picking up a quill to check its point when there was a knock on the half-open door and Mr Simley came in without waiting to be asked. She rested the hand wearing the wedding ring in her lap and covered it with her right hand.

He spoke with a touch of scorn. 'If you wish for a fire, miss, may I suggest you sit in the breakfast parlour, which has already got one?'

'I think we need one in here as well, Simley,' she said calmly, 'because people will be visiting the house, no doubt, to offer their condolences. Also I need to write a letter.'

'I don't think Mr Jannvier's papers should be disturbed until Mr Elkin has seen them.'

'My writing a letter will not disturbing anything. Are you refusing to light a fire for me in here?'

'I am merely trying to do my duty by my late master and by my new one, too,' he said stiffly, but his expression was far less polite than his words.

By now it had become a point of honour with her not to give in to this bullying. Bessie had often scolded Deborah for that stubborn streak, but she didn't to allow the two Simleys to treat her in this cavalier manner. 'Kindly do as I ask and send the maid in to light the fire.'

His breathed in deeply, then let his breath out again slowly. For a moment all hung in the balance, then he inclined his head and left.

However, when Merry returned she had lost her smile, had a red mark on her cheek and was looking distinctly tearful.

'Is something wrong?'

She sniffed. 'They're angry with me for showing you in here. And – and I've just been given my notice, miss. To leave after the funeral. If I do as they say till then, I'll get references, otherwise I won't.'

'Who told you that?'

'Mr Simley.'

'He has no authority to do that.'

Merry goggled at her. 'Well, it's him an' Mrs Simley what run the house and gardens, have done for years, an' they're the ones as allus hire the servants.'

Deborah chose her words carefully. 'That doesn't mean they can dismiss you. It'll be for the new owner to do that.'

Merry let out a snort of disgust. 'Mr Elkin? Him an' Mr Simley are as thick as thieves these days. Nor I'm not sure I'd want to work for him anyway. They say no woman's safe with him.' She gasped, realising she'd said too much, and turned her attention back to the fire. 'There, that'll soon be blazing up.'

Once she had gone, Deborah finished writing the letter, rang the bell and found herself faced with Simley not Merry. Before she could ask to speak to Jem, there was the sound of horses and a carriage drawing up outside, followed shortly afterwards by a thunderous knocking on the front door.

'If you will excuse me for a moment, miss?'

Simley hurried out of the room and she heard voices in the hallway but was unable to make out what they were saying. She folded up the letter quickly and slipped it through the placket in the side of her skirt into the capacious pocket hanging there. The voices continued. Who could it be? she wondered. Matthew hadn't expected Elkin to arrive until the afternoon.

There was the sound of footsteps and Simley reappeared, looking smugly triumphant. ''Tis Mr Anthony Elkin, ma'am, the new master, come to look after things as I told you he would.'

She was unsure what to do, could only hope Jem had heard Elkin arrive and was waking Matthew. Again she concealed her wedding ring, this time in the folds of her skirt.

A gentleman came in to join them. He was tall and thin, several years older than herself, as she judged, with deep crease lines down his cheeks and thin, bloodless lips. There was an underlying sourness in the set of his mouth and a dissolute look in his eyes, which were even now raking down her body in an offensive way. She wouldn't have ridden through the night with this man, felt uneasy at being alone with him, even.

'May I ask who *you* are, my good woman?' he asked, looking sharply at her as if assessing her clothes and status and finding them both lacking.

She spoke crisply, refusing to be intimidated. 'You may ask, sir, but it's really none of your business. I'm here at the invitation of the late Mr Jannvier and Mr Pascoe.'

'I think it *is* my business now.'

He moved forward to stand over her in a way that made her feel threatened and she took an involuntary step backwards.

'I'll ask you again who you are and I'll thank you for a prompt answer this time,' he snapped.

A voice from the door made him swing round sharply. 'The lady is my wife, Elkin, and I'll thank *you* to mind your manners when you speak to her.' Matthew stood there, his hair still rumpled, his expression stolid, betraying nothing of his feelings.

Deborah felt relief course through her.

'Wife! You're not married. She's your doxy, more like.'

Matthew moved to stand by Deborah's side. 'You're wrong, Elkin, but I'm sure Mrs Pascoe will accept your apologies for that insult. And this time, at least, I shall overlook it.'

Elkin ignored Deborah, hostility in every line of his body. 'It doesn't actually make much difference who she is. I'm here because we Elkins are the only relatives old Ralph had left and I'm his heir.'

'But you're not his only relatives,' was the gentle answer and now Matthew put his arm round Deborah's shoulders. 'My wife can claim an even closer relationship than you, for she's Ralph Jannvier's great-niece. Her name was, before our recent marriage, the same as his.'

Simley let out an audible gasp.

Elkin went red and fury built up swiftly in his face. 'I don't believe you!' he growled. 'This is just a trick to try to get hold of the estate. Ralph has never mentioned her

72

existence to *me*, not in all the years I've known him! What proof do you have of her identity?'

'Ralph has known of her existence ever since her birth.'

Elkin glared from him to Deborah. 'I don't believe you.'

'You can always check with Mr Downie. He too has been aware of her existence for a long time.'

'I shall do more than ask for his opinion – I shall demand proof of her identity.'

'Do that!' Matthew snapped. 'In the meantime, Mr Downie has put me in charge at Marymoor until after the will is read and my wife and I are not receiving visitors.' He moved towards the door as if to show Elkin out.

Deborah felt as if it would take only the smallest thing to set the men at each other's throats. She saw Simley look at Elkin questioningly and decided that if it came to a fight and the servant tried to join in, two to one against Matthew, she would snatch up the nearest vase and hit him over the head with it.

However, Elkin shook his head as if to tell his henchman to hold back and turned to her instead, forcing a sour smile which faded almost immediately.

'My apologies for the misunderstanding, *Mrs Pascoe*.'

She inclined her head slightly but cared little whether he apologised or not.

Elkin turned back to Matthew. 'My mother is outside in the coach, expecting to stay here for the funeral. Do you indeed intend to turn us away?'

Deborah watched her husband closely, seeing his hesitation. She knew it would look very strange if they turned Ralph Jannvier's only other relatives away, though she didn't look forward to having a man like this staying in the house.

After a moment Matthew said in a toneless voice, 'Pray ask your mother to come inside. No doubt we can find rooms for you both until after the funeral, but you will understand that we haven't many servants, so cannot guarantee you much attention, either in the house or the stables.'

'I've brought my own man and my mother's maid, so I daresay we can manage.' Elkin moved towards the door. 'I'll fetch my mother in. She's not in the best of health and the journey has tired her.'

When she and her husband were alone Deborah pulled her letter out of her pocket and held it out to Matthew. 'I've written to ask my mother to join us.' She gave him a wry smile. 'We shall be an interesting group of people.'

He took it from her and slid it inside his coat. '"Interesting" is not the word I'd have chosen to describe Elkin. "Dangerous" might be more appropriate. Best not mention this to him.'

'I can see now why you don't trust him. He makes me feel – uncomfortable. I wish he didn't have to stay here.'

'Unfortunately he's right: the local gentry *would* be scandalised if we turned him away. For your sake I don't want that.'

She glanced over her shoulder and lowered her voice still further. 'What do you think he'll do when he finds out about the new will?'

'That remains to be seen. For a man who stole some of the silver last time, Elkin has come here in style today. A carriage, no less, though it's a shabby one with only two horses. Did he think Ralph a rich man and borrowed on the expectations? If so, he'll be disappointed. When I came here, the estate and farm were run down and there's still a lot to do to the house. Ralph was rather

74

old-fashioned in his farming methods. As for Elkin — he wouldn't know how to manage the place and I doubt he'd even try. He just wants to milk it of its supposed wealth.'

She was quite sure Matthew didn't intend to do that. She could hear the love in his voice whenever he spoke of Marymoor, and indeed, she'd taken a liking to the house herself. It would make a wonderful home if it were properly run, without surly servants who neglected the housework, a perfect place to bring up children and... She didn't let herself finish that thought. This was no time for dreams. Those would have to wait until after Elkin had left.

There was the noise of footsteps in the hallway and they turned as one to face their visitors. Deborah found the nearness of Matthew comforting and tried to match his inscrutable expression as she stepped forward to greet a stooped, elderly lady who was weeping softly into a handkerchief.

But Elkin continued to look at her and Matthew as if *they* were interlopers and to act as if he were the owner. He was going to cause trouble when he found out the truth. Deborah was quite sure of that, even though she'd only just met him.

–

They kept country hours, with dinner at two o'clock and supper in the evening. Dinner was a very stiff affair, the atmosphere every bit as bad as Deborah had expected and the food poorly prepared. This didn't stop her husband from making a hearty meal, but drew complaints from Elkin and a declaration that he would change such things for the better when he was master here. He was allowed to speak unchecked, because Matthew addressed his food and Deborah followed her usual practice in new situations of watching more than speaking.

Mrs Elkin ate very little and still looked pale. She was, she confided to Deborah as Merry cleared the table, 'a poor traveller' and would be glad to seek her bed, if her hostess would excuse her. Which she did almost immediately.

After the meal, Matthew took Deborah for a stroll round the gardens near the house, then showed her the stables. At one point they saw Elkin coming towards the stable block and Matthew quickly pulled her round a corner. 'I think the less we see of that so-called gentleman the better.'

Mrs Elkin didn't come down to supper and the others didn't linger over the meal, which was very simple and again, not skilfully prepared.

After the meal, Deborah stood up. 'I'll say goodnight now. I'm rather tired.'

'I'll join you shortly.' Matthew watched Elkin pour himself yet another glass of port, but shook his head when the decanter was offered to him.

Deborah made haste to get undressed before her husband came upstairs, wishing she had a nightgown to wear instead of just her shift, which revealed rather too much of her body. Her legs and thighs were still sore and stiff and she groaned as she slid into the bed, closing her eyes and sighing in relief as she snuggled into the welcome softness of the feather bed.

She woke with a start as the door opened.

'It's only me.' Matthew set a candle down on a chest of drawers and began to take his clothes off.

'What time is it?' Deborah felt heavy-headed with sleep.

'Midnight. Elkin tried to persuade me to drink with him.' Matthew let out a soft snort of disgust. 'I know better than to let myself get fuddled when I have an estate to run and so I told him, but I thought it better to keep an eye on him.' He smiled at her in the flickering light of the candle. 'I'm looking forward to seeing his face the day after tomorrow when the will's read.'

'Wouldn't it have been better to have given him a hint?' she wondered. 'He's going to be very angry.'

'Let him get angry. He'll not be staying in this house after the funeral is over and he'll definitely not be visiting us again. The Simleys can leave with him, since they've tied their flag to his pole, or if he doesn't want them, they'll have to find themselves other work. I'm not employing them.'

'I must admit, I don't trust him. Or them.'

'Shows you've got good sense. Some folk are fooled by that gentlemanly exterior, but Elkin would do anything for money. I wouldn't put murder past him, even.'

'How can you speak so surely? He is, after all, a gentleman.'

'Hah! Gentleman or not, I've seen him act viciously time and again. While I remember – don't go out walking with him on your own, or linger anywhere with him where there aren't folk within call. Just to be safe.'

'If you say so. I don't enjoy his company anyway.' Deborah slid down in the bed and averted her eyes from Matthew's body as he finished undressing. Even in the dim light of one candle she could see he had a well-muscled frame. She wished they'd met in some other way, that there had been time to get to know one another properly, instead of being pitched into such a fraught situation.

As he blew out the candle and slid into the bed she wondered if he was going to claim his rights as a husband, but he simply sighed and yawned. Within seconds he was asleep and she didn't know whether to be glad or sorry. He was exhausted, poor man, but was he really so indifferent to her?

She hoped not because she was not, she found, at all indifferent to him. He was good looking enough to turn any woman's head. And she *was* his wife, after all.

5

In the morning Deborah woke to find that Matthew had already risen. Unsure of the time and not wanting to seem lazy, she got up immediately, but couldn't resist going to stare out of the window before she dressed. The slopes that led up to the moors were chequered by neatly-kept fields, dotted with white where sheep grazed, and edged by dry stone walls. Above them the duller greenish brown of the moors swept away into the distance, unfettered by walls or any other sorts of limitations.

She studied the sky, but to her relief the sun had only just risen. As she listened, she heard a few birds greet the dawn, sounding sleepy still as they chirped and cooed softly in the trees near the house.

Below her Matthew came into sight and she paused to watch him striding away from the house. He was wearing a pair of stout leather breeches and a sleeveless jerkin over his shirt and looked completely at home. He smiled up at the sky before disappearing in the direction of some barns and outbuildings. She hoped to feel at home here one day, she thought wistfully. She'd ask him to show her round properly as soon as the Elkins had left, which couldn't happen too soon for her. And one day she would like to walk across those moors. Perhaps Matthew would take her.

She clicked her tongue in annoyance at herself. And perhaps she should stop daydreaming and get dressed!

There was a knock on the door and Merry came in, carrying a ewer of hot water. 'I brought up your water now because Mr Matthew said you were stirring and Mrs Simley will be up soon, then it'll be hard for me to get away. I hope that's all right.'

'Of course it is.'

The maid looked at Deborah shyly. 'I wanted to wish you well of your marriage, Mrs Pascoe, if you don't mind me taking the liberty. Mr Matthew's a fine man, an' he allus treats folk decent.'

'Thank you.' As Merry turned to leave, Deborah asked quickly, 'Wait! Have the Simleys said anything further about your leaving?'

Merry's smile vanished and she nodded. '*She* said this morning I could stay on to help with the funeral, then I'd have to go. Said they wanted a maid as is more willing.' Tears welled in her eyes as she blurted out, 'But they couldn't find anyone who works harder than I do. You ask Mr Pascoe.'

'They can do nothing until after the will is read,' Deborah reminded her.

Merry sniffed and wiped the tears away with the back of one hand. 'I'd not have stayed here this long if I didn't want to be near my family. Them two aren't the easiest folk to work for. *She* leaves everything she can to me, she's that lazy. Oh, I'm talking too freely!' She clapped one hand to her mouth and looked at Deborah anxiously. 'You won't tell them what I said?'

'I won't reveal a word. Now, what usually happens about breakfast?'

'They allus served it at nine o'clock in the parlour when the old master was alive. I get Mr Matthew a piece of bread and cheese when he wakes, then he comes back later for a proper meal. He used to eat breakfast with the old master. The two of 'em never said much, but they looked right comfortable together.'

'Then I'll do the same, so perhaps you could bring me something to eat now – anything will do. I'm used to starting early as well and I want to sort out our clothes and things.' She looked round. 'I wonder what the time is exactly? Is there a clock anywhere? We definitely need one in here.' Setting the bedroom in order would help her avoid contact with anyone else until Matthew returned, but though she didn't want to be late for breakfast, neither did she want to go down too early and face Elkin alone.

'I know where there is one!' Merry left and came back with a handsome clock, which she set on the mantelpiece, saying cheerfully, 'This was the old master's but he isn't going to need it any more, is he?'

When the maid had left Deborah went through the drawers and the clothes press, noting that Matthew's things were neatly kept and were of good quality, but not of fancy materials. She smiled even to think of him in flowered brocade such as Elkin had been wearing yesterday. As she was putting away the few things she'd brought with her, she couldn't help wishing she had better clothes in which to do credit to her new husband – and to make him think well of her.

Just before she went downstairs, Deborah did the best she could with her appearance, combing back her hair and pulling it into as flat a bun as she could manage under the small cap of fine lawn. But strands would keep escaping – they always did – and she could do little about the crumpled appearance of her skirts. She had no hoops to wear beneath her simple, back-lacing gown, whose full skirts sat limply over the two petticoats she'd been able to fit into the saddlebag. Her uncle had forbidden her or her mother to try to ape the fashions of their 'betters', by which he meant her cousin and aunt, so she didn't even own a hooped petticoat. Not that she had minded that until now because such skirts would have constrained her movements too much when she was working round the house.

But it would have been comforting not to look so dowdy and old-fashioned now. She sighed as she twisted and turned in front of the small mirror on the chest of drawers. Still, she had brought along her best handkerchief, of fine muslin with a narrow lace edging, and she thought it looked well with the ends crossed and tucked into her bosom.

With a shrug at her own vanity, she left the bedchamber and walked briskly down the stairs.

To her dismay she found only Elkin waiting for her in the parlour, as immaculately dressed as ever, this time in a suit of grey brocade with embroidery down the front edges. The skirts of his coat were stiffened and he had wide cuffs, buttoned back and reaching nearly to his elbows. His wig today was a toupee with three horizontal roll curls on each side, tied back with a grey silk ribbon. But somehow its elegance only emphasised the narrowness of his face and the harsh lines of dissipation engraved on it. Or perhaps these were so engrained he always looked like that.

And for all his fine clothes he looked like a bird of prey, ready to pounce on an unsuspecting victim and seize what he wanted. She knew she couldn't trust him, knew it deep down in her bones.

When he offered both a bow and a smile, she felt instantly suspicious after the scornful way he'd treated her the previous day.

'A beautiful morning, is it not?' He waved one hand towards the window.

She noticed that his eyes were on her, however, studying, assessing. 'Indeed.' She inclined her head, wishing Matthew were here.

'Perhaps we could take a turn on the terrace until they serve breakfast?' He offered her his arm.

She hesitated, but could think of no polite way of refusing so allowed him to lead her outside via the front door.

'I must apologise for my ill-mannered behaviour towards you yesterday, cousin,' he said abruptly.

Oh? So she was a 'cousin' now, was she?

'I'm afraid Matthew Pascoe always rubs me the wrong way. No doubt you see a gentler side to him, but he has been no friend to me and my mother.'

She stopped walking. 'I shall not discuss my husband with you. Nor shall I listen to calumny about him.'

Elkin breathed deeply and shot her an annoyed look, which was wiped off his face almost as soon as it appeared. As they continued walking he found another topic. 'You don't have the Jannvier looks.' He stopped to study her features openly.

'Do I not?' She was itching to pull away from him, hated to be so close.

'No. But that is, perhaps, an advantage for a woman.' He touched one finger to his beaky nose with a rueful smile.

'Matthew has the Jannvier looks, too,' she said, thinking how much better-looking her husband was than this man, and wondering why, for he was not nearly as finely dressed.

'I am not myself convinced of his parentage,' Elkin said, 'though that is irrelevant now.' He gestured up at the house. 'I love Marymoor. It's been in the family ever since it was built. I know it's rather old-fashioned, but I've always wished...' He let his voice trail away and gave a soulful sigh, then went on, 'There's a roof walk, you know, built in the Great Queen's time. They don't make them nowadays, more's the pity, for it's a fine way to take the air. Look, you can see where it leads out. There.' His finger traced out a line across the edge of the roof. 'On fine days it gives one a splendid view of the moors. I always love going up there.'

Just then Matthew appeared in the doorway and Deborah let go of Elkin's arm thankfully to hurry across to her husband and kiss his cheek. 'Thank goodness you've come,' she muttered in his ear.

He draped one arm possessively round her shoulders and they turned as one to face their companion. 'You're up early today, Elkin.'

'So are you, Pascoe.'

'I have an estate to run.'

'Not for much longer.'

The air fairly crackled with hostility, though Matthew's face didn't betray his feelings as openly as Elkin's.

Deborah felt uneasy in spite of the beauty of the day, and leaned thankfully against her husband's arm, drawing comfort from the strength of the muscular body next to hers.

'Quite the loving couple, are we not?' Elkin sneered. 'Do you intend to stand there all day fondling one another like peasants or can we go and break our fast?'

So much for his politeness, Deborah thought. She wondered why he had even bothered to talk to her. Without a word she led the way inside to find a well-loaded table waiting for them and Mrs Simley herself standing in the doorway, beaming at Elkin.

The woman ignored the Pascoes but said ingratiatingly, 'I think you'll find all you need, sir.'

Elkin's smile returned as he went to sit at the head of the table. 'I'm sure everything will be fine, my dear Mrs Simley. You always look after me so well.'

Deborah glanced quickly at Matthew, who should be occupying that chair, but he shook his head and took a place beside her without a word of protest.

'Is your mother not joining us?'

'She usually takes breakfast in bed.'

The meal proceeded in silence, with Matthew eating as heartily as usual, Deborah picking at her food and Elkin making a leisurely meal.

The silence seemed to irritate him, however, and he said abruptly, 'What arrangements have been made for the funeral?'

Matthew continued to cut up his ham. 'Ralph made them himself before he died. Parson Norwood knows all the details.'

'The right people have no doubt been invited?'

'The people Ralph asked for have been invited. I'm no judge of who's a right or wrong person.' Matthew's voice was scornful and he took another mouthful of ham, as if the conversation were closed.

'I shall look into the arrangements myself, then,' Elkin declared. 'We can't have things done shabbily.'

Matthew looked up. 'Ralph *himself* arranged the funeral and I don't think you'll find Norwood going against his dying wishes.'

'So you say.'

'So Ralph arranged.'

As both men scowled at one another, Deborah intervened. 'Is your mother feeling any better this morning, Mr Elkin? Have you heard from her?'

'Sadly, her maid says she isn't at all well and will keep to her bed until later, if you don't mind.'

'I'm surprised you brought her here, if her health is so bad,' Matthew said, reaching out to cut himself another slice of bread.

'It was the right thing to do. She knows her duty. Do you always gulp your food like a hungry ploughman?'

'There's nothing like hard work and honest living for giving you a good appetite.'

Deep breathing was his only answer from Elkin.

When Matthew had finished eating, he sat on, saying nothing. Deborah toyed with the few morsels left on her plate, hoping for a private word with her husband.

In the end Elkin pushed his plate aside and stood up. 'Well, if you will excuse me, I'll take a stroll down to the village. One would wish for a larger centre with a decent inn, but this is, after all, the wilds of Lancashire.'

'Thompson at the Woolpack knows his trade as well as any,' Matthew said mildly.

'I'm sure you would know more about that than I would. Though I dare say he does his best. Mrs Pascoe, your servant.'

When his footsteps had faded away into the distance, Matthew muttered, 'Last time he visited, Elkin came here by stage coach, didn't even have a riding horse of his own. Now he has a carriage and pair, and is dressed like a lord. Where did he get the money for all that, do you suppose?'

'Gambling, perhaps?' Deborah had seen similar changes in her own father from time to time, though he'd never dressed so elaborately.

'Perhaps. Though Elkin has never been a successful gambler before.'

'Are the two of you always so hostile to one another?'

Matthew leaned back and grinned at her. 'We're not usually this polite, actually. Your presence must be having a calming effect on us. We came to blows once, but Ralph stopped it before we could do one another any real harm. Elkin strips better than you'd think, for all his damned finicky ways – though he prefers to let his man settle problems for him if he can.' His smile vanished. 'I'm sorry he brought Seth Bailey with him. The fellow's too free with his fists and usually manages to cause trouble in the village.'

'Well, I sincerely hope *you* won't fall to fighting this time – with Elkin or his man.'

'I shan't *start* anything.' Matthew hesitated, then lowered his voice. 'I think it's best if we continue to say nothing about how things are left until the will is read. I can't be with you all the time to keep an eye on you.' After a further hesitation, he added, 'If you like, though, we could go for a walk this afternoon and I could show you over the home farm. It's coming on nicely now, but it was very run-down when I took over.' He gave her a wry smile. 'If you're interested, that is. I don't think you'll ever turn me into a fine gentleman.'

'I am interested. I wasn't brought up to be an idle lady, either.'

'That's good.'

She looked down at their hands which were lying near together on the table. Two inches closer and they'd be touching. Did he want to touch her? She found she wanted to touch him. And she didn't want a fine gentleman to husband. She much preferred an honest man who wasn't afraid to work and get his hands dirty. Fine gentlemen weren't always easy to live with and were no help in hard times.

He stood up abruptly. 'I'll press on with my work, then.'

She went to the window to watch him go, noticing how his hair gleamed with a blue-black sheen in the sunlight, glad he wasn't wearing a wig. She wandered up to their bedchamber, wondering how to fill the rest of the morning. She wasn't used to sitting idle, but she didn't want to risk another encounter with their unwelcome and unsettling guest.

-

Anthony Elkin sauntered down into the village, which nestled in a narrow valley, its cottages and one or two slightly larger houses set neatly on either side of the only thoroughfare. He was itching to throw Pascoe out of Marymoor, and that stupid wife of his, too. Indeed, it was surprising Pascoe had stayed on so long. He must know he wouldn't be wanted from now on, however good a farmer he was. And yet, there were no signs of him getting ready to leave.

Why not?

And what had got into the fellow to marry Deborah Jannvier so suddenly? Had he thought it'd change Ralph's mind about who he left the estate to?

Elkin's footsteps slowed as he considered this. No, Ralph would never leave Marymoor to a chance-born bastard! He'd always insisted that the legitimate line must inherit the family estate. Pascoe should know better than anyone how stubborn Ralph was once he got an idea fixed in his mind.

But as he walked along Elkin could not get the thought out of his mind that Pascoe had had several years to ingratiate himself. There was no denying he was a hard worker, and a capable one, too. The estate had never looked in such good heart.

The thought returned: surely the old man hadn't changed his will?

He stopped to glare into the distance. Well, if there had been any trickery, if Ralph *had* changed things, it'd be easy enough to get rid of Pascoe. Seth was a strong fellow, loyal and could handle a pistol better than most. Men's bodies were very vulnerable things, easy to destroy.

Elkin turned to stare back at the big house, which sat squarely on top of a gentle slope overlooking the village. Here lay his only chance of getting land and property of his own. Status. Respect. He would do whatever was needed to keep his rightful inheritance.

As he turned to walk on towards the village, he bumped into someone and stopped to apologise. The fellow didn't look like a local, for he was too well dressed, yet he was no gentleman, either.

'Excuse me, sir, but would that house be Marymoor?'

The voice was soft and courteous, an upper servant's tone. Elkin chose to allow a conversation, wondering what a stranger was doing in the village today of all days. 'Yes. The owner has just died, my uncle, actually, so if you were intending to visit him, you're too late. Or is it Matthew Pascoe you want? He's looking after things until the will's been read.' He couldn't keep the hatred out of his voice as he spoke that name.

The stranger looked speculatively at him, then said, 'It's a Miss Deborah Jannvier I'm interested in, actually, sir, on behalf of her maternal uncle, who has been responsible for her this past year and more. He has been much concerned for her safety since she ran away from home a few days ago with a man called Pascoe.'

'Well, she's at Marymoor, and she's in ruddy health, so he can stop worrying. You've only to knock on the door and ask to see her.'

'Ah. Well, actually, I'd be grateful if you'd not mention to her that you've seen me, sir. If I am to serve my master to my best ability and find out what she's been doing, it'd be better if she didn't know I was here just yet.'

'I can tell you exactly what she's been doing. She's been getting married to Pascoe, who is the bastard-born son of the former owner.'

'Has she now?' The man stilled, blowing out his breath in a soft whistle as he considered this. 'Now why should she do that? Her uncle will be very interested in the news.'

It occurred to Elkin that it wouldn't hurt to find out more about the bitch. 'They brew good ale at the Woolpack. Let me offer you a mug of the best. I'm sure we'll both benefit from an exchange of information.'

'I'm grateful for your kindness and condescension, sir. Very grateful indeed. But pray let my master buy the drinks. He would consider it only right.'

Which Elkin agreed to by a regal inclination of the head as he led the way towards the inn. One never knew when fate would toss one a wild card to tuck up one's sleeve. He might have fallen lucky here.

—

Isabel Jannvier woke that same morning in the hay barn of the small farm from which they usually bought their milk. The owners had become friendly with Bessie and had seen them passing. They'd been horrified to think of two elderly women turned out of house and home like that, but because they were tenants of Walter Lawrence, they didn't dare house the fugitives openly.

The farmer's wife came to check that they were awake just before dawn, bringing some bread and honey and a jug of milk. She pushed a small parcel into Bessie's hand. 'Something to eat while you're travelling.'

'Thank you, love. We're grateful for your help.'

'I only wish we could do more. Do you – have any money?'

Bessie nodded. 'A little. But we shall have to husband it carefully.' She'd used up most of her savings during the past year to ease her mistress's burdens.

Their hostess was clearly on edge. 'I'll say goodbye, then. Just leave that platter here and I'll fetch it later. And – I'd be grateful if you could leave as soon as you've finished eating, before anyone starts work in the fields. You know what Mr Lawrence is like. I'd keep away from the main roads, if I were you, just in case he comes after you. He won't expect you to take the hill tracks and you'll be harder to follow across the moors, there's that many tracks crossing one another up there.'

'We won't be long. We don't want to get you in trouble.' Bessie walked to the barn door with her friend and whispered, 'He's threatened to have her locked away, you know, says she's losing her wits.' She hesitated, then added, 'I don't mind if you spread that around as long as you tell them she's as sane as anyone else. I *want* folk to know how badly he's treated her.'

Nell shook her head in disbelief. 'Eh, he's a nasty old devil, he is that. Well, I hope you have a fine day for your travelling.'

Bessie returned to her mistress, who lay smiling in a nest of hay. 'We have to hurry up, Mrs Isabel.'

The other woman nodded and stood up, trying to brush the hay off her clothes. 'I slept very well, you know, better than I have for months. I'm sure we're doing the right thing, Bessie. We should have left Newgarth long ago.' She chuckled suddenly. 'I wish I could have seen my brother's face when he turned up to check that you'd left the village and found that I'd gone with you. People will talk and he'll hate that.'

Serve him right, thought Bessie. But let's hope he don't come after us and try to drag you back.

They passed through the gate at the far end of the meadow and began walking through the woods, not hurrying, each of them enjoying the early summer morning.

'Nell's right, you know,' Bessie said abruptly. 'We'd better stay right away from the main highway. It'll be harder going up there on the moorland tracks, though.'

Isabel gave her a beaming smile. 'We can take our time. It's lovely in the woods, isn't it? Much nicer than a dusty old road.'

But the woods ended and then they had to follow the road on the other side until they came to a turning. When a cart overtook them, the driver slowed down to ask, 'Going far?'

'A good way,' Bessie said, not wanting to reveal anything.

'Want a ride? I'm going a good way, too.' He chuckled at his own joke.

She was too worried to smile. 'That'd be a big help. Thank you.'

'Hop up on the back, then.' He looked at them and his mouth fell open in shock even before they'd climbed on the cart. 'Isn't she Mr Lawrence's sister?' he whispered. His expression showed that this was not a point in their favour.

Bessie hesitated. 'She is.'

'Where's she going at this hour?'

She stiffened. 'She's leaving Newgarth against his wishes. If you don't want to give us a ride, we'll understand.'

He sucked his mouth into a twist for a moment, then shrugged. 'Who's to see you at this hour?' As Mrs Jannvier climbed into the back of the cart, he whispered to Bessie, 'I heard as how he were treating his sister badly. I'm right glad I'm not one of his tenants. Hurry up, will you? I want to be on my way. And keep your heads down if you don't want folk to know where you're going.'

As they lay down in the cart, Isabel's hand crept into Bessie's. 'It'll be all right. I'm sure it will.'

'I hope so.'

The man set them down three miles further along the road and pointed out a track that led up across the moors to Rochdale. 'That's the best way if you want to avoid the highway. It'll take you longer, but there won't be as many folk to see you. And most of them who live up there know how to mind their own business. As I do.' He tapped one finger to his nose. 'I shan't tell anyone I've seen you.'

'Thank you kindly.' Isabel stretched her hand up to shake his. 'But if my daughter or a messenger from her were to ask for me, you could tell her you've seen me, could you not?'

He looked a bit surprised to have a lady offer him her hand and wiped his own on his shirt before taking hers. 'My pleasure to help you in any way, ma'am.'

The two women stepped back, waving goodbye as the horses clopped onwards again, then turning towards the moorland track.

Shaking his head, he drove on. What was the world coming to when a lady had to take to the road for fear of her own brother?

'What if we can't find this Marymoor?' Bessie worried when they'd been walking for an hour. She wished she hadn't packed so many things in her bundle, which already felt heavy.

'Of course we'll find it. It lies to the north-east of Rochdale. It's a big house. Someone will know where it is.'

They continued in silence with Bessie covertly watching her mistress. Mrs Isabel looked better than she had in a long time. Far from seeming fearful or tired, she was walking steadily, looking round and clearly enjoying the scenery. Bessie chuckled suddenly. 'We're a bit old for running away like this, aren't we?'

Isabel smiled serenely. 'My husband always used to say that you're never too old to enjoy yourself. I'd forgotten that. I'd grown – over fearful of the world.' Of her brother, actually.

But Bessie couldn't stop worrying. 'I don't know what Miss Deborah will say about this, I really don't.'

'She'll say we were right to leave. My only regret is that we stayed in Newgarth so long and let my brother bully us. And her.'

Bessie could suddenly see again the lively girl who had run away to marry Paul Jannvier and to hell with what anyone else thought of that, the girl she had followed and helped, and who was not only her mistress but her dear friend. Her own spirits began to lift, too. It would turn out all right, she told herself. Anything was better than staying in Newgarth. It must be.

–

By late morning Deborah could find nothing else to tidy or re-arrange in their bedroom, and although she would have liked to give it a thorough clean-out, this was not the time. She decided in the end to go and explore the upper part of the house. After all, she was unlikely to meet Mrs Simley there, for the woman rarely seemed to leave the kitchen.

She peeped into the various rooms on this floor. There was a closed coffin in Ralph's room and the faint smell of death filled the air, in spite of a big vase of flowers on the table. She bent her head for a moment in prayer for her benefactor, then closed the door quietly. Outside Mrs Elkin's room she hesitated then tapped.

The maid opened the door, her expression unwelcoming. 'Can I help you, ma'am?'

'I came to ask how your mistress is.'

'Not at all well. She's been ill all night and she isn't dressed for receiving visitors yet.' Without waiting for an answer, the woman closed the door on the sound of someone vomiting.

Deborah didn't go near the room Elkin was occupying, but went to stand for a moment at the landing window looking out over the moors. The panes of glass were smeared and dull, making it hard to see clearly. Oh, she was itching to start setting this house in order and couldn't think what the Simleys did with their time to let things get so dusty and run-down. With the help of Bessie and a willing girl like Merry, Deborah would have kept the parts of the house that were regularly used in apple-pie order. And enjoyed doing it.

Not feeling like returning to her room, she was tempted up the attic stairs, just for a quick look round. Here were several closed doors. She pushed them open, closing two of them quickly as she saw that they were, as she had guessed, the servants' quarters. The biggest room, which presumably belonged to the Simleys, was untidy and smelled of an unemptied chamber pot. Wrinkling her nose in displeasure she closed the door again.

There was another door standing half-open at one side and behind it she could see another set of stairs. She suddenly remembered Elkin talking about a roof walk. It could upset no one, surely, if she went up there? She would really enjoy some fresh air and peace, and already loved gazing out at the rolling expanse of moors.

At the top of the final set of stairs was a smaller space than on the floor below, unwalled and showing the roof beams. It was filled with lumber and broken furniture. That would need sorting out, she thought, grimacing at its dusty disarray. How strange to think that she and Matthew owned all this now. Merry must have been airing the attic, and it certainly needed it, because yet another door stood ajar at the far end.

She pushed that open to find herself out on the roof itself, where a lively wind whipped more of her unruly hair from beneath her muslin cap. Taking a deep breath of the bracing air and smiling in pleasure, she moved forward across the roof walk that led out between the sloping tiles towards the edge. It didn't feel as secure as she'd expected, but she forgot that in the enjoyment of the space and freedom up here! Breathing deeply, she did nothing but hold her face up to the sun and let it warm her skin for a moment or two.

Which saved her life.

As she moved on again towards the stone rail that edged the walk, intending to lean against it and enjoy the view, someone screeched her name from below and yelled, '*Stop!* Mrs Pascoe, stop where you are!' She froze instinctively, staring down.

Merry was waving her arms furiously. 'Don't touch that railing!' she shrieked in a voice that could have been heard miles away. 'It's rotten. Pieces of it fell off in the last storm. And don't move from there. Some of the walk isn't safe.'

Deborah stared along the rest of this part of the roof, seeing the gaps in the stone railing which she hadn't noticed in her initial pleasure at the glorious views.

'I'll fetch Mr Matthew.' Merry rushed off towards the stables.

So Deborah stood there, feeling a shiver of apprehension in spite of the warmth of the sun on her skin. Elkin had waxed eloquent about this walk. Had he known it was in disrepair? Tried to tempt her our here on purpose? Surely not?

The wind tugged at her hair and when she put one hand up to adjust her cap, it whipped the piece of muslin off her head. It flew away, dipping and twisting on the breeze, then as the wind suddenly eased it fluttered to the ground. She would not have fallen so lightly. She would have dropped like a stone if she'd leaned against that railing and she'd not have survived. Her throat was dry with fear and she didn't dare move an inch.

Where was Matthew? It seemed a very long time before she heard footsteps and turned to see her grim-faced husband standing in the attic doorway.

'I'll not come out to you,' he said. 'Better not add extra weight to that roof. The whole of this section needs repairing and some of the joists are rotten. You were lucky not to have fallen through it.'

Which made her feel even more afraid to move.

His voice grew gentler. 'If you got out safely, you can get back safely too, Deborah. But I think you should move along the slope, not the flat part.' When she didn't move, he added softly, 'Don't think about what might happen and don't move jerkily. But whatever you do, don't bump against that railing. It's heavy and if it fell it could pull some of the roof with it.'

For a moment fear paralysed her, then she took two hesitant steps and stopped again. There was a creaking sound below her.

'Try to get to the sloping part,' he urged. 'Quickly!'

The wind teased her hair out to stream behind her and there was a grating sound from below her feet.

As the part where she was standing shook beneath her feet, she flung herself forward to the sloping part.

'Flatten yourself against it, Deborah!'

She pressed her body against the tiles as the tiles shifted behind her.

'Stay there.'

The creaking and grating noises stopped.

'Push yourself up a little and edge along the gutter,' he ordered. 'Slowly. Try not to move jerkily.'

Again she obeyed him, trusting him instinctively. It seemed to take a very long time and if it hadn't been for his low voice, encouraging and coaxing, she might not have had the courage to move again. But that voice was there, drawing her onwards. She didn't look sideways, just edged along carefully.

Behind her the rotten timbers were still groaning and once he shouted, 'Stop!' as they subsided again.

Then the slow movement began again.

When a timber snapped suddenly behind her, she moaned, but he reached out, holding the door frame with one hand and grabbed her upper arm. As he dragged her swiftly into the attic doorway, another piece of timber cracked like a whip, tiles shifted and with a sob she clung to him until the noise had stopped.

'It's all right,' he murmured into her hair. 'We're safe here. It's only that part of the roof that's rotten. Shh. It's all right.' For a moment he simply held her shaking body close, then he pushed her to arm's length and demanded harshly, 'Whatever got into you to come up here?'

She was hurt by his tone. 'I had nothing to do and thought I would enjoy the view. Mr Elkin said—'

'*Elkin?* What did he say?'

'He told me about the roof walk this morning, said there was a beautiful view from up here.'

'So he suggested you come up here?'

She considered that for a moment, then shook her head. 'No. He spoke about the roof walk, that's all. Modern houses don't have them. I was bored and interested to see one.' She shuddered again. 'Only I hadn't realised it would be so dangerous.' Her voice wobbled on the words and she began to shiver again as she thought of how close to death she had come.

With an inarticulate murmur Matthew folded her close and held her until the shaking had stopped. She clung to him gratefully.

'You could have been killed,' he said throatily. 'Dear God, you could so easily have been killed.'

She looked up at him, mute still with reaction, and he pressed a kiss on her forehead.

'But you weren't,' he said gently. 'And I'm glad of that.'

She was about to reply when they heard footsteps running up the stairs. Both turned instinctively to see who it was.

'Stay there!' Matthew called.

Elkin appeared at the top of the stairs, but did not move forward. 'Merry told me what had happened. Are you all right, Cousin Deborah?'

'No thanks to you,' Matthew snarled. 'Why did you set the idea of the roof walk in her mind?'

'I was telling her about the house. And if you're hinting what I think you are, you'd have more reason to see her dead than I would!' Elkin snapped back. 'You know now that you left it too late to win Ralph's favour and made a mistake marrying her – I've *seen* his will, don't forget, and it leaves everything to me. So now you wish to rid yourself of a burden.'

He turned to Deborah and moderated his voice, 'But I do blame myself in part. I'm sorry I even mentioned the roof walk. How could I know that part of the roof was in such a poor state? What a godsend the girl saw you and shouted a warning!'

Deborah could only stare from one to the other. Was there any truth in these accusations and counter-accusations? No, of course not. A very little thought reassured her. Matthew knew she was to inherit and had been a willing partner in the marriage, so why should he want her dead? And yet Elkin didn't know she was to inherit, so had no reason whatsoever for trying to kill her. It had been an accident, that was all, just an unfortunate accident.

Hadn't it?

Matthew moved away from her to study the outer door. 'Did *you* unlock it, Deborah? I gave strict orders that it was to be kept locked at all times.'

'It was already open.'

'Did you take the key out?'

She wondered why he was going on about that when all she wanted to do was get away from Elkin and spend a few minutes recovering. 'No. There was none.'

'Now how can that be?' Elkin wondered, his voice heavy with innuendo. 'Who could have taken it?'

'Who indeed? If we could trouble you to move from the stairs?' Matthew drew her with him. 'Come on, love. You'll want to rest until you're more yourself.'

Deborah managed a tremulous smile. 'I'll be all right soon. I just need a minute or two to compose myself. After all, I wasn't hurt.' But for all her brave words, she was still shaking and was glad to lay her hand on Matthew's shoulder and allow him to guide her slowly down the narrow stairs.

On the servants' floor Merry was waiting, her face lighting up as she saw Deborah. 'Eh, I'm that glad you're all right, Mrs Pascoe! I fair near died when I saw you standing up there.'

'I'm fine, really I am. But thank you for warning me. I think you saved my life.'

Matthew's voice still had a sharp edge to it. 'Mrs Pascoe would appreciate a tea tray in the library now and no doubt you have plenty of work to keep you busy, preparing for tomorrow, Merry.'

She left without a word, casting him a reproachful glance for his sharp tone as she turned away.

He took Deborah down to the library and sat with her on the sofa to wait for the refreshments, his arm curled loosely round her shoulders. She appreciated that, still needing the comfort of his presence.

Elkin followed them, throwing himself on a chair opposite to sprawl at ease and watch them with that cold gaze of his. They couldn't talk privately, but when she glanced sideways at her husband, he gave her a half-smile and she felt instantly reassured.

At the sight of that exchange the face of the man opposite them turned into a bitter mask, as if he hated the pair of them. It made her wonder suddenly what she would have done if Ralph Jannvier had asked her to marry Elkin. She didn't think she could have done it. Something inside her instinctively shrank from even touching his hand.

On that thought she almost reached out to clasp Matthew's hand, but stopped herself. Maybe he wouldn't want such a demonstration of her vulnerability in front of Elkin. She thought she could trust her husband, yes, of course she could.

But who had unlocked the door to the roof? And why? Surely no one would want her dead?

6

Not until Elkin left them did Matthew leave Deborah's side. 'I have to send for the local carpenter to replace the rotten roof timbers. Will you be all right?'

'Yes, of course.' But she missed him and was relieved when he re-joined her just before one o'clock.

Soon afterwards, Mrs Elkin came downstairs, assisted by Elkin. The older woman was walking hesitantly, as if unsure whether her legs would support her. She was pale enough to lend credence to the idea that she wasn't well, but it seemed to Deborah that she was nervous more than anything. She sat with them in the parlour waiting for dinner to be served, hardly opening her mouth. And whenever she did respond to a remark, she would flick a quick, anxious glance towards her son as if to check that she had not said the wrong thing.

His face remained bland and his remarks were all of the latest fashions in London or gossip about London figures of fashion of whom the rest of them knew nothing and cared even less.

But his eyes were watchful, Deborah thought, and his gaze moved from his mother to her then across to Matthew, as if he didn't trust any of them.

At two o'clock they were served a generous but plain dinner by Mrs Simley. Only the gentlemen did it justice, however. Deborah still seemed to hear the thumps of the pieces of masonry falling to the ground and the roof timbers cracking. Although she insisted she was all right, she felt on edge.

Matthew's servant, Jem, rode across the rear of the garden to the stables just as the meal was over. After he'd dismounted they could see him carrying a pair of saddlebags towards the house.

'Where has *he* been?' Elkin demanded. 'And who gave him permission to leave Marymoor when he should be working?'

'I did, because he works for me, not for the estate. I *do* have other interests than the farm.' Matthew spoke indifferently, not even watching as Jem vanished in the direction of the kitchen.

'Oh yes, I keep forgetting that you own a common alehouse!' Elkin laughed scornfully. 'Your husband will be able to support you in style, Cousin Deborah. I hope you enjoy the prospect of serving ale to ploughboys!'

'I don't disdain any honest work,' she said quietly, forcing herself to eat something, she could not have said what.

Elkin scowled at her and addressed himself to his food once again.

His mother laid down her knife and fork with a sigh. 'I find I'm not very hungry today. I feel a little – nauseous.'

When Matthew had finished eating, he looked at Deborah. 'If you've finished your meal, my dear, I'd like a private word with you.'

As she followed him outside, she couldn't help letting out a sigh of relief to be away from Elkin.

'Bear up. Only another day and we'll be shut of them for ever, because they live close enough to get home before dark. After that I shan't allow any Elkin into this house again. Now, I have something to show you, something pleasant, I hope, for a change.' He led the way, taking the stairs two at a time and she followed more sedately.

On their bed they found the saddlebags Jim had carried into the house.

'They're for you. Open them,' Matthew waved one hand in their direction, looking expectant.

Wondering what this was about, she unbuckled the first one, to find a bundle wrapped in a piece of plain linen. Inside was some silky material and when she shook it out, she found an open robe in black silk with a trained overskirt.

'I hope it fits you,' he said.

She held it against herself, looking down at it in delight, then up at him with a smile. 'It's beautiful!' The stomacher and petticoat were in figured black silk to contrast with the heavy silk of the main garment, and there was a black-edged handkerchief in delicate white muslin to fill in the rather low neckline. The skirts were full enough to support modest hoops and when she turned to the second saddlebag, she found a short linen petticoat with cane hoops sewn into it and another full-length petticoat in fine lawn.

Tears came into her eyes. 'Thank you.'

Matthew's voice was gentle and understanding. 'I thought you would wish to be suitably clad tomorrow when you meet some of our neighbours after the funeral, though I cannot guarantee these will fit properly, so you may have to alter them.'

'I doubt they'll need much attention.' Half-completed mourning wear was always in stock at dressmakers', ready for finishing quickly at need, and she had already noticed that the back of the bodice had a cunning placket for adjusting the size when lacing the gown up. She stroked the material, a good heavy silk which would last for years.

'Aren't you going to try them on?' He leaned against the door jamb as if he intended to stay.

She blinked in shock as the air seemed to vanish from the room. *Get undressed in front of him?* 'I – I can't...' Her voice trailed away and she flushed.

He gave her a heavy, considering look that sent heat rushing to her cheeks, then turned his back to the room, arms folded. 'Hurry up.'

Feeling nervous, she tried to untie the laces at the back of her bodice and in her haste got them into a tangle. The more she tried to loosen them, the bigger the knots seemed to grow. 'I – can you help me, please, Matthew?'

He turned round to stare at her, not as Elkin had been staring, but as a man looks at a woman he desires, with a warm light in his eyes. Aware of her half-bared shoulders and chest, she blushed even more hotly as she explained, 'It's the laces. They're in a knot.'

When he came across to stand behind her, his breath was warm on her shoulder blades, and she felt delicious shivers run round her body as he began to work on the laces.

'Stand still. I see my way.'

His fingers were as warm as his breath and she closed her eyes, trying not to show that she was responding instinctively to his closeness.

With a soft laugh he loosened the laces and patted her shoulder, but didn't move away. 'I make a fine lady's maid, do I not?'

She turned, letting out a shaky breath but saying nothing. He took a step away from her, his voice becoming harsher. 'There. Your ordeal is over, madam wife. I shan't need to touch you again.'

She could not bear him to think she disliked his touch. 'It wasn't an ordeal to have you touch me, Matthew. I'm just a – a little shy of – I've never…'

His expression softened again. 'You have nothing to fear from me, Deborah.' Moving slowly, as if trying not to frighten her, he drew her towards him. She knew instinctively that if she protested he would let her go, but she didn't want to protest. In fact, as his head bent towards her, she raised her lips to meet his.

His mouth was firm on hers and the kiss seemed to go on endlessly, till the world receded into the distance and everything felt to be floating around them. She hadn't guessed a kiss could feel so wonderful.

As he raised his head, she clutched him to keep her balance. But his lips were coming closer again and his second kiss was far more disturbing, for it seemed to make her whole body tingle and she found herself responding to it in a way that surprised her, pressing her body against his, giving back touch for touch. When he pulled away she couldn't help making a soft protesting noise in her throat, for she didn't want the embrace to end.

'I'm glad you don't dislike my touch,' he said, with a warm smile. 'For I intend to do more than kiss you as soon as this mess is settled. You're a bonny lass, Deborah, and I'm glad Ralph brought you here to be my wife.'

'I'm glad you're my husband.' She smiled up at him, then as he took a step backwards, she realised her unlaced bodice had slipped, uncovering one breast. Flushing hotly, she pulled the bodice up, not knowing what to say or do.

'No shame to let your husband see a body as fair as yours,' he said.

She noticed his breathing had deepened, knew she had affected him – and was suddenly fiercely glad of it! For he had certainly affected her.

His tone changed. 'But this isn't the time to take matters further, so let's see how the new clothes fit, eh?'

This time he didn't even pretend to look away, so she slipped on the hooped petticoat and tied the strings carefully at the side of the waist. The under-petticoat came next, then she turned her back as she adjusted the bodice. Finally the upper petticoat and the open robe which revealed an inverted V shape of figured silk at the front. She smoothed the material with one hand, enjoying its softness and admiring its lustre, wishing there was a mirror in the room. Turning to face him again, she spread her arms wide to invite inspection.

He smiled and nodded approval. 'You look very elegant and it doesn't seem a bad fit at all. A little long, perhaps.'

'It's the finest gown I've ever owned,' she confessed. Even when her father had been alive, money hadn't been plentiful and she and her mother had had to buy cheaply, sew their garments themselves, and choose practical, hard-wearing materials not silk. 'Thank you so much.'

Another of those long moments elapsed, where more seemed to be said without words than with them. They stood motionless, eyes searching eyes, then he said in puzzlement. 'The finest?'

She nodded. 'My father was a gambler. *He* needed fine clothes to make a good impression. My mother and I made do with anything decent.'

His eyes were understanding. 'That must have been hard.'

She shrugged. 'Sometimes. But we managed. Nothing was ever as hard as the past year under my uncle's rule. At least my father loved us in his own way.'

'I hope life will never be that hard again for you. We'll buy you other clothes with Ralph's money, clothes that suit your station in life, but these are my wedding gift to you, bought with my own money.'

'Thank you. But I don't have anything to give you in return.' She could feel herself flushing. 'I have very little money. My Uncle Walter gave us only enough to buy the bare necessities.'

'You yourself are gift enough for any man,' he said, then took a deep breath, stepped backwards and became very brisk. 'Well, then, if you'll put on your other clothes we'll go out for that walk, eh? I shall look forward to surprising Elkin with your elegance tomorrow.'

She felt a little hurt by his final remark. Was it the only reason he'd bought them, to spite Elkin? No, surely not. But a shadow of doubt still remained. Matthew Pascoe wasn't an easy man to read.

It was very difficult being married to a stranger.

—

The funeral took place the following day and although Deborah naturally didn't attend the interment with the male mourners, she did wear the new silk dress and see the surprise in Elkin's eyes as she came down the stairs. Satisfied with his reaction and delighted by the admiring look in her husband's eyes, she went to sit with Mrs Elkin in the threadbare drawing room where they would receive any neighbours who chose to pay their respects afterwards.

She had hoped to engage the older woman in conversation, perhaps find out more about her enigmatic son, but

Mrs Elkin responded to her questions in monosyllables and introduced no topics of conversation.

Since the churchyard was in the nearby village, the burial didn't take long. Matthew was first to return, riding in Ralph's old, rattletrap carriage, followed by another modest vehicle containing three gentlemen, neighbours who dressed like sensible men, not fops. He introduced Deborah to them and she found them pleasant enough, but they clearly didn't know what her position was to be, so they made no reference to their wives' calling on her.

The next to arrive were the parson, doctor and lawyer, whom she had met before, all riding in the latter's vehicle. Elkin's carriage brought up the rear of the small procession and disgorged only him, exquisitely dressed, from expensive tye-wig with three side curls (how many wigs did he own, for heaven's sake?) to silver-buckled shoes. His black coat had ridiculously large buttoned-back cuffs that nearly reached his elbows and a full skirt stiffened by whalebone, while his waistcoat was of embroidered grey velvet. But to her, the elegance was marred by the look of condescension on his face and she couldn't help wondering where he had found the money for such finery, if he had been reduced to stealing some of the silver on his last visit.

She offered the guests wine and light refreshments, taking it upon herself to play hostess, which brought a frown from Elkin. The three neighbours looked more at ease as they chatted quietly to Matthew, seeming to respect him. They were monosyllabic with Elkin. After a single glass of wine apiece, they made their farewells.

Neighbours, she thought wonderingly. I shall have neighbours now, shall not need to move on, may even be able to make friends once the will is read and we are settled here. Modest ambitions, but they'd been out of her reach while her father was alive, and even more so under her Uncle Walter's strict control of their comings and goings.

And so will my mother! she added mentally. Perhaps now Isabel would lose that dreadful vagueness that had so worried Bessie and Deborah. Yes, she thought looking round, the risk of answering Ralph's summons had been well worth it.

As soon as the neighbours' carriage had driven away, Mr Downie cleared his throat to gain everyone's attention. 'May I suggest that I read the will now?'

Elkin, who had taken it upon himself to see the neighbours to the door, sat down beside his mother, eagerness showing in every line of his body, though his expression was calm. Matthew came to stand behind Deborah's chair with his hands resting lightly on her shoulders.

'I have here the last will and testament of my late client, Ralph Jannvier,' Mr Downie hesitated, then said in a rush, 'dated the nineteenth day of June, 1760, and signed on his deathbed.'

Elkin jerked to his feet. 'Then it's a damned forgery. I have a copy of his will, his *real* will.' He strode forward. 'Show that to me!'

Matthew pressed Deborah's shoulders in a signal to remain where she was and as she nodded her understanding, he moved forward to stand beside Mr Downie. The lawyer was holding the piece of parchment with its single paragraph and the black slash of a signature showing clearly at the end.

Elkin snatched it from him and studied it, rigid with fury. 'It *is* a forgery! No one writes a will one paragraph long.'

Mr Downie was spluttering with dismay, so Mr Normanbie stepped forward to join him. 'Indeed, it is not, sir! I myself witnessed Ralph Jannvier's signature three nights ago.'

Matthew nipped the will out of the enraged man's fingers and handed it back to the lawyer.

Elkin stared from one to the other, his eyes blazing with fury. He opened his mouth as if to say something, then snapped it shut again.

'If you gentlemen will please resume your seats, I shall continue to read the will.'

Deborah felt sorry for Mr Downie, whose hand was shaking as he again raised the piece of parchment. Matthew had remained near him and she felt the lack of her husband's solid presence behind her. When she glanced sideways towards Elkin, who had flung himself down on the sofa again, she saw that his mother, who was sitting beside him, had a look of near terror on her face and was clasping her hands so tightly in her lap they looked like bloodless claws.

Mr Downie took a deep breath. 'The will is very simple, ladies and gentlemen: I, Ralph Jannvier, being of sound mind, leave everything of which I stand possessed to my great-niece, Deborah, née Jannvier, now married to my natural son, Matthew Pascoe. God grant them a long and happy life together.' He coughed and cleared his throat as he looked up. 'That is all.'

'I shall contest the will,' Elkin snapped.

'On what grounds?'

Matthew's voice was calm, but Deborah could see how watchful his eyes were.

'Undue persuasion brought to bear on a dying man. As Ralph's nearest relative—'

This time it was Dr Lethbury who interrupted, drawing himself up to his full five feet six inches and bristling with icy dignity. 'I resent that slur on my professional behaviour, sir. I would never allow anyone to coerce one of my dying patients into doing anything. You will find no case to answer.' The look Elkin gave him was so threatening he added quickly, 'In fact, fearing there might be some questions about a deathbed will, I have already made a written deposition before the nearest magistrate, stating that Ralph Jannvier was in full possession of his faculties right until the moment of his death. Which is the solemn truth.'

Elkin swung round to stare at Matthew. 'You wasted no time.' His expression was so malevolent Deborah could fully understand why her husband had deemed it wise to keep silent until now to protect her. With a chill she realised Matthew was right: he and she were both in danger from this man.

Light as a whisper came another thought: she couldn't bear it if anything happened to her husband, not now, just when personal happiness and a settled home life seemed within her grasp.

The lawyer cleared his throat and spoke again. 'In point of fact, you are not Ralph Jannvier's closest relative, Mr Elkin. Mrs Pascoe has that honour.' Mr Downie bowed to her. 'But even if she were not, she would still be the true beneficiary, because my late client had every right – *every right in the world!* – to leave his property where he wished. Nor will you be able to overturn the will because everything was done with due care and attention to legal processes, and there are three of us to bear witness that Matthew Pascoe in no way coerced his father to sign.

Indeed, there was obvious affection between the two of them.'

Elkin made a sound of disgust in his throat.

Life never let you do things easily, Deborah thought sadly, watching them. Something as wonderful as being left Marymoor had already been marred by Elkin's reactions.

Matthew broke the silence by saying coldly, 'I'd be grateful if you'd leave the house at once, Elkin. You've plenty of time to get home before dark.'

'It's getting late and my mother is frail. Do you really intend to turn us out?'

Mrs Elkin, who had been standing there with a look of sheer terror on her face, let out a whimper and muffled her face in her handkerchief. 'Anthony, perhaps—'

'I shall not let them harm you, mother. You know how poor your health is.'

She looked at him, shivered and turned to Deborah. 'So sorry. I don't feel at all – at all—' She slid to the ground in a faint.

Deborah shot a quick glance at Matthew, then knelt down to check the older woman's pulse, which was thready and irregular. She was sure this was a ploy, but the poor woman was so white she couldn't find it in her heart to turn her out. 'I think we must let her stay until morning,' she said in a low voice.

Matthew's face was grim and it was a moment before he responded with an equally quiet, 'Very well.'

Deborah sat back on her heels. 'If someone can send for her maid, we'll take her up to her room as soon as she recovers.'

'I'll carry her. She's prone to these fainting fits, I'm afraid, and needs to lie quietly for a few hours.' Elkin stepped forward, bending over his mother, his face only inches away from Deborah's. 'You'll not remain Mistress of Marymoor,' he whispered.

His expression hadn't changed, his lips had scarcely moved and his voice had been so low that no one else could have heard it. She couldn't move for shock as she watched him scoop up the frail, elderly woman in his arms, behaving calmly, as if he had not just made a threat to her life. She didn't feel calm, however, and pressed one hand involuntarily to her breast, for her heart was beating fast with sudden fear. Yes, fear. Elkin might dress like a fop, but there was a strength beneath the fine clothes. And an evil purpose.

Unaware of what had happened, Matthew opened the door and Elkin paused for a moment as the two men's gazes met, neither attempting to hide his true feelings. Then he moved on, carrying his mother with exaggerated care.

Deborah thought she saw Mrs Elkin's eyes flicker open and close quickly. With a shudder she turned back to the room, relieved at how normal it all seemed now Elkin had left.

The lawyer was shuffling his papers together. Dr Lethbury was speaking to the parson in a low voice and Matthew was still standing in the hall, just outside. He looked as if he were carved from stone and didn't move until she walked across the room to ring the handbell.

Mrs Simley answered the bell herself, looking round for Elkin and seeming surprised not to see him.

'Mrs Elkin has been taken ill,' Deborah told her. 'Can you please send her maid up to her bedchamber.'

'Just a minute.' Matthew came across to join them. 'You may also wish to know, Mrs Simley, that your former master left everything he owned to my wife, who is now mistress of Marymoor. And since you're so fond of Elkin that you must needs forget where your loyalties lie, when he and his mother leave tomorrow, you and your husband may leave with them.'

The housekeeper gasped and clutched one hand to her ample bosom. She said nothing, but the look she threw at them was filled with hatred.

Another person who bears us ill-will, Deborah thought wearily.

'Don't forget. You're to leave tomorrow morning,' Matthew repeated.

'And please send Merry to see me,' Deborah called after the housekeeper.

Mr Downie came forward to join them. 'I think I can leave you to explain to your wife exactly what she has inherited, can I not, Mr Pascoe?'

Matthew nodded. 'Yes, of course. And thank you for all your help.'

'I was fond of Ralph. He was more than a client; he was a dear, dear friend.' He bowed to Deborah. 'I shall take my leave of you for now, Mrs Pascoe, but if you or your husband need my help...'

The parson and doctor left with him and as they drove away, Merry came in to clear away the wine glasses.

She looked so downcast that Deborah asked, 'Did Mrs Simley tell you what's happened?'

'No, ma'am.'

'Matthew and I have inherited Marymoor, not Mr Elkin.'

Merry let out a stifled shriek, clapping one hand to her mouth then beaming at them. 'Eh, I wish you well of it, I do that.'

Deborah smiled back, glad of the young woman's simple friendliness after the tensions of the past hour. 'Mr and Mrs Simley will be leaving tomorrow, but I hope you'll stay on to work for us. It'll be a bit difficult at first till we've hired other staff, but I'm not too proud to dirty my hands, so it won't all be left to you.'

Matthew came to stand beside them. 'I know what a good worker you are, Merry, and have told my wife so.'

The girl's eyes filled with tears. 'I'll be happy to stay, sir, madam. Eh, to think of it!' She bustled out with the laden tray, still beaming.

'Well, one person is pleased, at least,' he commented. 'Are you not?'

'I shall feel better once Elkin has left. Until then I shall keep careful watch on his comings and goings.' He looked at Deborah very seriously. 'Stay near me at all times until he's left.' A minute later, he said thoughtfully, 'And I think we'll keep a careful watch tonight. Who knows to what lengths that man is prepared to go?'

'But he has no right to the house now. Surely once his anger has cooled down, he'll realise that?'

'*He* has no right to it. But *you* do. If anything were to happen to me, you'd be at even greater risk for as the only other relative he'd be your heir – or he could obtain Marymoor by marrying you.'

She remembered Elkin's words, 'You'll not remain Mistress of Marymoor.' That was what he'd meant. 'I could never marry that man.'

'People can be forced into marriage.' He shook his head regretfully. 'I wish we hadn't sent for your mother. I'd like to send you away somewhere safe until—'

She didn't hesitate. 'I'd not go! My place is here now, with you.'

He gave her a wry smile. 'I knew you'd say that. But I'd take you away by force if I had to, to save your life.' His voice softened. 'And not only because of the money. There is no time now, but afterwards...'

'Afterwards,' she echoed, adding her own promise to his.

It was so easy to love him. She started to move away, then stopped to marvel at what she had just realised – she loved him. So quickly. So easily. And though he might not love her in the same way, he wasn't indifferent to her, she was quite sure of that.

–

When they went up to bed that night after a tense and mainly silent dinner in Elkin's company, Matthew made no attempt to get undressed. 'Jem and I will be keeping watch tonight,' he told his wife. 'I've had word from John Thompson at the inn that there's a stranger in the village, who's been sitting drinking with Elkin, their heads close together like conspirators. We need to find out who he is, what they're planning.' He looked at her steadily. 'You're not to leave this room tonight, not for any reason. Promise me.'

She nodded agreement.

'Lock the door after me, then remove the key. I have another.' He smiled briefly. 'In fact I have keys to all the rooms and if Elkin leaves the house, I intend to search his bedchamber.'

Danger seemed to swirl round them again as if the very shadows held menace. She had to bite back a plea to him to take care.

He patted her shoulder. 'Open the door to no one but me or Jem, Deborah, whatever anyone tells you. *Whatever they say!*'

Again she nodded.

When he had gone, she was left with the flickering candle and the sure knowledge that she couldn't possibly sleep, so sat upright on the bed waiting for she knew not what.

She must have dozed eventually, however, because she jerked awake as some small noise disturbed the stillness of the night. She glanced quickly round the room, lit only by moonlight now, for the candle had burned down. She was still alone. What had woken her? Slipping from the bed she went to stand by the door, wondering if it was Matthew coming back.

The handle of the door turned – silently, slowly, making not a sound.

Matthew would not need to be so quiet!

She watched the handle hardly daring to breathe. It stopped moving as the person on the other side found the door locked, then turned back just as slowly and carefully.

She heard only the faintest of sounds as someone crept away. Was it Elkin? Well, who else could it be? If he had wanted something honestly he would have knocked, so what had he intended to do if he found the door unlocked? *You'll not remain Mistress of Marymoor.* The words came back to her again.

She shivered and stayed where she was, continuing to listen, but hearing only the usual night noises. She jumped in shock as an owl hooted in the distance then told herself not to be silly and went to sit on the bed again. For a while she struggled desperately to stay awake, then decided she might as well lie down and rest, at least.

When she awoke, the first light of dawn was turning the room into a grey blur. Beside her, Matthew lay sleeping peacefully. She hadn't even heard him come in, though she was usually a light sleeper.

She sighed and relaxed into sleep again. With him there she felt safe.

–

The two elderly fugitives spent the night with a packman and his wife in a shepherd's shelter on the moors. It stayed fine and once again Isabel Jannvier slept soundly to wake looking rosy and refreshed. It was Bessie who was feeling the strain, for she was a buxom woman and not used to walking so far.

'We could give you a ride into Rochdale for sixpence each,' the packman's wife said as they shared a simple breakfast. 'The baskets are mostly empty and 'twouldn't take much to rearrange them. Our horses don't go fast, but they're steady. Better than walking.'

'That would be delightful,' Isabel said at once. 'I haven't ridden for years, but I'm sure I haven't forgotten how to.'

So they bumped along on the sturdy little packhorses and Bessie listened in amazement as her mistress held a lively conversation with the rough-looking woman. Mrs Isabel didn't seem at all concerned about what they were doing, but Bessie couldn't help worrying. It had just occurred to her that they'd both left most of their worldly possessions behind. Would Mr Lawrence destroy them out of spite? Would they ever get them back? They'd only been able to bring a few necessities with them.

And what had happened to Deborah? If she sent a message to Newgarth now, there would be no one to receive it except her uncle. They could only hope that she'd still be at Marymoor.

Gradually the mild sunny day lulled Bessie and she let herself bounce along, enjoying the fine vistas as they started to make their way down towards Rochdale. Funny old way of travelling, this, but Walter Lawrence would be hard put to follow them, she was sure.

They'd better be careful once they got to Rochdale, though. Conceal who they were. Behave circumspectly. She must impress that on her mistress.

If he heard where they were, they would undoubtedly find themselves in trouble.

7

When Matthew awoke he saw Deborah lying on her side, looking at him and smiled. 'You're a sound sleeper. You didn't even stir when I came into the bedroom.'

She pulled a wry face at him. 'That's because I stayed awake a long time in case you needed me.'

'Jem and I are quite capable of keeping an eye on things, my dear. No one left the house or entered it during the night, I promise you.'

'But someone did creep along the landing and try the handle of our bedroom door.'

'They knocked?'

'No. Just turned the handle. They didn't speak, but must have made a noise coming here because something woke me and I went to stand by the door in case it was you returning. There was enough moonlight for me to see the door handling turning. I could also hear faint sounds, as if someone were creeping away again after they found it locked.'

He half-closed his eyes as he thought this through. 'Elkin could have seen us watching the outside of the house. You *must* be careful of him, Deborah.'

'Why were you watching the outside?'

'Because we thought he had an accomplice. There's a stranger staying in the village and Elkin sat drinking with him.' He took a step backwards. 'Perhaps you'd like to get up now? I'll wait for you on the landing.'

As soon as he'd left she got up and made a hurried toilette, dressing in the simple gown she'd brought with her.

When she went out to join him, he locked the bedchamber door. 'Let's go down and eat.'

Mrs Simley was nowhere to be seen.

'She's packing up her things,' Merry said apologetically. 'Shall I get you something?'

'I'll help you,' Deborah said.

Matthew watched her work with a half-smile on his face. 'You seem at home in a kitchen.'

'You know how small our house in Newgarth was.' She looked round. 'We'll eat in the dining room, I think. This table needs a good scrubbing.'

'We'll get someone in from the village to do that,' Matthew said firmly.

When they'd eaten their fill, he rang the handbell for Merry to clear the table.

'What's Seth Bailey doing?' he asked as she began to collect the pewter platters together.

'Sitting in the kitchen feeding his face and talking to Mr Simley.'

'And Mrs Simley?'

'Getting them all something to eat.'

'I think I'll go and speak to Bailey while his master's not around,' Matthew said abruptly and followed the maid back to the kitchen.

After the briefest of hesitations Deborah followed, stopping in the doorway to listen.

'What time does your master usually rise?' Matthew was asking.

Seth, a large man with a broken nose, stood up with obvious reluctance, casting him an unfriendly look. 'I never know, sir. I just wait till he rings. Not an early riser, Mr Elkin.'

The maid Denise came rushing down into the kitchen by the back stairs, squeaking in shock as she nearly bumped into Deborah. 'Oh, Mrs Pascoe, my mistress is very ill this morning. Please can the doctor be fetched? She keeps being sick and she has the flux. She thinks it's something she ate.'

'I'll come up and see her myself first. Though how it can be something she ate when the rest of us are fine, I don't know.'

'All I know is she's very ill, poor lady, and her not strong to begin with.' Denise noticed Seth scowling at her and shot him a frightened glance before edging back towards the servants' stairs.

Wondering at this, Deborah accompanied her to Mrs Elkin's room, using the nearby stairs to save time, not caring about her dignity. She found their guest in great distress, definitely not faking illness.

She came back down and reported this to Matthew. 'We'll have to call in Dr Lethbury, I'm afraid.'

'Damnation! We can't turn her away if she's really ill.'

She looked at him anxiously. 'This means Elkin will have to stay on as well, doesn't it?'

'Yes, I'm afraid so. You're sure this illness isn't being faked?'

'Absolutely sure. I saw her vomiting myself.'

He sighed. 'Then I'll send Jem for the doctor and ask him to come immediately. Excuse me a moment.'

Deborah walked across to stare out of the parlour window, admitting to herself that she was worried sick about Elkin staying on. It wouldn't take much to set him and Matthew at each other's throats, and they were both tall and strong so who knew which would win if it came to a fight?

Or Elkin might have some dirty tricks planned. In fact, the more she thought about it, the more sure he would have. He wasn't going to give up Marymoor without a struggle.

Well, neither was she.

-

Elkin rang for his servant half an hour later, but it was a while before he came down. He was dressed with his usual elegance and professed himself greatly upset that his mother was still ill. 'I do hope you're not going to turn us out?' he said to Deborah.

'No, of course not.'

'Is that man of mine around? I asked him to make sure there was some breakfast ready for me.'

'I'll ring.'

He was at the door already. 'No need. I'll go and say good morning to Mrs Simley while I'm in the kitchen. She's an old friend of mine, distantly related to Seth. I've known her since I was a boy.'

'She's upstairs packing.'

'Ah. I'd forgotten your husband dismissed her. Shall you turn her into the street or shall you need her services to look after your guests?'

As if he didn't know the answer to that, Deborah thought angrily. He was just mocking her, as usual.

'I believe she's come down now to join her husband.'

'I'll go and speak to them, ask them to stay on.' Deborah found the Simleys in the kitchen, sitting at one end of the table eating some bread and cheese.

'We're waiting for Mr Elkin,' Mrs Simley said, without waiting to be addressed.

'Mrs Elkin is ill. We need you to stay on for a day or two longer.'

The woman opened her mouth, clearly about to refuse, but a voice behind Deborah said softly, 'We'd be very grateful, Mrs Simley.'

There was another heavy silence, then the housekeeper said graciously, 'Well, since *you* ask me, Mr Elkin, I shall be happy to do so.'

Deborah could only accept this as calmly as she could manage. 'Thank you. I'll see that you're paid for the extra work. And now I'd like some polish and some rags.'

Merry got them for her and she went back to the small parlour, which she intended to use, rather than the larger drawing room.

A short time later Deborah heard voices in the hall. Tiptoeing to the door, she saw Elkin speaking to his man in a low voice near the door into the kitchen. Both had their backs to her. Standing very still she watched them, seeing the servant give his master a small silver flask, which Elkin slipped into the pocket of his fine brocade coat.

'When I've seen my mother, I'll stroll into the village.' Although he spoke quietly, his words carried clearly to the listener.

When he went up the stairs, Seth went back to the kitchen, so Deborah went out into the hall and walked quietly up the bottom few stairs, pausing where at the bend to listen. Upstairs she heard Denise trying to keep Elkin out of her mistress's room.

'Your mother's just fallen asleep, sir. Please let her rest a while.'

'Get out of my way, if you value your job!' he said with sudden acid in his normally drawling tone.

This was followed by a squeak of shock, as if he'd pushed the woman aside, and a door banging open. Then it banged shut again and Deborah could hear nothing else. But she stayed where she was, hoping to hear more and praying no one would come and catch her eavesdropping.

When the door above her opened again, she heard the sound of Mrs Elkin sobbing in the background, but didn't wait to hear more. Tiptoeing quickly back into the small parlour, she began to polish the wood panelling, a task which pleased her, because it seemed a positive step towards setting her house in order. As soon as the Simleys had gone, she would take stock of the larder and set the kitchen in order, she decided.

'Can the maid not see to that?' Elkin asked from behind her. 'It's demeaning to see a Jannvier doing menial work.'

Deborah jumped in shock, not having heard him come in. 'Merry has more than enough to do and the whole house has been let run down. Mrs Simley isn't good at her job.'

'And you *are* a good housekeeper?' His lip curled scornfully.

'Yes. And I'm not ashamed of it, either.'

'Fine mistress you'll make for a house like this!' he scoffed and swung on his heel. 'You'll be working in the dairy next or serving ale at your husband's inn.'

'If he asks me to, I will. There's no disgrace in earning an honest living.'

He made a scornful noise and left.

When she heard him go outside, she went to peep through the window. He was pacing up and down in front of the house, irritation in every line of his body. Sighing and wishing Matthew were around, she went back to the polishing, taking pride in bringing a sheen to the wood. Beeswax and elbow grease, as Bessie called it.

It helped to keep yourself occupied when you were worried sick about your husband's safety.

–

Dr Lethbury arrived an hour later. When Elkin went forward to greet him, ignoring Deborah, the doctor stepped back, snapping, 'It is my custom, sir, to deal with the mistress when I visit a female member of any household.'

'Mrs Pascoe knows nothing whatsoever about my mother!'

'She does own this house, though, and it would be greatly discourteous of me not to greet her first.'

Deborah smiled and moved out of the parlour to join them. 'Dr Lethbury. How kind of you to come so quickly.'

'Dear lady, it's my pleasure.' He made her a bow and suggested, 'Perhaps you would accompany me upstairs to see your guest?'

Elkin again stepped forward, this time going close enough to the doctor to loom over him in a threatening manner. 'It's *my* mother who is ill, so naturally it is *I* who will accompany you.'

He does it on purpose, Deborah decided. Uses his height and strength to browbeat people. For all his airs and graces, and his pretence of being a gentleman, he's an arrant bully.

The doctor puffed out his chest and glared at Elkin. 'I'm afraid, sir, that I prefer another lady to be present when examining a female patient. It isn't at all seemly for a son to be there when I'm examining his mother.'

Matthew appeared at the back of the hall, his skin flushed with fresh air and sunshine. 'Pray go upstairs with the good doctor, Deborah. Our *guest* can wait in the parlour with me.'

'This is outrageous!' Elkin snapped.

Why was he so angry about this? Deborah wondered as she led the way up the stairs. It hardly seemed worth making a fuss about.

The maid opened the door, her eyes going automatically to check that there was no one behind them. With a sigh of what sounded like relief she greeted the doctor, who approached the bedside.

'I hope you don't mind my being here, Mrs Elkin,' Deborah said.

'No. No, of course not.'

Deborah stood at the foot of the bed while the doctor questioned Mrs Elkin about her symptoms. The old lady looked white and frail, and was definitely not pretending to be ill.

'It's merely a summer flux,' Dr Lethbury pronounced in the end, his eyes much shrewder than his gentle words. 'I shall send my man to bring you a draught which will help greatly, I promise you, my dear lady, but you mustn't think of leaving your chamber until you are completely recovered. At our age we cannot take these reverses in health lightly.'

There was a heartfelt sigh of relief from the patient, who then looked across at Deborah and said in a faint voice, 'I'm sorry to be so troublesome, Mrs Pascoe.'

'You can't help it, Mrs Elkin. And your maid is doing most of the work of caring for you, after all, so it's no great trouble.'

'But you don't want us here.' She dabbed at her eyes with the edge of the sheet. 'Anthony is disappointed about Marymoor, and – and he can make things a bit uncomfortable sometimes when he's crossed.'

Deborah tried to think of a reassuring response, but couldn't find anything to say. Was Mrs Elkin trying to give her a warning? she wondered.

'The draught will be here within the hour,' Dr Lethbury said as he turned to leave.

Deborah noticed that the maid had taken hold of her mistress's hand and was patting it. The woman was hatchet-faced and surly, but clearly cared greatly for the old lady, which was good to see.

'Please don't worry about things,' she said from the doorway. 'Just try to rest and get better.'

But it worried her greatly to think of Elkin staying on at Marymoor for longer and she prayed the old lady would recover quickly.

–

When she came back inside after seeing the doctor on his way, there was no sign of Matthew. Elkin was alone in the small parlour, sipping a glass of wine, his long legs stretched out before him, his brow furrowed in thought. He hadn't seen her, so she tiptoed away and went into the kitchen instead to see what was happening about food that day.

She made a few changes to what Mrs Simley had planned, changes that were received with a scowl and deep breathing. After which, tired of fusses and botheration, Deborah went out through the back door to look for Matthew, breathing in the fresh air with relief, but looking up at the sky and wondering if rain were on its way.

She thought she heard voices near the stables, so went that way, then stopped in shock as the words sank in.

'Don't tell my wife about this, Jem.'

'Don't you think she should know, Matt lad?'

'No. Not yet, anyway. George isn't badly hurt and will take more care how he goes next time.'

Deborah stepped backwards, feeling as if she had moved on to quicksand. What did he mean *George isn't badly hurt?* She had been thinking that the young groom would have arrived in Newgarth by now, that her mother and Bessie would know she was well and would be starting to pack.

Matthew might be trying to keep bad news from her for her own good, but she would have preferred to hear the truth, however bad.

She hesitated, debating whether to go and confront her husband and demand to know what was happening. But just as she was preparing to do that, a hated voice spoke softly behind her, startling her, and the moment was lost.

'Enjoying the morning air, Cousin Deborah?'

Elkin walked up to her. He must have been watching her, seen her stop and listen! She made sure her voice was loud enough to be heard by Matthew and Jem. 'I'm looking for my husband and am far too busy to stroll about aimlessly, as you must surely realise.'

'Ah, yes. The fair châtelaine,' he drawled, 'taking possession of her new kingdom.'

'Is there any reason I should not do that?' she demanded.

'No.' He smiled. 'Enjoy your triumph while you can.'

Was he threatening her again? But before she could challenge him, she heard footsteps coming towards them.

'Ah, behold, your lord and master approaches,' Elkin drawled. 'I'm desolate that our pleasant chat is to be interrupted.'

Matthew frowned at these words, looking narrowly at Deborah, and she realised Elkin was deliberately trying to giving him the impression that they had been chatting for a while.

'I was taking a breath of fresh air when our guest joined me,' she said curtly, 'and now must return to my duties.' She exchanged glances with her husband, then turned on her heel and marched back to the house. She would speak to Matthew later about what she'd overheard.

'Will you tame her, do you think?' Elkin asked. 'There's more fire beneath that practical exterior than is immediately obvious. She's lovely when she's properly dressed. I wonder you can bear to see her clad like a maidservant – and working like one, too.'

'Some of us look beyond the clothes,' Matthew said shortly. 'And see no shame in honest toil. Enjoy your stroll.' He turned on his heel, his eyes going for a moment towards his wife, who was just disappearing into the house.

Elkin gave a short laugh. The fool really was fond of her. It was a weakness to bear in mind. 'Get on with your *work* while you can, oaf!' he muttered as he swung round to stare at the house, its grey-gold stone lit up by the morning sun. 'I shall *not* give up what is mine by right.'

Behind the barn, Matthew picked up the fork, then slung it down again so that it landed in the muck heap, tines firmly embedded, handle quivering. 'God damn the bastard! He's counting on the fact that we don't want to be seen throwing him out when his mother's so sick. But if he continues to taunt me, he may find how little I care about what people think.' It was only for Deborah's sake that he was paying attention to appearances – and because at least he could keep an eye on Elkin while he was at Marymoor.

Jem watched him sympathetically. 'His man's been nosing around the stables. I don't know what he expects to find here, though.'

'Well, keep an eye on him and I'll watch the master.' Matthew grunted and walked off. Not even to Jem could he say that what upset him most was to think of Deborah alone with Elkin. The idea of that scoundrel filling her ears with his lies made him want to grind his guest's face into the ground, then drag his wife off to the bedroom to make her his own in more than name. He should have woken her last night when he went to bed, had wanted to because she had looked so beautiful lying there in the moonlight.

But then he'd remembered how tired and sore she was from their ride through the night, and that she was a virgin. She deserved better than a tired fumble the first time they made love.

Had he been mistaken in her? Would she ally herself with Elkin against him? Was she impressed by fine clothes and fancy manners? No, surely not?

–

Elkin strolled on towards the village, hoping he had stirred up suspicion between that clod Pascoe and his wife, ignoring the stares and mutters from those he passed. Let them gape as much as they wanted. Gentlemen dressed with style and elegance, and he would not lower his standards to suit the villagers. What did he care about these yokels, who had never made him welcome here? It was the house and land that mattered. Without land you were nothing. And even if you bought land, it wasn't the same as inheriting it from your family. In his new life, he needed the status of landed gentry, hungered for it.

Would kill to get it, if that's what it took.

As he passed the inn, he saw Walter Lawrence's manservant, Chadding, come out, which suggested the man had been watching out of the window. Elkin slowed down and inclined his head in greeting, noting the bruise on the man's forehead with a grim smile. Seth said the fellow knew how to handle himself. His groom and Chadding had shared the money they'd taken from the young groom, which should keep them both happy for a while. As for the stable lad, he should be grateful they'd let him live.

Pascoe was stupid to send someone so young and inexperienced to fetch the old women. The young idiot had been easy to capture and rob.

'If you have a moment, sir, perhaps we could have another little chat?' Frank asked.

'Certainly. Walk on briskly and I'll meet up with you on the other side of the village. No need to show everyone that we're continuing to do business with one another.' Elkin went into the inn on the pretence of expecting a letter by the mail, but the dolt of an innkeeper showed him no respect, so he left again without ordering anything to drink. He sauntered down the street as if he hadn't a care in the world, smiling gently even though rage simmered within him – as it had done ever since that damned will was read.

The landlord watched him go and summoned his son with a snap of the fingers. 'Mr Pascoe wants to know what that fine gentleman does with himself when he comes into the village. Can you follow him without being seen, Sam lad? I daresay you'll win yourself a copper or two if you find out what Elkin is doing.'

Young Sam brightened up and left at once by the back door.

John Thompson went back to stand at the front of his inn and watch that peacock figure saunter away. You got them in every family, wrong 'uns. They were all glad Elkin hadn't inherited Marymoor House, because he'd not have made a good landlord.

–

The young groom spent the day lying down in Jem's room above the stables, nursing an aching head, a black eye and a sore spirit. George had been set upon by two rogues and robbed of all the money he was carrying just after he'd left the district, and the shame of that still smarted. Fine way that was to serve his new master.

Jem said you only learned to be careful by getting caught out. Well, George would know to take a lot more care next time. He couldn't imagine Jem Newton, a man he admired greatly, ever falling into an ambush so easily.

George had been so surprised he hadn't even given a good account of himself when two men jumped out at him, which added to his shame. Though he'd struck a blow or two, of course, and had heard one of them curse when his fist connected. But after that someone had hit him over the back of the head, the coward, and everything had turned black.

He'd not regained consciousness for a while, until the sun was quite low in the sky. Then he'd turned and made his way back on foot, to find that his horse had got home before him and Jem was pacing up and down behind the stables, worried sick.

But his master and Jem trusted him enough to send him off again tonight and he wouldn't let them down this time, he swore to himself. He'd find the two old ladies and bring them back safe, or die trying.

Jem peeped in a little later and saw that George's colour was better and he was sleeping soundly. If the matter weren't so serious, he'd smile at what had happened. It was a pity there wasn't an older man to send on this errand, but there were two old ladies who needed rescuing quickly, it seemed, and there were people who didn't want them rescuing. The whole situation was far more serious than anyone had realised.

He saddled a horse and chose his moment carefully, when the folk at the big house were eating supper and even that Seth was sitting stuffing himself in the kitchen like the pig he was. He walked the animal out to the stream and tethered it to a convenient tree. George could set off from here during the night without waking anyone in the house or village.

Like his master Jem didn't believe the attack had happened by sheer chance. Masked men didn't suddenly appear from the bushes and drag a young man off his horse near Marymoor. This wasn't London, after all. He reckoned someone had known George was on an errand for his new master and had set out to stop him. Which made him think immediately of Seth.

And the stranger at the inn was sporting a bruise on his cheek today, young Sam had told him when he brought a message from his father, so likely the stranger had been the second robber.

He and Matthew hadn't told anyone what had happened, but Jem was worried about his master's safety. Elkin had brought one ruffian with him, planted another in the village. How many men did he have at his disposal? Even a strong man like Matthew couldn't fight off several others.

And anyone could be shot at from a distance.

–

Deborah sat up in bed, an old shawl she'd found in Ralph's room around her shoulders, waiting for her husband to come up to bed. It seemed a very long time.

She'd checked on Mrs Elkin before retiring and found the maid a trifle more helpful this time. But the old lady still seemed afraid to speak to her. However, the doctor's draught was helping, so Deborah was hopeful that the Elkins would be able to leave soon.

When she heard footsteps she leaned forward, but they lacked Matthew's briskness and sure enough, they stopped at Elkin's door.

It was a while before her husband came up to bed.

'You're still awake, then,' he said as he set down his candlestick.

'Yes. I wanted to talk to you.'

'Oh?'

'I wasn't walking out with Elkin today,' she said bluntly. 'He followed me. Before he joined me, I overheard you and Jem talking. Matthew, what happened to George? I thought he'd have reached Newgarth by now.'

He sighed and sat down on the bed. No avoiding telling her, then, but the information would only add to her worries. 'He was attacked and robbed.'

She gasped and stared at him. 'A highwayman? Near Marymoor?'

He shrugged. 'Who knows? We haven't had any attacks round here before, though there have been several over Rochdale way.'

'Who knew George was going?'

'Half the village, I suppose. We didn't make any secret of it, though we told him not to say exactly where.'

She was silent. 'Then my mother's been at the mercy of my uncle for several days. And he'll have been in a foul mood.'

'I'm sorry. George is leaving again tonight. Secretly. He'll fetch her back in a day or two.'

She nodded. After all, her uncle couldn't stop his sister leaving Newgarth. Could he?

'Are you still stiff?' he asked.

'A little. Nothing to worry about.'

'And how's Mrs Elkin?'

'Somewhat better.'

'Good. Maybe we can get rid of them tomorrow.'

He began to take his clothes off, putting on a nightshirt, then easing into bed beside her. She was hoping he would take her in his arms, kiss her – maybe seal their marriage. But he only sighed and slid down under the covers.

Within a minute or two he was breathing deeply. He seemed to fall asleep very easily. She felt tears come into her eyes. Was he so indifferent to her?

When he heard her breathing deepen, Matt stifled a sigh. It was hard to pretend indifference with such a lovely young woman lying beside him – and that woman his wife! His body was crying out for her, and his spirit was, too. He was growing more fond of her each day. A woman after his own heart, Deborah.

He eased himself into a more comfortable position and waited for sleep.

–

In the middle of the night, Jem woke George with food and a glass of ale and took him to where the horse was patiently waiting.

'Take care how you go this time, lad.'

George nodded, his young face serious in the moonlight. 'I'll die before I fail again, Jem.'

'Don't you dare get yourself killed. Just do what you've been asked carefully. Mrs Pascoe is worried about her mother. But you should stay out of the way of her uncle, if you can, and whatever you do, tell him nothing and offer him no incivility. He's a nasty type, by all accounts.'

So George trotted off into the darkness, burning with determination to do better this time, while Jem made his way slowly and carefully back to the stables, where a fellow he trusted was waiting for him, eager to earn extra money by keeping watch for them that night.

–

George arrived in Newgarth at eleven o'clock in the morning, having travelled through the night and pushed on as fast as his horse could manage. He made his way straight to the cottage on the green, which had been described to him, and knocked on the front door. While he waited for an answer he kept his eyes open. People had stared at him open-mouthed as he crossed the green.

Why? And an old woman had stopped to watch when he tied up his horse outside the cottage.

But no one had come near him. Why not? Normally people exchanged greetings with strangers and asked their business.

When there was no answer he knocked again and this time heard footsteps shuffling towards the door. An old man opened it and scowled at him.

'Yes?'

'I'm looking for Mrs Jannvier.'

'She isn't here.'

'Is this her house?'

'Used to be. Isn't any more.'

'Well, how can I find her?'

The man shrugged. 'How should I know? You'll have to go and ask Mr Lawrence. He's her brother.'

George backed away, puzzled. He had instructions to avoid the landowner, if possible. After standing outside for a moment, he took hold of the reins and led his horse across to the inn. The poor beast was tired and would be the better for a feed and rest, as would he.

Ross Tucker hadn't failed to note the arrival of a stranger, or where he went. He chose to serve the young man himself. 'Were you looking for Mrs Jannvier?' he asked.

George studied his companion. An open face, eyes that didn't flinch from yours. 'Yes. Do you know where she is?'

'I could probably find out.' He went to bring back a tankard of ale and set it down before the young man, choosing to approach his subject obliquely while he assessed the newcomer. There had been such goings-on in the village in the past few days! Strangers riding off with young women. Old women sneaking off secretly without telling anyone where they were going. Well, most of the villagers, including Ross, were on Mrs Jannvier's side against Mr Lawrence, though they didn't dare show that, of course. What sort of man talked about his sister being deranged, about locking her away in a lunatic asylum, as Mr Lawrence had been doing for the past two days?

Shameful, that's what it was. If Mrs Jannvier really was deranged, then there was enough room at the manor to look after her there.

And Ross's cousin Bessie definitely wasn't deranged, so if she'd left secretly there had to be a good reason for it. What's more, if anyone tried to lock her up, the Tuckers would want to know why, whether he was the landowner or not. By hell they would. They looked after their own, the Tuckers did.

'I'm a cousin of Mrs Jannvier's maid Bessie,' he announced suddenly, deciding to trust the open-faced young fellow. 'She'll be with her mistress.'

'Ah.' George looked at him, then admitted, 'I have a letter to deliver to Mrs Jannvier from her daughter. I was told she lived at that cottage across the green.'

'She did, but she left two days ago.'

George stared at him. 'Left? What do you mean?'

Ross lowered his voice. 'She and my cousin Bessie ran away.'

It took George a minute to digest this. 'Why?'

'Because of that brother of hers, Mr Lawrence.'

George took a good pull of ale, then looked sideways at the innkeeper. 'Do you know where she's gone? Her daughter's married my master and is living at Marymoor now. I'm supposed to take Mrs Jannvier and her back there.'

'Married? Miss Deborah's married?' the innkeeper gaped at him and was about to ask for more information when he noticed two horses stop outside and their riders dismount. 'Be careful. This is Mr Lawrence,' he muttered, then said loudly, 'Something to eat, did you say, young sir?'

A choleric gentleman erupted into the inn even as he was speaking and marched across to George, shoving the innkeeper aside.

'What does Deborah want?' Walter Lawrence demanded, slapping his riding crop on a table.

'I beg your pardon, sir?' George said cautiously.

'You were inquiring for my sister. You could only have come from my niece, so I want to know what Deborah wants, and I want to know now, or you'll find yourself in the stocks for insolence.'

'I don't know what you mean, sir.'

Walter poked him in the chest with the riding crop. 'Answer me at once.'

'I'm on my master's business,' George said stolidly, already looking for the best way to get out of the room, as Jem said you should do in a sticky situation. 'It's not up to me to say what that is. I just do as I'm told.'

'Insolence!' The crop thwacked down towards the side of George's head and he put up one arm to defend himself, feeling its sting.

'The fellow's attacking me!' Walter yelled at the top of his voice. 'Stop him!'

The groom moved forward, anticipation gleaming in his eyes.

But before they could catch him George dived for the back door.

The innkeeper, who had been eavesdropping on the other side of the door, shoved George in the direction of the kitchen and hissed, 'Tell 'em to hide you!' then fell through the doorway as if he'd been pushed, yelling in supposed shock and getting in the way of the two pursuers.

George ran in the direction of the pointing finger and dived through the door at the back of the room. 'The innkeeper says to hide me!' he gasped.

A man sitting by the fire gaped for a moment, then jumped to his feet and led the way outside at a run.

By the time Walter Lawrence's groom came in, the two of them were across the stableyard and out of sight.

He glared at the innkeeper's wife, who was placidly stirring a stew. 'You! Where did he go?'

She stopped stirring to look at him disapprovingly. 'Who?'

'The fellow as ran through here.'

'Oh, to the privvy, I suppose. I thought he'd been took short. I wasn't watching. I didn't want this stew to burn.'

He grasped her arm and shook her, making her drop the spoon and cry out in shock. 'You're lying! Where did he go?'

Her son Ben, who was bringing in some more firewood, dropped it to go to her aid, yelling at the top of his voice, 'You let go of my mother!'

Which made his father run into the kitchen and place himself between his family and the Squire, hands clenched into fists by his side.

By the time Walter Lawrence had got them all to be quiet, precious minutes had passed and Judith had started sobbing into her handkerchief and asking what the world was coming to when an honest woman was pushed around in her own kitchen.

Walter Lawrence said with savage restraint, 'If I find you've been sheltering that young man, a brute who attacked me in broad daylight, as my groom here can witness, then you'll be in serious trouble, woman. It's a hanging matter, attacking a member of the gentry is.'

'How could I be sheltering him, sir?' Ross asked, adopting a witless look he'd perfected for dealing with the Squire. 'I was with you all the time.' He kept silent until the two men had left the inn, accompanying them to the door with a smile on his face and much bowing and scraping.

As he watched them ride off, however, the smile vanished and he muttered, 'He's getting worse, that one is. I won't stand for anyone treating my wife roughly, damned if I will.'

When he repeated this to his wife in the kitchen, she turned on him sharply. 'You can't do anything about that. He's the Squire and you aren't. And what's a bit of a shake? I'm not even bruised. What I want to know is: what's that poor young man done to upset Squire?'

'Tried to deliver a message from Miss Deborah to her mother and refused to say what it was.'

There was silence while she wrinkled her brow in puzzlement. 'Is that all?' she asked eventually.

'Aye. That's all.'

'Did he really attack the Squire?'

'No. As I shall bear witness if asked.'

She gasped and seized his arm. 'No! You can't go against Squire.'

'I'm not having my cousin Bessie treated like that, no, nor Miss Isabel, neither. Nor I won't let them hang a young man as did nothing but try to deliver a message from his master. And nothing you can say will persuade me different.' He walked outside, shoulders hunched and a mighty scowl on his face.

Judith sighed, knowing Ross had reached the sticking point about the situation in the village, which was an unhappy place to live these days. He was easy-going to a fault, her Ross was, and it was only occasionally that something roused his ire. Hurting his family was one thing which would make him see red. He cared a lot about family, did Ross. All the Tuckers did.

And he was right when he said Mr Lawrence had gone from bad to worse lately, 'deed he had. But Mr Lawrence was gentry and they weren't, so he'd get away with it and they'd land themselves in trouble if they got involved.

She began to weep in earnest as her husband went outside to speak to the young man who had inadvertently brought all this upon them. What had the world come to when a woman wasn't even safe in her own kitchen, and her husband was threatened in his own inn?

–

Outside, Ross's anger rose still further when he found Mr Lawrence's groom searching the inn's stables. 'What are you doing here?' he demanded. 'You've no business in my stables.'

'My master's orders. I'm to keep watch on the young man's horse. He's bound to come back for it. You'll get about your business and keep your nose out of Squire's affairs, if you know what's good for you.'

Swelling massively that a foreigner from London could treat him like this in his own home, Ross strode forward.

'No, *you* get out of my stables and leave me to go about my business,' he roared. He didn't wait but gave the groom a mighty shove that sent him staggering back. 'And don't you go bullying my wife again, either. Lay one finger on her and I shall be the one laying complaints, not you!'

'You wouldn't dare!' But the groom backed away from the huge, red-faced man, who followed him step by step.

'I'd dare do anything to protect my family and don't you forget it. My family have owned this inn for nigh on a hundred years. I live in this village and can get as many witnesses as I need to prove I've done no harm. Half the folk round here are related to me. You're a foreigner. You might be working for Squire, but you have to come and go in the village. We'll be watching you from now on. You should spare a thought for your own safety.'

'Squire'll be furious when I tell him what you said.'

Ross looked down at him, arms akimbo. '*I'm – furious – already!*'

The groom went to wait in the back lane. He'd say nothing of this to his master, he decided. A man couldn't do the impossible. And he did have to come and go in the village.

Judith, who had heard her husband's voice booming out, wept still harder, sure that they'd all be clapped into jail for upsetting Squire.

But Ross set his son Ben to sweep the inn yard and keep watch for anyone approaching, then went whistling into the stables. 'You there, young fellow?' he called softly.

There was a rustling in the hay loft and a head poked out. 'Yes, I am. Thank you for hiding me.'

'I'll do more than hide you. I'll get you away tonight. The groom is outside keeping watch, but we'll outfox

147

him, don't you worry. He isn't one of us. Bessie and Mrs Jannvier are.'

He grinned as he walked back to the kitchen. It'd be a poor lookout when a man from Lancashire couldn't best a soft-arsed foreigner from the south, by hell it would!

8

Ross went out into the stableyard of the inn after dark, taking care that no light showed as he opened the little-used side door. He knew his way well enough to make no noise and entered via the tack room. He called softly and when George peered over the edge, beckoned him down. 'Here. I've brought you some food and while you eat it I'll saddle your horse.'

'Haven't they got someone watching the inn?'

Ross grinned. 'Aye, but I'll make sure he's distracted while you get away. He's allus hungry, that one is. You'll have to walk the horse for the first bit, keeping to soft ground. I've a man who'll guide you but it'll cost you a shilling or two. That all right?'

'Yes, of course. Guide me where? I still have to find Mrs Jannvier and her maid.' George was determined not to go home without them.

'The guide will take you to the first place they stayed after they left the cottage and you can ask where they went from there. That's all anyone knows. Crying shame them two having to run away like that at their age – and one of 'em Squire's sister, too. You be careful of him.'

'I will. But I'll not let my master down, if I can help it.'

Ross clapped him on the back. 'That's the way, young fellow. And give the old ladies my best regards if you find 'em.'

I will find them, George vowed to himself as he strode off into the night. I'm not going back till I do.

–

Bessie and Isabel eased their weary bodies off the pack horses near the ford in the centre of Rochdale, thanking the packman and his wife for their help. The string of horses splashed across the shallow river, heading uphill towards St Chad's Parish Church and the Pack Horse Inn, which was where they always stayed on their visits to town.

The two women picked up their bundles and looked at one another.

'What now?' Bessie asked, for to her surprise her mistress had shown more decisiveness on this journey than she had since her husband died, whereas Bessie felt overwhelmed by having to run away like thieves in the night and live so roughly.

'We'll have to ask directions to Marymoor, of course,' Isabel said serenely. 'But for tonight, if you have enough money, I think we'll find an inn and sleep in a proper bed. I want to wash myself and change into my other clothes. I don't want to shame my daughter by turning up looking like a dirty old beggar woman.'

'Dare we risk it?' Bessie worried. 'What if your brother has sent people to look for us? What if he's carried out his threat to…' Her voice faltered and she looked at her mistress and friend because she was secretly terrified of what would happen to them if Walter Lawrence caught them. She had seen examples of his revenge in Newgarth, families destroyed, men thrown in prison on Walter's word of their misdeeds to a magistrate friend.

'Not even Walter would do that to his own sister,' Isabel said, though less confidently. 'It's just a threat he uses to frighten me.' And the thought of being locked away in an asylum did frighten her. Very much.

But Bessie wasn't so sure it was only a threat, not when you were dealing with Walter Lawrence. However, she too was feeling exhausted and longing for a wash, so she allowed herself to be persuaded and they found themselves a room in The Peacock, a small inn near the centre of the thriving, grey-stone town. There they ordered warm water to be brought up to their room, a request which seemed to surprise the landlady, and then enjoyed the luxury of a thorough wash.

When the chambermaid took the dirty water down again she slipped out to empty it into the drain then carried the town constable's supper along the street to him, a regular task. She'd been waiting impatiently to do this because she'd heard there had been a reward posted that very day for information on two older women.

At the constable's Jane set down the tray of food, then went to look at the new poster carefully, studying the sketch and asking him to read her the details.

She knew he humoured her in this, but she dreamed of one day earning one of these rewards and then finding herself a good, hard-working husband with the proceeds. As he described the two women who were wanted, she thought of the old ladies in the back bedroom and her excitement rose, for they answered the description of the latest poster perfectly. The thin one was better spoken than the fat one. The poster said she was the poor mad sister of a landowner. She didn't seem mad, but you could never tell. And they were finicky about washing, weren't they? So they must be gentry.

The constable listened gravely to her claim to have seen them. 'I'll come and look at them after I've eaten.'

'But what if they run away?'

'Why should they do that? They've hired a room for the night, haven't they?' He picked up his knife and fork and cut himself a chunk of roast lamb.

The girl hurried back to the Peacock, but couldn't resist boasting to the landlady of what she'd done and the reward she'd earn if these were indeed the right women.

Furious that the wench hadn't shared the information with her, the landlady went into the big common room to stare at the two women eating their supper. They were the same age as herself and both looked deep down weary. She felt sorry for them if the information was true, for who would want to be shut away in a lunatic asylum? Was the thin one really mad, as the poster said? She had such a gentle smile it was hard to believe. Edging closer, the landlady tried to listen to what they were saying, pretending to wipe clean the next table.

Bessie couldn't afterwards have said why she felt suspicious of the way the landlady was staring at them, but she did. When the woman had gone back into the kitchen, Bessie followed her. The landlady and maid had their backs to the door and were arguing furiously. What Bessie heard made her insist Isabel abandon eating and come up to their room.

'They know about us. Your brother's put out a poster saying you're mad and offering a reward. That chambermaid has reported our presence to the constable.'

Isabel's bright new confidence faltered. 'Are you sure?'

'Yes.'

They looked at one another in dismay.

'I'd never have believed Walter would...' Isabel's voice trailed away.

'I know he's your brother, but he'd do anything to get his own way. He's worse than your father ever was. We'll have to slip out quietly, as if we're going for a walk. We'll put on as many of our clothes as we can and we'll leave the rest, because if we took our bundles it would give us away. Quick! The constable may be on his way already. Perhaps we can slip out the back way while they're still busy with that crowd of customers? They won't expect us to do that.'

They went upstairs and put on every piece of clothing they could squeeze into.

'I'll leave the money for the room on the mantelpiece,' Bessie decided. 'Then they can't accuse us of theft.'

When she turned round she saw the vague, distant look on Isabel's face again and couldn't bear it. Without thinking she shook her friend hard. 'Keep your wits about you. We *can* escape!'

Isabel swallowed and nodded.

The two of them crept down the back stairs, watching from the dimly-lit landing as the maid rushed past in the corridor below carrying platters of food.

'That door leads into the back yard,' Bessie whispered. 'You go first. I can't move as quickly as you, so if they catch me, you run for your life.'

They both froze as the door to the dining room swung open again and the maid returned, but she was too intent on her task and she didn't glance up.

As soon as the kitchen door had shut behind her, Bessie hissed, 'Now!' and they picked up their skirts and ran.

When Elkin returned to Marymoor for dinner at two o'clock, he was unshakably affable. The food was plain and plentiful, but neither Matthew nor his wife spoke unless addressed and even Elkin's conversation faltered after a while before this wall of determined silence.

'I must go and look in on your mother, Mr Elkin,' Deborah said as soon as she could politely leave the table.

He gave her one of his cat-like smiles. 'That's very kind of you, but I looked in on her myself just before dinner and she was sleeping. The draught your good doctor sent seems to have done her a great deal of good.'

'Oh. Yes, well, all right then. I'll wait until later. Perhaps she'll be well enough to travel tomorrow?'

'She's a frail old woman and I don't want to risk her life by rushing her away. I trust you're not going to turn us out?' He raised one eyebrow at her.

'I wouldn't send anyone away who was ill,' she said obliquely.

'The minute she's fit to travel, you can leave,' Matthew said, tired of this mock civility. 'And I'll thank you not to come back again.'

'Ever the gracious host,' sneered Elkin.

'Never the gracious host where you're concerned,' Matthew snapped. He pushed his chair back. 'I have things to do.'

'So do I.' Deborah fled to their bedroom and stayed there, mending one of Matthew's shirts and wishing Elkin would leave.

But two hours later Mrs Elkin's maid came and knocked on the door in great distress, begging her in to come and see her mistress, who was vomiting again.

When she saw how bad Mrs Elkin was Deborah realised with a sinking heart that they would have to continue to entertain their enemy for a day or two longer.

She went to look for Matthew, but couldn't find him. Jem thought he was out 'talking to someone' but was very vague about who and where, so she didn't press the point, just left a message for him that Mrs Elkin was worse.

On the way back she saw Elkin come to stand in the front doorway, looking out thoughtfully across the gardens. Hoping he hadn't seen her, she ducked behind some shrubs until he went in then made her way to the kitchen for another confrontation with Mrs Simley, who was being as awkward as she could with everyone but Elkin.

When Matthew came up to change his clothes for supper he said abruptly, 'Elkin went into the village today and spoke to this stranger who's staying at the inn again. Thompson sent his lad to follow them, but young Sam couldn't get close enough to overhear what they were saying.'

'Is Elkin planning more mischief, do you think?'

'Undoubtedly. I'm going to hire a couple of fellows to help me keep watch here tonight. If he can bring in reinforcements, so can I.'

'Is that really necessary?' She blushed at what she had been hoping for that night and hoped he hadn't noticed.

'I think so.' But he had guessed what she was thinking. Hell, he had been thinking about it, too. Only – if he had to choose between saving her life and making love to her, he'd save her life, of course he would. He didn't dare let himself be distracted, so he deliberately kept his voice curt.

After an interminable evening of stilted conversation and long silences, Deborah went upstairs to their bedroom. When Matthew joined her, he saw she'd made no attempt to undress.

'You might as well get some sleep,' he said gruffly, standing with his arms folded and his back against the door.

'What about you? You look so tired.'

'I shall be all right.'

He looked across at her. 'I didn't like to see you walking with Elkin.'

Her heart lifted just a little, because that sounded very much like jealousy. She risked going across to lay one hand on her husband's arm. 'I don't like to be near him. His touch makes my flesh crawl, as if his very skin is unwholesome.'

He looked down at her hand. 'And my touch does not?'

'You know it doesn't.'

He raised one hand to caress her cheek briefly. 'If it were not so important to keep watch, I'd stay and prove that. Would you object?'

She blushed, but shook her head. 'No.'

He looked her very directly in the eyes. 'Will it be your first time?'

She nodded.

'I thought so. That's why I don't intend to rush things. It must be right between us, now and in the years to come, if we're to make a good marriage.' He took a determined step sideways and grasped the door handle. 'Get you to bed. No need for you to stay awake as well as me.'

But when he'd gone, she couldn't bear to get undressed, she knew not why, so changed back into her everyday garments, laying the new black gown carefully in the press before she got into bed. These clothes were so crumpled already, it hardly mattered if she slept in them, but if anything happened, she intended to be ready to help.

–

Just before midnight Seth made his way down the stairs and slipped out of the house, using a spare key he'd purloined from the big rack of keys near the kitchen door. Only trusting fools left keys lying around like that and they deserved all they got.

The farm labourer Matthew had hired to keep watch at the rear blinked in shock as a man crept out of the house. He had not believed his new master about there being mischief plotted, but he did now. He began to follow the man, trying to make no noise.

Just outside the village, Seth met Frank as arranged and the two turned back towards the house. 'You've got the pistol?'

'Yes. Loaded and ready primed. Don't worry. I know how to use it and am accounted a good shot.'

'Well, if you blow Pascoe to eternity tonight, you'll be well rewarded.'

Frank smiled. Knowing the situation, he'd be well rewarded by his own master as well, but he didn't share that information with Seth. He'd made sure no one had followed him from the inn and when they were nearly at Marymoor, he stopped Seth and insisted on checking that they were not being followed now.

'Who's the hell's going to follow us?' Seth growled. 'Jem's keeping guard on the stables and Pascoe's watching the house. One man can't watch both my master and me at the same time.'

'Better safe than sorry. Walk on slowly.' Frank slipped away into the darkness.

A couple of minutes later there was an exclamation and a grunt, followed by a dull thud, which sounded like a body falling. Seth stiffened, not liking to be proven wrong.

Frank appeared beside him, grinning, his teeth showing white in the light of the waning moon. 'We *were* being followed, but the poor man had an accident and won't wake up for a while.'

'Let's get on with it, then.'

They made their way in silence towards the house, avoiding the stables and entering by the kitchen door. But the second man hired by Matthew to patrol the boundaries of the gardens saw them coming and was more careful how he followed them than his companion had been, waiting in the shrubbery until they'd gone inside.

Once they were indoors Seth led the way slowly towards the hall where Matthew had been keeping watch. Seth paused, with a soft exhalation of annoyance.

Behind him, Frank tensed.

'The bastard isn't here,' Seth mouthed close to his ear.

'Let's wait a few minutes. He may only have gone out for a piss.'

There was the noise of footsteps from the direction of the library and both men fell silent again, moving back into the shadows. There was enough moonlight in the hall for Seth to be sure of his victim. No one else at Marymoor was as tall or had as broad shoulders. His own master was tall, too – it ran in the family – but he was much thinner built than Pascoe. He nudged his companion.

Frank cocked his pistol, but the click made the intended victim jerk round, and at that moment the watcher who had followed them inside called out, 'Look out, master! He's got a pistol.'

Matthew threw himself to the side and the ball buried itself in the wood panelling where he had been standing. 'Get him!' he roared. The labourer dived towards Seth while Matthew tackled Frank.

A desperate struggle ensued, because although the labourer was willing, Seth was more skilled at close fighting and not afraid to use dirty tricks. Frank was also skilled, but he made heavier weather of his encounter with Matthew, who was a strong man and much bigger than him.

The noise brought Deborah out of her bedroom holding one flickering candle aloft and Elkin out of his, wearing a banyan unfastened over a nightshirt.

'What the hell is going on?' he demanded.

'I think we have intruders,' she said.

'I must help!'

Before she could say anything else, he ran down the stairs, barrelling into Matthew and Frank just as Seth punched the labourer on the chin and sent him staggering backwards to thump against the wall and fall over a chair. Glancing towards the stairs, he saw Deborah coming down, muttered a curse and edged quickly out of the hall, using the servants' stairs to hurry up to his room.

Somehow Elkin got in Matthew's way and thanks to his intervention, Frank was able to wrench himself free and turn for the kitchen just as Deborah reached the foot of the stairs.

She caught a brief glimpse of him, not enough to identify him, but enough to make her feel there was something familiar about him.

By the time Matthew had got to his feet and rushed out after the intruders, all he found was the kitchen door open but no sound of flight outside. He yelled, 'Jem! Intruders!' but kept himself out of sight, not wanting to attract another shot.

Frank, standing in the deep shadow of the stable wall, smiled as Jem stared round, saw nothing and ran towards the house. Swiftly but cautiously Frank then made his was back to the inn. On the way he heard the man he had thumped staggering along the lane long before he reached him, and moved to stand behind a tree as the other stumbled past him. Another fool! he thought as he back slipped into the inn.

He stood by the window of his bedroom for a while, keeping watch on the street to make sure no one had pursued him, but when nothing happened to disturb the peace of the night, he got undressed and lay down on the bed. It was galling to have his shot spoiled like that. It would not be nearly as easy to get another chance at Pascoe from such close quarters now that he was warned that someone wanted him dead.

–

In the big house Matthew was glaring at Elkin. 'You allowed them to escape.'

'I was trying to help.'

Deborah, watching, thought how ugly he looked without his wig. The shaven head with its light stubble seemed to emphasise the viciousness of his character and the deep lines of dissipation on his face.

'Then please refrain from helping us in future,' Matthew snapped. He could prove nothing, but he was quite sure that Elkin had let the man go on purpose. 'Where's that manservant of yours?'

'In his bed, I expect. He sleeps very soundly.'

'Through a noise like this?' Matthew gave a disbelieving laugh and turned towards the stairs. 'I intend to check on that.'

'Do so!' Elkin waved one hand languidly. 'I need a brandy to restore my spirits. Do you have such a thing, Cousin Deborah? I beg you to pardon my state of undress.'

She could hardly bear to speak to him, as sure as Matthew that he had deliberately made it possible for the man escape. 'I don't know whether we have any brandy or not. You'll have to ask Matthew when he returns.' She turned to the labourer who was standing by the wall. 'Are you all right, Peter?'

'Yes, mistress. Just a few bruises and such. I was sorry that fellow got away. He fights nasty, he does.' He fingered a deep scratch across his cheek. 'He was going for my eye.'

'I'll bathe that for you in a minute. If you go into the kitchen, perhaps you could get the fire going to heat some water?'

Jem spoke from the doorway. 'The intruders got clear away, Mrs Pascoe. Not a sign of them. What happened here?'

'Someone got into the hall and shot at Matthew. He's gone to check on Elkin's man, who seems to have slept through the whole thing.'

'Oh, did he?'

Jem sounded as disbelieving as she felt.

Upstairs Matthew was first accosted by the Simleys, demanding to know what had happened. As they were speaking Seth came out of his bedchamber, wearing a nightshirt and yawning, while Merry peered out of another door.

Seth was overdoing the sleepiness, Matthew thought grimly, but as with Elkin, you couldn't prove that he'd been involved in the attack. 'We had intruders break into the house, but we drove them off,' he said curtly.

Mrs Simley screamed and had to be comforted by her husband.

Merry listened wide-eyed but said nothing.

'Does my master need me?' Seth asked.

'I can't say. You'd better find out.' Matthew turned on his heel and made his way downstairs again.

Deborah was waiting in the hall, with several candles lit now. She came to meet her husband at the bottom of the stairs. 'Well?'

'Nothing can be proved one way or the other. I know what I think, though.'

'Me, too. Elkin wants a brandy.'

'Let him serve himself, then. There's some in the library.'

'You're not hurt in any way?'

'No. The bullet missed me completely, thanks to Peter's warning.'

She breathed a sigh of relief. They looked at one another, then he said softly, 'Go back to bed now, Deborah.'

'I want to tend your man's scratches. And I doubt I'd sleep anyway.'

They went through into the kitchen, but just as Deborah was picking up a bowl there was a sound outside. Matthew stiffened and put one finger to his lips.

However, the person was making no attempt to be quiet and it turned out to be the other labourer, still groggy from the blow to the head.

By the time they'd tended to both men and got their versions of the night's events, which suggested that Seth had indeed left the house, the sky was lightening. They left the man who'd been knocked out sitting in the kitchen while the other continued to patrol the outside.

'We can prove nothing,' Matthew said when they were alone in their bedchamber. 'No one saw the faces of the two attackers, well, not clearly enough.' He saw that Deborah couldn't hold back a yawn and put his arm round her. 'I think we should both go to bed now. I must get an hour or two's sleep or I'll be good for nothing today.'

But he lay awake for a while listening to her breathing slow down as she fell asleep, feeling the warmth and softness of her body against his and the hardness of his response to her presence. He was very tempted to wake her up.

He didn't. He wanted more out of their marriage than a sensible business arrangement. Much more. And a hasty coupling was no way to start off.

–

In the library Elkin poured himself a brandy and when Seth joined him, said in a savage undertone, 'You bungled it.'

'He had extra watchers outside we didn't know about.'

'Make very sure you don't bungle it next time! Is that fellow in the village worth dealing with again?'

'Aye. He gave a good account of himself and he's the one who noticed the man following us – and dealt with him efficiently. His aim was good and Pascoe would be dead now if we hadn't been interrupted.' He heard footsteps passing through the hall and raised his voice. 'I'll see you in the morning, then, sir.'

'Aye. But not too early.'

Elkin sat on in the library, sipping the brandy and considering his options. He wasn't going to give up now. He wanted Marymoor more than he'd ever wanted anything in his life, but to that desire was now added a grim determination to best Matthew Pascoe. And then deal with that stupid bitch the man had married, the bitch who'd brought Marymoor to his enemy.

Elkin was still undecided whether to kill her or marry her himself after he disposed of her husband.

9

In Marymoor village news of what had happened the previous night had spread rapidly and John knew what he thought about it all, oh, yes. But if Chadding had sneaked out of the inn to take part in the rumpus at Marymoor House, he hadn't noticed, and that annoyed him even more.

It was Anthony Elkin's fault, he was sure. No one liked the man. He'd been bad enough before but now had such scornful, foppish ways it made an honest man want to puke. Such behaviour might do for London – southerners were soft folk, everyone knew that – but northerners wouldn't put up with such a patronising attitude. The villagers were glad to see the big house go to anyone but Elkin. John's niece, Merry, said Mrs Pascoe was as nice a lady as you could hope to serve and they all knew what a hard worker Matthew Pascoe was and what a difference he was making to the run-down manor.

A young man who looked like a groom rode up to the Woolpack Inn and asked if a Mr Chadding was staying there. John offered him only a nod, still suspicious of his guest, as he would have been of anyone who was spending time in earnest conversation with Elkin.

'Then could I see him, landlord? I have an important message for him from his employer.'

'I'll fetch him down. You stay here.' What John didn't understand was why a man who had an employer was sitting around in his inn all day. It didn't make sense.

When he knocked on the door of Chadding's room, a voice called, 'Just a moment.'

He waited, wondering why the fellow couldn't just open the door, then, as the seconds stretched into minutes, wondering what was he hiding?

The door opened a crack. 'Yes?'

'There's a man come to see you, says he's got a message from your employer. He's waiting in the common room.'

'Right. I'll be down in a minute.'

The door was shut in his face. What was the man doing, John wondered. Something was going on, something that involved his inn, and John didn't like it. He hurried back to the kitchen where he instructed his wife to listen to what the two men were saying if she could. He intended to have a quick look round Chadding's room while he was talking to the stranger.

He beckoned his son over. 'Once Mr Chadding's come downstairs, you keep watch at the foot of the stairs, Sam lad. If he looks like coming up before I come down again, bump into him then say you're sorry – loudly – to give me time to get out of his room.'

Sam nodded, excited to be involved in all this.

But their unwelcome guest took the stranger out walking, so Mrs Thompson couldn't listen to what they were saying. She was, however, able to see how carefully Chadding looked up and down the street before he left the inn and how quickly he and the stranger left the main street to disappear up the back lane. She had thought her husband was making a fuss about nothing, but now she also began to wonder what was happening.

Upstairs John found the pistol and its box of powder and shot almost immediately, because it was in the top of the stranger's saddlebag. He stared at them in disapproval. A man had a right to defend himself on lonely roads, but Chadding didn't need such protection in his inn. He raised the weapon to his nose and could smell a faint trace of gunpowder. He prided himself on having a fine nose, else how could a man select decent wines and brew his ale properly? The pistol had been fired recently and had not been fully cleaned. Was that what he had interrupted when he knocked?

He went out of the chamber and beckoned his son up the stairs. 'What's Chadding doing now?'

'Gone out with that man who came looking for him.'

'Right, then. Go and stand near the front door and keep a sharp watch for him coming back down the street. Give me a yell if you see him.'

John searched through the saddlebags, shocked to find that the clothing of the respectably clad stranger included a mask. He scowled at it. What did an honest man need with a mask? Was this a highwayman staying in his inn? There had been a few daring robberies over Rochdale way a year or so ago, then they'd stopped. No, more likely Chadding was one of the gang who had attacked Mr Pascoe last night.

Scowling, he put everything away again and went downstairs to tell his wife what he'd found, then laboriously penned a few lines to Mr Pascoe asking him to come to the inn on a matter of urgency 'connected with your present troubles'. He gave the note to Sam and instructed him to deliver this in person either to Mr Pascoe or to Jem, but to *no one else*.

'You can rely on me.' Sam puffed out his chest.

'Mmm.' John watched him go, then had another idea, so nipped out to the stables to look at the newcomer's horse.

'Good piece of stock, this one is, Mr Thompson,' his ostler said. 'Looks more like it belongs to a gentleman. Been ridden hard, though. I wouldn't do that to any animal.'

'Did the fellow say anything about where he was from?'

'Not a word. Surly devil, if you ask me.'

Chadding had been similarly evasive about why he was in Marymoor. Well, John intended to keep a careful eye on the fellow from now on. No one was using his inn to harm Matthew Pascoe.

–

Deborah was unable to get the memory of the intruder out of her mind. What was there about him that seemed familiar? If only there had been more light.

'Shall you hire watchmen tonight?' she asked Matthew over breakfast, for which their guest had not joined them, thank goodness.

'Aye. And for every night Elkin spends here. I've no mind to be shot at again.'

She shivered. 'You will take care from now on, won't you?'

'As much as I can. And you too. Remember: don't go out alone or with *him*.'

'No, I won't. I'll go and see how Mrs Elkin is as soon as her maid comes downstairs. Surely the poor woman will be better this morning? Dr Lethbury sent another bottle of his special draught and if that doesn't do the trick, I'll ask him to come back again. I want to go into the village to the market later, though, because we're low on fresh food. I'll take Merry with me.' She didn't tell her husband, but she also intended to see if she could catch a glimpse of the stranger staying at the inn, in case he was one of her Uncle Walter's men. Merry said he was called Chadding, but that name meant nothing to Deborah.

Unfortunately Mrs Elkin wasn't better. Deborah left the sour smell of vomit behind, glad of a walk in the fresh air. She'd call in at the doctor's house while she was on her way to the village and ask him to call. The weather looked like being fine again, thank goodness.

As they walked along she asked Merry about her relatives and when she found out that the girl's uncle was the innkeeper, decided to confide her mission.

'I'll take you to see Uncle John,' Merry said at once. 'He'll help us.'

Deborah hesitated. 'Is there some rear entrance to the inn? I don't want the stranger to see me going in.'

Merry frowned in thought then her face brightened. 'I know. We'll buy our provisions, then I'll take you to meet my old auntie. We can go out of the back door of her cottage and get to the inn through the gardens without anyone seeing us.'

'That would be very helpful.'

There were only half a dozen sellers at the market, but the two women filled their baskets with so much fresh produce that one man offered to take everything back to Marymoor for them on his cart.

'Thank you. I promised I'd take Mrs Pascoe to call on my Auntie Jane.'

As Merry led her mistress across the green, the bystanders stopped talking to watch them.

'The new Mrs Pascoe's not too toffee-nosed to speak to ordinary folk, then,' one woman said approvingly.

'Got a pretty face on her too,' an old man added.

'And Matthew Pascoe's all right, too,' the man taking the baskets to Marymoor said.

'Old Ralph Jannvier did the right thing by us, I reckon,' the old man said and several folk nodded agreement.

—

The old woman who opened the cottage door to Merry's knock seemed at first over-awed by her visitor, but Deborah's easy manner soon relaxed her, and when Merry explained what they wanted, she nodded, thrilled to be part of the conspiracy.

'You go over and see our John, Merry. Tell him what your mistress wants.'

The girl came back a couple of minutes later. 'The man's still there. My uncle says if you come over now you can peep into the common room and catch a glimpse of him, because there's a right old crowd in there and he's sitting in a corner looking sour and talking to some fellow as turned up with a message for him.'

Deborah followed her through a neat little garden and was then whisked into the inn kitchens by John.

Mrs Thompson offered her an apron and mobcap. 'If you'll put these on, begging your pardon, Mrs Pascoe, no one will notice you when you peep into the common room. But if they see that hair of yours – real pretty it is – they'll all turn and stare.'

So Deborah let them dress her quickly and went to stand by the kitchen door, staring into the busy common room where people who'd been to market were now taking their ease and enjoying a few mugs of ale after doing their business.

What she saw made her gasp aloud and press one hand to her throat in shock. At the other side of the room sat Frank, her uncle's henchman, and with him one of her uncle's grooms. She closed the door quickly before they saw her.

'Know him, do you, Mrs Pascoe?' John asked, studying her shrewdly.

She nodded. 'I know them both. They're employed by my uncle. The older one does the dirty work for my uncle, turns folk out of cottages, collects rents, even beats people if my uncle fancies himself slighted.'

There was silence in the kitchen as they struggled to take this in.

'Then what's a fellow like that talking to Mr Elkin for?' John asked.

'I don't know, but nothing good, I'm sure.' Deborah looked round the room, seeing only friendly faces and tried to smile at them, but could not. She hated the thought of her uncle trying to interfere with her new life. Pulling off the mobcap and apron, she tried to tidy her hair. 'Thank you for your help. I'd better hurry back and tell my husband what I've seen.'

–

On the other side of Rochdale, young George's guide knocked up the farmer and his wife, who were at first reluctant to talk about Mrs Jannvier and Bessie. But after his companion had reassured them several times that George was to be trusted and the innkeeper would vouch for him, they said he'd better come inside. They could only tell him how they had sheltered the two old women and set them on their way early the next morning.

'Dear knows where they'll have gone,' the farmer's wife said. 'I didn't like to think of them tramping across the moors on their own, not at their age, but we didn't dare be seen helping them. Mr Lawrence is a bad man to cross and although this isn't one of his farms, he knows our landlord and we don't want to be turned out. So we'd be grateful if you didn't mention us to anyone, young man.'

'I promise I won't,' George assured her.

'You'll not get far in the dark, so you can spend the rest of the night in our barn like they did if you want. They left before dawn and Bessie took Mrs Jannvier through the wood, that I do know, so you should try in that direction first.' She pointed out the direction to him. 'That path there. But who can tell where they went afterwards? I reckon they must have gone across the moors, because we know he's sent men out looking but we haven't heard of him catching them.'

George decided not to stay, wanting to get as far as he could before it grew fully dark. He turned to his guide. 'Can you set me a bit further on my way? I'll pay you for your trouble.'

The man nodded. 'I'll take you through the wood, but after that it's up to you. I don't want Mr Lawrence knowing I've been out at night, or he'll be accusing me of poaching.'

So they set off again. After a while the guide looked up at the sky and announced, 'Looks like it'll rain soon.'

'Aye.' But George wasn't going to let rain stop him.

As they walked on, darkness fell and they slowed down, but the guide seemed to know his way, even with no moon showing through the clouds. When they came to the edge of the woods, money exchanged hands, then he slipped away.

George tied up his horse and sat down on a big rock to wait for dawn, since he couldn't see a hand in front of his face. He shivered in the damp, chill air and when it started to rain, moved back a little, to stand beside his horse beneath one of the larger trees then, as he grew tired, sit on one of its large exposed roots. Slowly the rain eased and it grew light enough in the false dawn for him to set off again, but the sky was still heavy with clouds.

Within the hour it was raining again, hard enough this time to soak him to the skin and depress his spirits. Was this a wild goose chase? he wondered. How did one find two old ladies who were avoiding the main roads and trying not to be seen?

Only – he just couldn't go back and face Jem until he'd tried everything.

–

The same rain was making going hard for Isabel and Bessie. They seemed to have run out of luck entirely and with no baggage, they were looked on suspiciously by some people when they asked the way to Marymoor.

Eventually they found a woman working stolidly at weeding a field of cabbages. She was clad in a big smock, with a sack round her shoulders to keep off the worst of the rain. At their hail she stopped work, wiping the moisture from her face, though that only streaked it with mud from her hands.

'Hard work, that,' Bessie said.

'Aye.'

'We're looking to find our way to Marymoor, but we're lost. Can you set us on the right road?'

'You're on it already. Just follow it to the end. It only leads to Marymoor.'

'That's good news. Thank you.'

She nodded but didn't speak again, just bent over her weeding.

'Life's hard,' Isabel said softly. 'We should have given her a penny.'

'We can't afford to, Mrs Isabel.'

'We seem to have been travelling for ever.' She sighed and swiped at the moisture that was running into her eyes. 'And we look like a pair of beggar women, Bessie.'

'We're well on our way and Miss Deborah won't care what we look like. Everything will be all right when we get to Marymoor.' It had to be. They couldn't go back to Newgarth. It would be the death of Mrs Isabel to return to her brother and that damp cottage, Bessie was sure, even if he didn't carry out his threat to lock her away.

They came to a tiny inn and knocked on the back door to check again that they were on the right road. 'Better safe than sorry,' said Bessie.

'Oh, yes. Marymoor is about seven miles away if you could go straight across the tops,' the innkeeper's wife told them, 'but the road twists about something shocking. Come and sit down by the fire for a minute. You look chilled to the marrow. Come far, have you?'

It was hard to leave the warmth of her kitchen and the simple kindness which had made her give them a place by the fire and provide a bowl of porridge for each of them without asking any payment.

'Should we perhaps hire a trap?' Isabel whispered as they left.

'I *daren't* spend the rest of our money,' Bessie whispered back. 'What if Deborah isn't there? What should we do then if we'd nothing left?'

They were both silent, then Isabel nodded agreement. If they were found wandering without any money or possessions, they'd be accused of being vagrants and sent to the poorhouse, because parishes were very careful not to let beggars settle and become a charge on the poor rates. 'I'll make it up to you one day, Bessie.'

'Ah, get on with you! We've stayed together this long. Did you think I was going to leave you now just because I'm a bit uncomfortable? Besides, I don't have anyone left except you and Deborah.'

But although they both tried to keep up a cheerful face in front of the other, they had nearly reached the end of their strength and they knew it. Each mile seemed longer and each hill steeper as they trudged on.

When they found a shepherd's shelter, Bessie said firmly, 'It's time we settled down for the night. No use pressing on in the dark. We don't want to break an ankle.'

'Yes. Yes, of course.'

They lay down in the most sheltered corner, huddling together for comfort as much as warmth, glad of their extra layers of clothing.

Bessie prayed that the next day would be their last on the road. It had to be. They were both exhausted.

Isabel prayed they would find Deborah in happier circumstances and never have to ask her brother for help again.

Neither slept well.

-

On the way back to Newgarth, Walter Lawrence's groom stopped to rest his horse and warm himself up a bit in Rochdale. He chose a quiet inn and found a bench near the fire, flirting idly with the maid who served him.

'We been getting a lot of strangers here lately,' she said. 'Nearly caught two fugitives yesterday. Fancy two old women being wanted like that!'

He stiffened. 'Two old women?'

Nothing loathe, she told him the story of the reward she had nearly earned and the way the old women had left half their possessions behind – which just showed they were guilty – and how the landlady had taken the things and not given her anything, though she'd been the one to recognise them for what they were.

When her mistress called her over sharply and told her to get on with her work, she tossed her head and slouched away. The groom sat lost in thought. He didn't know whether to go back and tell Frank what he'd heard or go straight to Mr Lawrence. In the end he plumped for Frank, because he'd be the one who did what was necessary.

With a sigh he bought himself a lantern on a stick and got ready to ride out again, awkward though it was travelling after dark. Dusk was falling and it looked like being a wet, cloudy night, so he'd make slow progress. But he'd travelled the road before and knew it was clearly marked. He didn't want Mr Lawrence thinking he'd shirked his duty.

His master would be very pleased if he and Frank caught the two old women for him. And if you served him well, Mr Lawrence always rewarded you.

–

Deborah didn't manage to get Matthew on his own until they retired for the night.

'I found something out today,' she said as soon as he had closed and locked their bedchamber door.

'Oh?'

'The man staying at the inn is my uncle's henchman. I know him as Frank Netton, but he's calling himself Chadding here.' She saw she had his full attention and went on, eager to share all she knew with him. 'He's a nasty sort. Every now and then he rides off and doesn't come back for several days, and when he does my uncle always looks smug. I can only suppose he was sent after me.'

'He's also been seen talking to Elkin,' Matthew said, 'and he's carrying a pistol and has a mask in his luggage.' He grinned at her shock. 'John just happened to notice them when he was checking the man's room.'

He sat down on the bed and patted the space beside him, putting his arm round her shoulders as she joined him, then wondering if this was wise when every time he touched her his wits scattered. 'Do you think your uncle will come here to visit us?' He gave a short laugh. 'We shall be a happy household if he does – him *and* the Elkins.'

'He might come, though to what purpose I can't imagine now that I'm married.' She leaned against him, sighing and resting her head on his shoulder.

Matthew didn't allow himself to pull her closer. 'His interests and Elkins coincide there. If I were not here, you'd own Marymoor and either of them might take advantage of that.'

'I wouldn't let them.'

'You might not be able to stop them.'

'Matthew, why do you let Elkin stay on here? We all know he wants you dead and has tried to arrange that. We could let his mother stay and ask him to leave. I don't care what people may think. I want you safe.'

He gave in to temptation, picked up her hand and carried it to his mouth. 'And I want *you* safe as well, my dear.' His eyes held hers as he added, 'Above all I want our marriage and life together to prosper. Therefore I think it better if we eliminate all threats now. If Elkin is here under my roof, I can at least keep an eye on his comings and goings. He isn't aware of it, but I have one or two friends in the village who are keeping me informed. Though only you could know Chadding's real identity.'

Another silence, then he added, 'I wonder when he and Elkin will find their interests no longer coincide? It'll be interesting to see what happens then.'

As she shivered involuntarily, he gave her a quick hug. 'Let's go to bed, Deborah.'

She looked at him and decided to risk saying it. 'Together? As man and wife?'

His breath stopped in his throat and for a few seconds he could only stare at her. 'Is that what you truly want?'

'Yes.'

'Even now?'

'Oh, yes. Especially now.' She wanted no one to be able to declare the marriage invalid because it wasn't consummated, but most of all she wanted him. Just – wanted him.

He pulled her closer and used one fingertip to raise her chin and kiss her. As she stared at him, innocent but willing, his breath caught in his throat and he realised how fond he had grown of her. So quickly and easily had it happened that it filled him with wonder. 'I want it too, lass. Very much.' He smiled into her clear eyes. 'Let *me* undress you, then,' he said softly. 'And trust me. I shall deal with you very gently this first time.'

Her breathing quickened as she nodded. She did trust him. In the midst of danger and deceit she had found him and she wanted to be his true wife more than she had ever wanted anything in her life before.

Delicately he removed her clothes one by one, kissing her, caressing her, making her whole body hum with anticipation.

'Should we not put out the candles,' she whispered, feeling her cheeks grow hot as he exposed her breasts and bent to kiss them, too, an act which had her writhing beneath his touch.

His voice was low and husky. 'No, my little love, we should not. I want to see you as I make love to you. It's part of the pleasure. I hope you want to see me, too.'

She knew not what she wanted, but when he led her onwards she followed willingly. She had expected pain, but got none, had expected it to happen quickly and found long, languorous pleasure instead, until she found herself begging him to take her.

With a groan of both pleasure and relief, he thrust inside her, feeling her stiffen for a moment, then relax with him into the age-old rhythms of love.

Afterwards, he pulled her back into his arms and held her close. 'We're man and wife now, Deborah Pascoe. Body and soul.'

'I'm glad of it. It was – wonderful. I didn't realise...'

He could easily have taken her again, for she roused his manhood more quickly than any woman he had ever met, but he restrained himself, afraid of making her sore and uncomfortable. He wanted her to find their couplings a thing of joy.

She fell asleep quickly, nestled trustingly against him.

He took longer to fall asleep, because he had so many things to consider. So far he had let Elkin have his head. Now he wanted this mess over and done with, wanted his wife safe.

It was time to set a trap, to flush out the conspirators.

10

Dr Lethbury came out of Mrs Elkin's room with a puzzled frown, holding the bottle containing the remainder of the draught he had sent. Deborah followed him out and watched him walk to the end of the landing where he held it up against the window. He squinted at the contents through the dark green glass, shook the remaining liquid and took the stopper out to sniff it.

'I can't understand it,' he said in a low voice. 'This mixture has never failed to help before and I'm always extremely careful to use the best ingredients. But the liquid looks – well, thicker. Maybe I'm imagining things.'

Out of the corner of her eye she saw the door of Elkin's room move slightly, almost but not quite closed.

'Perhaps we should go and talk privately in the library,' she suggested, tugging at the doctor's arm to get his attention, then indicating Elkin's door with a jerk of her head.

'Hmm? What? Oh, yes. Of course.'

As they moved towards the stairs, Elkin stepped out of his room to block their way, radiating anger. 'Ah! The very man I wish to see. I have to tell you, sir, that I am dissatisfied with your treatment of my mother. Grossly dissatisfied! And as for this!' He snatched the bottle out of the doctor's hand and brandished it at him. 'It's useless. Absolutely useless! Hasn't helped her in the slightest.'

As the doctor reached out to take it back, Elkin took a step backwards and stumbled. The bottle flew out of his hand, hit the top step and slid over the edge, bouncing down the stairs and gathering momentum to smash to pieces on the hall floor.

'Damnation!' Elkin exclaimed. 'I cry pardon, Cousin Deborah, for making a mess.'

'It can be cleared up,' she said quietly. She had not missed the gleam of triumph in his eyes as the bottle smashed, nor did she think he had dropped it by accident.

Elkin turned back to Dr Lethbury. 'I want to talk to you about how you've been treating my mother.'

The doctor regarded him coldly. 'Later, if you please. At the moment Mrs Pascoe and I are in the middle of an important discussion.'

'I would have thought your patient came first,' Elkin sneered.

'This is Mrs Pascoe's house, not yours,' the doctor snapped. 'Kindly remember the duty we both owe to our hostess.'

Elkin glared at him, swelling with anger.

'I'll send Merry to fetch you when we've finished, Mr Elkin,' Deborah said hastily, gesturing to the doctor to lead the way downstairs. Avoiding the shards of broken glass and splatters of milky fluid at the bottom, she ushered him into the library. 'Please excuse me for a minute. I'll get Merry to clear up the mess.'

Dr Lethbury went to stand by the window, fingers drumming on the sill. He had no doubt that some emetic agent had been added to the draught, but there was no way of proving it now. There was only one person who could have done it, but to treat one's own mother like that was beyond shameful. He saw Elkin come into view outside, pacing up and down the terrace outside their window. 'Look at him!' he muttered to himself. 'You can dress a person up in fine garments but cruelty shows on the human face. Ralph was right not to leave Marymoor to that one.'

When Deborah returned she closed the library door carefully and joined the doctor by the window. 'One would think Mr Elkin was trying to intimidate us by pacing up and down outside this room.'

'I'm sure he is. But I hope I am not so easily intimidated.'

'I sometimes wonder whether I'm too suspicious of Elkin.'

'If you are, then so am I,' he said quietly. 'Dropping that bottle today was no accident. In my opinion, my dear lady, you cannot be suspicious enough – given the circumstance – or too careful of your own safety and health. Do not eat anything with which he could have tampered.'

She sighed. 'We can't *prove* anything against him, though! And if we turn him and his mother out without proof, ill as she is, people will cry shame on us. I'm a newcomer to the district, while the Elkins have lived nearby for a long time.'

'They may have lived in the district, but they haven't been good landlords and the family fortunes have been in decline for the past two decades. They have no land left now, beyond a barren moorland acre or two, and they even had to sell their house, so now live in a crumbling place that used to belong to the bailiff. The father, James Elkin, was heartily disliked and things have gone from bad to worse with the son, who is, I am told, another unlucky gambler.'

'And yet Elkin doesn't appear in need now. Look at his clothes. They're new and very fine, must have cost a great deal.'

'This change has only occurred in the past year or so. Before that his clothes were shabby, then suddenly he seemed to have money again, explaining it as some lucky gambling in London. But he hasn't moved from the bailiff's house, which they tell me is in a parlous condition, so one has to wonder.'

He smiled at her look of surprise. 'We doctors hear a great deal of gossip, you know.' Then his smile faded. 'I pity Mrs Elkin, I do indeed. That poor woman had a miserable marriage and is now in her son's power, for her jointure was all spent by her husband.' He shook his head in strong disapproval, then asked, 'What exactly does Matthew say about him?'

'He thinks it's better to have Elkin here, where we can keep an eye on his comings and goings at least, than leave him free to see anyone he pleases and plot in secret. I'm not sure I agree.' After all, someone had shot at her husband inside their own home and she still shuddered when she thought of that. 'What are we going to do about Mrs Elkin now?'

'Nothing. I feel her best chance of getting better is to take no potions at all. And you should tell her maid to be careful what her mistress eats and drinks.'

'Her son enters her bedchamber regularly, though. How can we stop him from putting things in her food and drink?'

'Is the maid working with him, do you think?'

Deborah chewed at one fingernail as she considered this, then shook her head. 'I don't think so. Both she and her mistress seem terrified of him.'

'This is a difficult business. I'll have a word with Matthew before I leave.'

'If you can find him. He's been very busy today.' She couldn't keep the sharpness out of her voice, because although he hadn't told her what he was doing, she was sure he was planning something with Jem. Pulling herself together, she said more temperately, 'Well, Elkin cannot stay here for ever, can he?'

Her words seemed to echo prophetically round the room. Staying for ever was exactly what that man wanted, what he was trying to arrange by fair means or foul.

'I suppose I'd better speak to him about his mother now,' Dr Lethbury said with a grimace.

'I'll go and tell him you're free.'

When she went outside, Elkin sauntered across to her, standing so close she took an involuntary step backwards. 'You said you wished to see Dr Lethbury. He's waiting for you in the library.'

'Thank you, Cousin Deborah.'

Oh, so she was 'cousin' again this morning, was she? And spoken in a caressing tone, too. Did he think she was a total fool?

The interview didn't last long and there were no raised voices, though Deborah lingered nearby, just in case the doctor had need of an interruption.

When Dr Lethbury had ridden away, she saw Elkin go outside again but luckily he didn't see her. He seemed unusually restless this morning and she couldn't help wondering why. She prayed he wasn't plotting something else, knew he must be.

Once he'd left the room, she went into the library and pulled a few books out to make it look as if she were tidying the bookcase, then went to stand by the window, hidden by the curtains, to continue watching him.

Her patience was rewarded half an hour later when she saw his manservant come running across from the stables. Elkin, who'd been pacing to and fro in the garden, moved swiftly to meet him and the two men disappeared in the direction of the gate in the dry stone wall which separated the grounds from the moors.

What had sent the man running for his master? She wondered whether to follow them, but resisted the impulse. Not only was there no way for her to hide her presence on the moors, but Matthew was right. It was too risky for her to be alone with Elkin.

Even in the house he made her feel ill at ease and she sincerely pitied anyone who was in his power.

—

The two men left the grounds and walked along a path that led towards the moors. When they were about a hundred paces from the house Elkin stopped and looked at his companion. 'Well? It's not often I see you moving in such haste, Seth. What's happened?'

His companion grinned. 'Chadding's just told me the mother's been seen with her maid. The groom who brought a message from Mr Lawrence stopped in Rochdale on the way back to Newgarth and heard that two old women had left the inn suddenly when a maid recognised them from Lawrence's wanted poster. They got away, but they can only be making for Marymoor. The groom returned to tell Chadding, who acts for his master in such situations.'

'Ah!'

'He's very anxious to find them and has asked for my help.' Seth grinned. 'I've said I'll have to ask your permission first, but I think we should help him find her. After that, we may discover that we have greater need of the old dame than his master does.'

'We may indeed. Having her in our power will enable us to persuade that woman to do as we wish – *exactly* as we wish – once Pascoe is disposed of. Hire any help you need, but find those old women before they get to Marymoor and stow them safely away in the cottage.'

'I'll do my best, but it won't be easy. They could be taking any route to get here from Rochdale.'

Elkin frowned in thought, then shook his head. 'Not if they're trying to avoid being seen. They'll be coming across the moors not using the main highway. And anyone heading for Marymoor across the tops has to take North Edge Way for the last part of the journey. That's where we'll catch them. I'm sure of it.'

Seth had seen his master sure of something before, especially when he was gambling, and didn't share his optimism. 'Dare we restrict ourselves to watching the one route?' he ventured.

Elkin threw back his head and laughed. 'Oh, yes, we dare indeed, because even if they get through to Marymoor, we can still seize them. But we need to keep Chadding out of the way, so see if you can persuade him to watch the main highway from Rochdale. And the minute we have the old women we'll deal with Pascoe permanently. This time he won't escape.'

'You'll have to marry her to be sure of obtaining Marymoor House.'

'That'll be no hardship. She's a cosy enough armful if somewhat pert in manner. Once I've schooled her to be obedient, I may decide she's just what I need, especially if she proves fertile. A man needs an heir, after all. But if she proves an uncomfortable wife, well, we have ways of removing annoyances, do we not?'

Seth nodded. 'Will there be enough money to stop doing the other thing?' he asked, after a thoughtful silence. 'We've been lucky so far in our dealings, but luck can run out, as I warned you at the beginning. They hung my former partner for highway robbery. I don't want to follow him to the gallows.'

Elkin was silent, staring into the distance as he thought this through. 'Marymoor isn't a rich estate.'

'Then maybe once you've secured your inheritance, you'll have to dispose of your poor wife and find yourself an heiress.'

'I suppose you're right. Pity. Heiresses are always so ugly and they have to be wooed with great care or they fly away to nest elsewhere. And they usually have damned relatives who want to interfere.'

Seth decided it was time to change the subject a little. His master had already tried and failed to woo two heiresses. 'And your mother?'

'Oh, she's served our purpose here. It's more than time she recovered from her indisposition. When I move into Marymoor, she and that maid can stay on at the bailiff's house. They needn't cost us much.' He gave a mirthless snort of laughter. 'From what she said last winter, the dampness is like to kill her.'

Seth kept silent. He knew Elkin was always in two minds about his mother. He treated her ruthlessly, but had once revealed that he had pleasant memories of her from his childhood. Lucky him! Seth had no pleasant memories of his family and if he never saw any of them again, he'd be happy.

The only thing that counted, as far as he was concerned, was money and for the moment Anthony Elkin was enabling him to get some of that precious commodity for himself. When Elkin was no more use to him, he'd leave and find someone else who needed the services of a man who wasn't afraid to dirty his hands when paid well enough.

When Matthew went into the village to see the innkeeper, he made his way across the fields and slipped through the back gardens. He made no attempt to enter the inn, but went into the stables, startling the ostler.

'Eh, Mr Pascoe, you nearly frit me out of my skin.'

'I want to see your master but I don't want anyone to know I'm here. Can you go and fetch him for me?'

'Aye, sir.'

Matthew nodded. 'You get yourself a glass of ale and a bite to eat now, lad, but keep your mouth closed about my visit, eh?'

When John went out to the stables Sam moved to follow his father but was shooed back inside with a genial, 'Not this time, lad.'

Matthew had been leaning against the half-door of one stall, lost in thought, but he straightened up when John came in. 'I got your note. What exactly's been happening?'

John explained about the surly messenger who said he'd come from Chadding's employer. 'He left yesterday, then returned very early in the morning, looking as if he'd been up all night, as did his poor horse, so I thought,

"Something's afoot." And since Elkin's been seen talking to Chadding a couple of times, I thought you'd want to know. My Sam tried to get close enough to eavesdrop, but didn't manage, more's the pity. I never did take to that Chadding, not from the start, though he's always civil enough. But anyone as takes up with Elkin is up to no good as we've all seen many a time, even when he was a lad.'

Matthew patted the horse absent-mindedly as it nudged him. 'I was coming to see you anyway. I think the time has come for us to take more direct action. I'd been hoping that if I gave Elkin a long enough rope, he'd hang himself, but he's treading very carefully, damn him!'

'He always was clever at protecting himself.'

'Can I count on your help if I need it, John?' He didn't really need to ask. There had been a time when the two of them had worked in the same trade of inn-keeping, when Matthew hadn't hesitated to ask John's advice on wine and ale, yes, and follow it too. Later, when he came to Marymoor, he'd hired a distant connection of John's to run the inn, and he was a good man, too.

Elkin had never learned how useful country networks could be, but Matthew knew and was glad of them now. If anything happened to Deborah... He suppressed that thought. He wouldn't *let* any harm come to her.

'You know you can count on me, lad,' John said. 'What are you going to do?'

'I don't know yet, but I'm not going to sit around worrying about whether someone's going to take another shot at me. It's time to flush Elkin out into the open and end this affair once and for all.' He turned to leave, then stopped to add, 'If you receive any message from me, it'll say "for old time's sake" or it'll be false.'

John nodded and watched Matthew slip out the back way. He hoped his friend knew what he was doing. Elkin was a tricky devil.

–

Isabel and Bessie set off the next morning but made even slower progress. They were walking slowly and wearily along the moorland track, trying to avoid the worst of the mud, when a gentleman rode past them on horseback. He was exquisitely dressed, but with a haughty expression on his face. He slowed down enough not to splatter them with mud, but stared at them indifferently and made no attempt to offer a greeting.

'Doesn't hurt a body to pass the time of day,' Bessie grumbled as they stopped to watch him ride on and turn down a side track to the left.

'Never mind. He must think we're vagrants, we look so bedraggled.' Isabel looked down at herself and sighed. 'I wish a cart would come past and give us a ride. My feet are hurting.'

'Do you want to rest again?'

'No. I just want to get to Marymoor. You're exhausted, too, Bessie, and don't pretend you're not.'

'We're getting old, Mrs Isabel.'

A sigh was her only answer.

When they were a little way past the same side track as the rider had taken they heard a rumbling sound and turned to see a cart coming along it towards them. Both women stopped automatically to watch it.

'Will the cart turn our way, do you think?' Isabel asked. 'Or will it go back towards Rochdale?'

When it turned their way, she could not hold back a sob. 'Dear God, let the driver be of kindly disposition. If he refuses us a ride, I don't think I can bear it.'

The cart came towards them and when Bessie waved one hand, the driver reined in his horse alongside them. 'We're heading towards Marymoor. Would you be kind enough to give us a ride?'

He studied them thoughtfully. 'You ladies look tired,' he said. 'Have you come far?'

'From near Rochdale.'

'Well, I'm heading towards Marymoor and I don't mind giving you a ride, but I have a call to make on the way, so I hope you don't mind a little detour. Got relatives in Marymoor, have you?'

'My daughter,' Isabel said before Bessie could stop her.

'Would I know her?'

'She's called Deborah. Visiting Mr Jannvier.'

'Oh, yes. I've seen her.' He smiled at them. 'Well, can't stay her chatting all day, can we? Climb up behind and let's get moving.'

Eagerly the two women scrambled up on to the tail of the cart and made themselves as comfortable as old bones can on bare boards.

As they set off again, the driver threw over his shoulder, 'The place I have to stop is a farm. They want me to take some stuff into Marymoor for them. It'll only add an hour to our journey. I'm sure the farmer's wife will offer you a bite to eat while you wait for me. She's a kindly soul.'

'That'd be very welcome,' Isabel admitted.

Bessie didn't say anything. The man was being kind to them, but she just couldn't take to him and she wished Mrs Isabel hadn't mentioned Deborah. It hadn't escaped her notice that he hadn't given them his name or asked theirs. But it was such a relief not to be walking. And she was probably being foolish to be so suspicious.

As the cart rattled along, the driver began to whistle cheerfully but made no further attempt to engage them in conversation.

Within minutes, Isabel had fallen asleep and Bessie was dozing. They were sheltered from the wind by the sides of the cart and the rain was holding off.

Seth smiled as he tugged on the reins so that the horse turned off towards the right. Never caught a pair of pigeons so easily, he thought. You're right. Things are definitely going our way, master. These two have even told me they're the right ones.

–

When Deborah went up to see her, Mrs Elkin was dozing but looked a little better, with more colour in her cheeks.

'The doctor suggested you take care what your mistress eats and drinks,' Deborah told the maid. 'Perhaps you should keep some food out by the bed, but eat only what you've kept safe elsewhere?'

Denise stared at her, then clapped one hand to her mouth and glanced towards the bed. 'You know, don't you?' she asked in a low voice.

'About your mistress's son deliberately making her ill? Yes.'

The maid started wringing her hands together. 'He'll kill me if he finds out I've been talking to you. Or turn me off without a character and then what will my poor mistress do?'

'Has he – done this sort of thing before?'

Words poured out. 'He uses her all the time, whether she's well or not, but for all she's afraid of him, she won't hear a word against him. And yes, she fell ill unexpectedly at a cousin's house two years ago. It bought us a few days of comfort when we didn't know where to turn for our next meal.'

Deborah made a soothing murmur but didn't interrupt the flow of confidences. She hadn't realised Elkin had been so short of money – and so recently, too. He didn't seem short now. The maid's next words echoed her thoughts.

'All that one cares about is himself. He's got money from somewhere now, probably from his gambling. Well, just look at those clothes he's wearing! But he won't spend it on making the house more comfortable, will he? No, he just leaves us there and it's like to fall down about our ears. The roof leaks, there isn't enough wood to last the winter and I'm at my wits' end how to look after her properly, I am that.' She began sobbing, muffling the sound in her apron.

Deborah patted her on the shoulder, thinking furiously. 'If you should happen to have any useful information about what he's planning, my husband and I would make sure you were all right afterwards, give you a place here if he turned you off.'

Denise pulled away. 'I wish I could. Oh, I do wish I could tell you everything. But he'd do more than turn me off. He'd kill me if he found out I'd been talking about him.' She turned away, blowing her nose and making obvious efforts to stop weeping. 'I'm sorry, Mrs Pascoe. I daren't talk to you any more.'

She moved across to the door as a signal that Deborah should leave, but didn't open it immediately. 'If you don't mind my saying so, you ought to be very careful of crossing him. He's ruthless. And more than that I dare not say, for my life I dare not.'

—

When Matthew returned from the village he went to find his wife, marvelling at how even the thought of seeing her made his spirits lift. He found her in the small linen room and stopped in the doorway for a moment, enjoying the sight of her with a pinafore tied round her slender body and a slight flush on her cheeks. He'd have hated to marry a woman who was too fine to apply herself to honest toil. He smiled at the thought. A funny thing to find attractive, wasn't it? But his money had been too hard won to idle around as Elkin did, and he didn't want a wife who just sat around primping and being a burden to him.

She was going through the yellowed linen, muttering to herself as she moved things to various piles.

'The linen doesn't please you?' he asked with a smile. 'Do we need new sheets?'

She jumped in shock, then relaxed and smiled at him.

'Everything is in such a muddle, I don't know what we need. Mrs Simley has been a terrible housekeeper. Wait till Bessie takes over here. She'll turn the house upside down and have us all running to do her bidding till it's to her liking.'

He smiled as he remembered the suspicious old woman who had opened the door to him in Newgarth. He hadn't had time to be polite, so would probably have to mend his fences with her when she came to live here. 'You're very fond of your maid.'

'Yes. Bessie's stayed with us through good times and bad, and she's more like family than a servant. I don't know what my mother would do without her and since my father's death we haven't been able to pay her a penny piece in wages.'

The maid rose still further in his esteem. That was another thing he valued highly, loyalty. 'You can remedy that when she comes here.' He frowned. 'I'd expected to hear from young George by now. He's had time enough to find them.'

Deborah's smile faded. 'You think – something might be wrong?'

'I wondered if your uncle might have stopped your mother leaving. Would he do such a thing?'

'If he saw a profit in it for himself.'

'Then as soon as we've dealt with Elkin, we'll go and fetch them ourselves.'

She beamed at him, clutching a pile of linen to her breast. She was caught in a stray sunbeam that lit up the glory of that beautiful hair which was already escaping from the confines of the cap and hair pins.

For a moment they stood there staring at one another. The man she'd married, Deborah thought, might appear stern to others, but he had a way of smiling at her that made something inside her melt. She wished they had time to get to know one another properly, instead of having to deal with one crisis after another. Still, at least they'd been able to snatch precious moments like these every now and then. That helped bring them closer.

'Did they tell you in the stables that Elkin's man came to find him this morning and they left together?' she asked.

'Aye.'

'He came *running* across to the house, so it must have been something important. And the two of them rode out together soon after.'

Reluctantly Matthew dragged his thoughts back from contemplation of last night's pleasures to the present crisis. 'Did you see where they went?'

'They rode across the moors. I didn't think there was anything in that direction.'

She put down the linen and would have moved past him but he caught her in his arms and pulled her close, bending his head to kiss her.

She didn't even try to pull away, giving him back kiss for kiss and twining her arms round his neck.

Only the knowledge that he had important things to do made him end the embrace, but he couldn't help smiling down at her and lingering for long enough to say huskily, 'Once we have got rid of Elkin…'

'Yes.' Her voice was a breath only but her eyes were full of smiling promise.

'I had a message from John only a few minutes ago that Seth had been speaking to Chadding, after which the fellow rode out along the main road to Rochdale. He's left his things at the inn, though, so he's coming back.'

'Do you think the groom who came back to speak to Chadding had discovered something about my mother? Why else should he return here so quickly? He didn't have time to get back to Newgarth or see my uncle.' She shook her head in bewilderment. 'I can't work out what's happening. I only know I'm worried sick about my mother and Bessie.'

Matthew paused for a wary glance sideways, then risked saying, 'I think it's time to set a trap for Elkin.'

'How shall you do that?'

'What better bait than myself?'

'*No!* Matthew, no, I forbid it!'

'It's the only bait he'll take, Deborah.'

'But you may get hurt.'

'If I do nothing, someone will definitely get hurt.' He pulled her into his arms and said into the warmth of her neck, 'I shall take the greatest care of myself, I promise you. I have a lot to live for.' But he pushed her aside quickly before he lost himself in kissing her. He needed all his concentration if he was to come out of this alive.

After he'd gone back outside she tried to settle to work again, but couldn't. The thought of Matthew deliberately putting himself in danger terrified her. She'd only just found him, couldn't bear to lose him now.

—

As the cart drew up with a jangling of harness and much snorting from the horse, Bessie woke with a start and looked around. They'd stopped in front of a tiny, tumbledown cottage which stood alone in a dip in the slope leading up to the moors. Wind whistled around them and no other habitation was in sight. This place definitely wasn't a farm. She nudged her mistress, feeling suddenly anxious, and when Isabel woke with a start, helped her sit up.

'I don't know where we are, but it doesn't feel right,' she whispered. 'Oh, why did I let myself fall asleep?'

The driver jumped down and came round to the back of the cart. 'Why don't you come inside, ladies.'

'I think we'll wait here,' Bessie said quickly, feeling more nervous by the minute, she couldn't understand why. 'You see to your business and we'll just sit here quietly.'

'How can I load the cart with you on it?' He held out one hand imperatively just as a horseman came riding along the track.

The fine gentleman who had passed them earlier reined in his horse and sat staring down at them. 'Are you Deborah's mother?' he asked Isabel.

'Yes. Yes, I am.'

'Good. If you'll come inside, I'll send her a message to say you've arrived. She'll want to come and see you.'

But Bessie didn't trust him any more than the driver, for the look in his eyes was cold and he was staring at them in a way that was insulting, as if they were of no account, dirt beneath his feet. He might dress like a gentleman, but he didn't act like one in her opinion.

Isabel looked at her uncertainly, then back at the rider. 'Can we not go to her? This man promised us a ride to Marymoor.'

'You can't see her quite yet.' Elkin dismounted and left the reins dangling as he strode across to offer them a hand down and say imperatively, 'Come!'

Isabel edged forward and took the help he offered. When she was down, he led her off towards the house.

The driver of the cart came to help Bessie down.

'Who is that man and how did he know Mrs Isabel was Miss Deborah's mother?' she asked.

'You'll find out when you're inside.'

When she didn't move, he dragged her off the cart, taking no care about whether he bumped her or not. That proved her suspicions were not groundless and something was very wrong indeed. Miss Deborah wouldn't associate with men who hurt folk like that. Nor would she want to keep her mother hidden in a lonely cottage on the moors.

So who were these people and why had they brought them here?

But Bessie knew better than to shout out her suspicions. As she stumbled along by his side, the man kept hold of her arm. A cold wind whistled about her ears and she could see no other habitations. She didn't protest about what was happening. What was the use? Two strong men could do as they wanted with two old women like her and Mrs Isabel. No, she must keep her wits about her and pretend to be weaker and more stupid than she was.

No one knew they were here, so no one else could come and rescue them. They would have to help themselves. If they could.

And if there was a way, any way at all, she'd find it.

–

George rode along the moorland track only an hour after the two women had been abducted. He had spoken to a woman weeding a field, who had definitely seen them, and knew he was getting close. He touched the butt of his pistol, which he had ready loaded, praying he might find them before others did.

When he passed a cottage, he knocked on the door. 'I'm sorry to disturb you, mistress, but I'm seeking two old women who have been travelling across the moors towards Marymoor. Have you seen them today?'

The woman shook her head. 'No women have passed this way, only two riders heading in the other direction.'

'Are you sure of that?'

She nodded. 'Very sure. I was out working in the garden all morning. It's near the road and I'd have seen anyone who passed by.' She laughed. 'There are so few travellers along this road we watch for them and call out for news if they look friendly. I didn't call out to Mr Elkin, though.'

'Elkin? He was one of the riders?'

'Yes. He lives a few miles away now in the old bailiff's house, but he used to live closer before the family lost all their money.' She eased her back with both hands, then repeated, 'No, I'd definitely have seen your old ladies if they'd passed by today.'

George frowned at her, then looked back along the track, shaking his head. 'Thank you for your help.' He rode a short distance along the track in the direction of Marymoor, then turned back. He believed the woman.

But where could Mrs Jannvier and her maid have gone? He had grown up on the other side of Marymoor and only recently started working for Mr Pascoe, so he didn't know this side of the village very well at all. There didn't seem to be many farms round here, just the moors and a few fields on the higher side of the road and who knew what on the downhill slopes, which had more trees growing on them.

In the end he decided, with great reluctance, that it was time to return to Marymoor and tell Mr Pascoe all he knew. He hated to admit that he hadn't found the old ladies, wanted Jem to think well of him, wanted to keep his job at Marymoor. But he'd done all he could on his own, especially if Mr Elkin were involved. Jem knew the district far better than he did and would work out what to do next. And George would be right next to him, helping.

11

When the man who called himself Chadding rode out of Marymoor village, he searched for a place to tie up his horse, so that he could keep watch for travellers without being seen. He found a perfect place, a small grove of windswept trees, behind which the ground sloped down so that he could tether the horse out of sight. As long as it didn't rain, he could sit on the ground with his back against a tree and watch who passed by.

He settled down to wait, getting quickly bored because there were so few travellers, mainly farm carts going from one field to another. Easy enough to see who was driving them. The only trouble would be if the old ladies were inside a vehicle or hidden under something. From the way they'd fled from Rochdale, they must know that Mr Lawrence was pursuing them.

He grinned as he wriggled into a more comfortable position. Things couldn't have suited him and his master better. Mr Elkin intended to kill Pascoe, then a widowed Deborah would have land and money. He was quite sure the master would find a way to get hold of it and that some of it would fall his way. Mr Lawrence wasn't a generous man, but knew to a nicety how much he needed to pay to keep the loyalty of those who served him in special ways.

Elkin thought Frank was going to deliver his master's niece and the estate she'd inherited into his hands, which just showed how stupid the man was.

Frank kept watch all day, though at one point he rode to a nearby inn for a quick sup of ale and a bite to eat, making sure he sat where he could keep an eye on the road. The innkeeper tried to find out his business, but he knew how to keep his mouth shut. Good ale, it was, though.

As darkness began to fall he debated whether to stay on a bit longer, but decided the old ladies would have found shelter for the night by now. If they hadn't, if anything had happened to them, his master would not be entirely displeased. They were more trouble than they were worth, really, for there was no profit to be made from them.

Mounting his horse he rode slowly back to Marymoor, looking forward to a good dinner at The Woolpack and hoping Seth would pop in for a chat. He'd watch the road for another day or two, then if he didn't see any sign of the old dames, he'd try something else. There were times when you had to be patient and this was one of them. The groom would have reached Newgarth by now, with news of what was happening.

–

Seth turned up just as Frank was finishing a hearty meal of lamb stew in the common room of the Woolpack. He gestured to the other man to join him, but Seth gave a small jerk of the head to invite Frank to follow him outside instead, so regretfully he left the rest of the food and heaved himself to his feet.

The two men strolled along the street.

John gestured to young Sam to follow them.

'Have any luck today?' Seth asked.

'No. Did *you* see anything?'

'Yes, we did actually. We captured both of the old biddies.'

'Ah! My master will be grateful.'

Seth stopped to grin at Frank in the light of a lantern hanging outside a house. 'No, he won't.'

'What the hell do you mean by that? You haven't killed them, surely?'

'Of course we haven't. It's just that we need them ourselves, so I'm afraid your master will have to manage without his dear sister. And in case you have any idea of making trouble...' Without warning Seth punched Frank in the jaw and watched in satisfaction as the other man went sprawling. He pulled a dagger out and flipped it from one hand to the other. 'Let me warn you now that it'll be safer for you to get out of the village at once – far safer – or you might find yourself in even worse trouble.' He rapped the blade of the dagger on his palm, then turned and walked briskly away.

Seth had disappeared into the darkness before Frank managed to haul himself to his feet, for he was still feeling muzzy from the well-placed blow. He was furious that he'd been taken for a fool. 'We'll see about that,' he muttered and went back to the inn to look for the landlord.

Sam had enjoyed the sight of Chadding measuring his length on the ground, because the man had shoved him out of the way several times, as if a mere boy didn't count for anything. He hurried home, eager to tell his dad what had happened and what he'd overheard.

When Chadding came back into the inn, he ordered a pot of ale.

'Eh, that's a nasty bruise. Fall over, did you?' John said.
'Yes.'

'I'll get your ale.' Grinning broadly, John walked across to the current barrel. Served the rascal right.

When he carried the tankard across, Chadding looked up at him and said abruptly, 'I need some information and I'll be happy to reward you for helping me with it.'

'If I can do owt to help, you've only to ask.'

'Tell me about that fellow Elkin. Where exactly does he live? Tell me everything you know about him.'

—

The young groom arrived back at Marymoor in the late afternoon and found Jem and his master talking earnestly in one corner of the stables. They stopped speaking as they heard his horse snorting its pleasure at being home, then when they saw who it was, they both strode forward.

'Did you find them, George?' Matthew asked, even before the traveller had dismounted.

'No, sir. They'd run away from Newgarth before I arrived there.' George explained what had happened and how he'd lost the two old women somewhere along the moorland track that led to Marymoor. 'Mr Elkin had passed by, though.'

'Had he, indeed?' Matthew stood frowning. 'He and that rogue of his have been out of the house since this morning. Do you think he could have found the old ladies?'

George shrugged. 'Someone did. But I saw no sign of Mr Elkin myself, though the woman I spoke to was quite sure no one else had passed her cottage. But another woman I saw earlier weeding a field had definitely seen the old ladies heading towards Marymoor. She said they looked tired and were walking slowly.'

Matthew frowned into space for a moment and the others waited respectfully.

'Elkin's own house isn't on the Rochdale road, though he can ride out anywhere he chooses, I suppose.' He came to a decision. 'I want you and Jem to ride along that track as soon as it's light tomorrow morning. See what you can find, but try not to let Elkin or his man see you. Come back here as soon as you can, though. We have a trap to set.'

'Are you going to tell Mrs Pascoe what's happened?' Jem asked when George had gone to stable his horse.

'No. It's only guesswork at the moment and I don't want to worry her unnecessarily. We're only supposing the two old women were her mother and maid, only guessing that something's happened to them.' Though he had a strong feeling that this was Mrs Jannvier, and that Elkin had been involved. It was too much of a coincidence for two other old ladies to be making for this isolated village.

After a further silence, he added slowly, 'Set watch tonight round the house again and inside it, too, Jem. I'm not having Elkin creating mischief in my own home. As for tomorrow, make sure his man finds out I'm going to buy some stock and which direction I'll be taking. Let's see if they'll take the bait.'

'You're putting yourself too much at risk, Matt lad,' Jem protested.

'How else can we draw them into the open? But I've chosen a lane which doesn't have any shelter close to it, so I don't think the risk is great. We'll keep watch on it from dawn to prevent anyone getting near, and we all know how unreliable pistols are from a distance.'

But Jem couldn't help worrying as he went about his business. He didn't like this at all. If anything happened to Matthew, Mrs Deborah would be in serious trouble.

And so would he and the other inhabitants of Marymoor. In such a small place what people did affected their neighbour's lives as well as their own, especially what the landowner did.

—

Mrs Elkin looked so much better when Deborah went to check on her that evening that she asked gently, 'Do you think you'll feel well enough to leave tomorrow?'

The older woman's face crumpled and she stared pleadingly at her hostess. 'Another day, perhaps? So that I'm truly rested?'

Deborah found herself unable to refuse this plea and nodded.

Both mistress and maid sighed in relief.

'Will your son be taking you home in his carriage?' Deborah asked.

'I suppose so.'

'We should let him know how much better you are.'

'Tomorrow?' Again, it was a plea.

'Very well.'

Deborah went away to see about supper, then changed into her one good gown and waited for Matthew in her room. She heard him come running up the stairs, no mistaking his tread. When he stopped in the doorway, he smiled at her in that way she was beginning to recognise. The smile crept across his face slowly, as if he hadn't done much smiling in his life, lighting up the sombre planes and making him look younger. She hadn't seen him smile at anyone else like that.

'Wait and talk to me while I wash and change my clothes?' he begged.

'Of course. I wanted to speak to you anyway, to tell you Mrs Elkin is much better.'

He frowned. 'So she's leaving tomorrow?'

'She begged to be allowed another day here and I – well, I found I couldn't refuse her. She's a very unhappy woman and seems terrified of her son.'

He looked at her in resigned exasperation, but didn't protest her decision, because it suited his current plans. Besides, it was already clear to him that Deborah was not the sort to turn away from someone else's troubles and he liked that in her.

'George has returned,' he said abruptly, changing his mind about telling her.

'Did he see my mother?'

'No. It seems she and Bessie had run away by the time he got to Newgarth.'

She could only gape at him. '*Run away?* But why would they do that?'

'Your uncle apparently dismissed Bessie and told her to leave the village before nightfall, so your mother went too. George followed their tracks for a while then lost them.' Matthew hesitated, then added, 'And it seems your uncle's put up posters saying your mother has lost her wits. He's offering a reward to anyone who finds her and returns her to his care.' He watched the colour drain from his wife's face and reached out to grasp her hand.

'He's threatened to have her locked away before,' she whispered. 'It terrified her. I think he'd do it, too.'

'Well, from now on, we'll take her in charge and make sure no one frightens her. Who better to look after her than her own daughter?'

She looked at him numbly. 'If we find her in time. If she's all right.'

He pulled her into his arms and held her close. 'We *will* find your mother, love, I promise you.'

She nodded and watched him finish dressing in the one good suit he had, made of fine dark grey broadcloth, instead of the brocades and silks Elkin wore. She knew which she preferred. As she watched it occurred to her that he had called her 'love'. Did he really mean that, or was it simply the casual form of address used by Lancashire folk?

It was with reluctance that she moved forward to accompany him downstairs for supper. She didn't want to share him with anyone else, especially Elkin. They'd had so little privacy since their marriage. 'I wish we could stay here and not go downstairs,' she murmured.

He stopped in the doorway, turning to look at her. 'Do you?'

She nodded.

He pulled her into his arms again for a quick embrace. 'So do I.'

His lips were close to her ears, his breath warm on her cheek. And when he raised one hand to twist a strand of her hair round his finger, she felt herself sag against him.

'Ah, Deborah!'

Her name was the merest whisper then his lips moved against hers and she lost herself in his kiss.

His breath came unevenly as he pushed her away from him. 'Later.'

She nodded and tried to pull herself together, but it was difficult with desire for him still swirling round her body. She hadn't realised how much you could hunger for a man's touch, how love came from the body as well as the heart and mind.

It was a moment before he reached for the door handle and even then he hesitated before saying quietly, 'When I invite you to ride out with me tomorrow, please refuse.'

The warmth inside her was replaced abruptly by fear.

What was he planning to do? She'd have asked him, but he'd already left the room and was waiting for her on the landing.

–

Elkin was determinedly affable over supper, but Deborah noticed a gleam in his eyes, as if he were mocking them while play-acting the polite guest. She wished she had hardened her heart to Mrs Elkin's pleas to stay. It was too late to do anything about that now, though.

'Did you enjoy your ride out?' she asked as she picked at her food, feeling duty bound to introduce one or two topics of conversation into the leaden silence that didn't seem to worry Matthew at all.

'Greatly,' Elkin said. 'There's nothing like rational exercise for keeping up the spirits and maintaining a healthy body. I apologise for not letting you know I'd not be here for dinner, but I went further than I'd intended.'

'You can *maintain a healthy body* even better with hard physical work,' Matthew said dryly.

Elkin's sneer became pronounced. 'I'm afraid some of us were not cut out to be *farmers*. Gentlemen do not work with their hands.'

Deborah stared down at her plate, suddenly finding herself without appetite for the food on it.

'Well, some of us lowly fellows enjoy being farmers, and you'd not have much to eat if we didn't. Deborah, I'm going to inspect some beasts I'm thinking of buying in the next village later tomorrow morning. Do you want to ride with me?'

She pretended to consider his invitation for a moment, tempted to accept in spite of what he'd said earlier. 'No, I think not. I have too much to do here.'

After forcing down another mouthful she looked at Elkin. 'Your mother was much improved today. If she keeps up this progress, she'll be ready to leave the day after tomorrow.'

Matthew paused in his eating. 'Good.'

'One should never outstay one's welcome, should one?' Elkin sneered.

Deborah ignored that. 'There is also the question of the Simleys. I hope you're prepared to employ them, Mr Elkin, because they seem quite devoted to you. Whatever your decision, I've told them to leave when you do.'

He laughed, a snarl of sound. 'Oh, I'm sure I can find something for them to do. But it won't look well, your turning off your uncle's servants so soon after his death.'

Matthew said in chill, emphatic tones, 'They've been in your pay for a while now, and I won't employ disloyal servants.'

'I simply wished to keep myself informed of my uncle's health and since he didn't write to me, it seemed easiest to ask the Simleys. I'm still not convinced that he changed his will of his own accord.'

Both men stared at each other across the table and the tension rose palpably until Matthew waved one hand dismissively. 'Well, as long as the law is convinced he did and *I* know it's the truth, *you* can believe what you want.'

Elkin's expression was, for a moment, murderous.

Deborah's heart was in her mouth as she waited for something to happen, but it didn't. Both men turned to their food and addressed it in silence, as if neither was ready for a confrontation. Gradually the tension eased a little, but things were never truly calm when these two men were in the same room.

After the meal was over she rose, unable to bear any more. 'I'm tired. I think I'll retire now.'

Matthew waited till she'd left to say to Elkin, 'You'd be wiser to accept what's happened.'

Elkin shrugged ever so slightly. 'When was I ever wise?' he asked the ceiling.

As the door slammed shut behind Matthew, he smiled down at his glass of port. 'Enjoy your possession while you can, Pascoe. Tomorrow it'll end.'

–

Deborah woke up the next morning with a feeling of apprehension that deepened when she found herself alone in the bed. That fact that Matthew was nowhere to be seen worried her even more than usual because it was barely dawn. What was he doing? She prayed he was being careful.

She got up at once, washing and dressing in cold water, not wanting to waste a minute. Then she went down to the kitchen, determined to make sure the Simleys understood they were to leave the following day with the Elkins. After that she didn't care what happened to them.

She found only Merry in the kitchen. 'Where's Mrs Simley?'

'Oh, she never gets up this early. I usually start things off. If I'd known you were awake, I'd have brought you some hot water. The master said to let you sleep.'

'I couldn't sleep and cold water is no hardship in summer.' She decided to remind the maid of the situation. 'The Simleys will be leaving tomorrow with the Elkins, but we're happy for you to stay on in our employment.'

Merry beamed at her. 'I'll be glad to see the back of them and happy to stay on here. You won't regret it, Mrs Pascoe, I promise you.'

'I'm sure I won't.' Deborah cut herself a slice of bread and went out to the stables, but the sight of Seth lounging in the yard watching Jem work made her turn away. Where was her husband? Surely he hadn't set off to buy the stock yet?

She couldn't settle to anything, so took herself off to the linen room to continue sorting out the yellowed sheets and tablecloths. It still amazed her that a house should have a room solely devoted to linen and other household items, though it was, of course, very convenient – and that all these rooms should belong to her and her husband. How happy she could be here if Elkin would only go away!

Hearing a sound she looked up, to see him standing in the doorway watching her. He was dressed in a nightcap and banyan, the loose indoor garment fastened only by a sash around the waist. 'Did you need something?' she asked crisply. 'I'm rather busy, I'm afraid, so if you'll just ask the Simleys.'

'So I can see. I was enjoying the sight of my pretty cousin working so assiduously. You have beautiful hair, Deborah.'

'I'd prefer you not to talk to me like that.'

'I talk as I please.'

'You wouldn't if my husband were here.'

'He does cramp my style somewhat,' Elkin agreed. 'And he certainly doesn't deserve a lovely woman like you.'

She would have left, but that would have meant pushing past him, so she concentrated on the linen, counting it carefully, but forgetting the total when Elkin cleared his throat. Reluctantly she looked towards him again.

'I shall look forward to seeing you at breakfast,' he said, his eyes full of innuendo as they raked her body. 'Maybe today we can sit next to one another.'

She shuddered, couldn't hide it.

He scowled for a moment, then forced a laugh, though it was a mirthless sound. Turning, he strolled off.

The encounter only added to her worries. How dared he accost her like that? It must mean he was sure Matthew wasn't in the house. Had her husband left without saying farewell even?

He still hadn't appeared when it was time for the formal breakfast at nine o'clock and Deborah wondered whether to stay in her room and ring for Merry to bring her something. But she didn't want Elkin to think that he'd frightened her, so she checked that her clothes and hair were neat, pinning up some stray wisps of hair before she made her way down the stairs.

Her guest was already in the dining room, standing by the window looking out. To her relief he was more formally dressed now, wearing garments suitable for riding.

He turned as she came in and swept her a mocking bow. 'We meet again. And it seems we're to break our fast tête-à-tête today.'

He spoke with his usual mocking intonation, waving one hand towards the table and she wondered why he never seemed to speak normally, even to his mother. There was always some hidden meaning lurking behind his words, usually unpleasant.

She stared at the table, noting it was set only for two, and her heart sank. 'Matthew was going to buy some beasts,' she said – calmly, she hoped.

'Yes. Our noble sovereign would be very impressed by him and his devotion to farming. But then we can't all be like Farmer George, can we?'

She ignored that, but in her opinion a king who set a good example to his subjects should not be mocked for his interest in agriculture by ne'er-do-wells like Anthony Elkin.

She took care to sit opposite her guest and promised herself that if he started making personal remarks she would leave the room at once. But he didn't. He spoke of life in London, the perils of travelling on bad roads, his pleasure that his mother was recovering. If it hadn't been for the mocking tone, it might have been interesting to hear of such things. But always the mockery was there and with it, to her, a sense of malice or downright evil. She listened with half an ear, wishing herself anywhere but here.

It was a while before she realised that Elkin was deliberately prolonging the meal. Good manners forced her to stay until he'd finished eating, but she replied only briefly to his flow of small talk and raised no topics herself.

'Tsk! Tsk!' he chided after a while. 'This is no way to conduct yourself in polite society, my dear Deborah. A lady should be able to maintain a light conversation with her guests.'

'I do not consider this "polite society",' she countered, letting her annoyance show for once.

For a moment she saw clearly the vicious brute behind the smiling face, the brute whose actions had, she was sure, set the dissolute lines down the cheeks and the chill world-weariness in the grey eyes. She wished she'd minded her tongue, though. It did no good to rile him.

When the meal at last came to an end, she stood up. 'I have a great deal to do and no doubt you will wish to start your man packing your clothes ready for your departure tomorrow.'

He rose swiftly and barred her way to the door. 'First come outside and take a breath of fresh air with me.'

'No, thank you.'

'I have news of your mother,' he said very softly. 'But if you mention that to anyone I shall deny it. What I have to say is for your ears only and there always seems to be someone hovering nearby inside the house.'

She froze, staring at him. 'I don't believe you.'

He pulled out a thin gold band and held it out between forefinger and thumb. When she reached for it, he pulled it back. 'You recognise it?'

'It's my mother's wedding ring.' She felt as if she were choking suddenly. 'How did you get it? She never normally takes it off.' And even her father had never tried to pawn that. The ring must have been taken forcibly from her mother.

'I shall tell you when we're away from the house, and only then.'

She hesitated, knowing this was to put herself in his power, something strictly forbidden by Matthew. But her husband wasn't here and that *was* her mother's ring, so she didn't dare refuse to go. 'Very well. I'll just go and fetch a mantle.'

'It's not cold. You don't need one. Either you come now or I toss this away and forget about the old lady. And Bessie. What do I care how uncomfortable they are?'

He knew the maid's name! She couldn't refuse to do what he wanted any longer. 'Very well.'

As they walked outside she looked for someone to see her go, but there was no one, and that in itself was strange. No gardener, no groom, no sign of Merry working about the house. What had happened to everyone?

Almost she turned back. But the thought of her mother in this man's power kept her moving on. When Elkin offered his arm, she took it and, heart thudding with anxiety, accompanied him across to the path across the moors, the one he had taken yesterday with his manservant.

She resolved not to go far, though, not out of sight of the house.

12

Elkin set a cracking pace, but after a while, since he didn't say anything further, Deborah stopped walking. As he scowled at her, she raised her chin and said defiantly, 'Tell me about my mother now or I'm returning to the house.'

'I don't think you can afford to make threats, Cousin Deborah.'

'I can do as I wish.' Suddenly she felt vulnerable and turned to go back. She shouldn't have come, whatever the threat he made. But he grabbed her arm and twisted it behind her back, making her cry out in pain. She tried to kick him, struggling against both him and her full skirts, but he only twisted harder, so that she cried out involuntarily and stopped struggling.

'That's better.' He increased the pain still more so that she had difficulty biting back another cry. 'You need to understand that I'm much stronger than you, Deborah – not only physically but in the cards I hold in my hand. I have your mother and Bessie, you see.'

Her breath caught in her throat. 'Where are they? Are they all right?'

'They're safe enough.' He paused and waited for a few moments before adding, 'For the moment, anyway.'

She stood there motionless, not struggling. She knew he was going to continue hurting her, whether she obeyed him or not, because he had the same expression in his eyes as her uncle, who also enjoyed inflicting pain on people. But she was quite sure Elkin would go much further than her uncle ever did, for Walter Lawrence was always concerned to maintain his public image as a gentleman, however badly he behaved in private.

'I'll take you to them,' Elkin offered when she didn't speak, 'as long as you behave yourself.'

'Why can't you bring them here?'

'Because they're useful bargaining counters to me. It should be obvious even to you that only a fool gives away his advantages for nothing.' He jerked her forward so that she had to start walking again.

It was no use screaming or she'd have done so, for Elkin had chosen his spot well and there was no one close enough to hear. 'I don't understand,' she said, though she would guess he wanted money from her in return for her mother's safe return.

'You don't need to understand until we get there.' He shoved her again, making her stumble and smiling as pain in the arm he was still holding twisted behind her back made her gasp.

She didn't try to reason with him any more, but stole the occasional glance sideways, trying to work out what he intended before he did it. She noticed that he was scanning the horizon every few paces, as if keeping a careful watch for something. She also managed to glance towards the house. Surely someone had noticed them leaving? But at this distance she couldn't make things out very clearly.

Without warning Elkin threw her to the ground and she couldn't help moaning as she scraped her arm on a stone.

He flung himself down beside her. 'Keep still. I have excellent eyesight and we don't want Merry to notice us as she picks some vegetables, do we?' As they lay there among the tussocks of wiry grass, he laughed softly and reached out to squeeze her breast. 'Next time you lie down with me, it'll be to serve my needs as a woman should.'

'I'm married to someone else!' She tried to pull away, but his hand was like iron clamped around her wrist.

'Keep still, I said!'

As she lay facing him in a parody of an embrace, he tweaked her nipple so hard it brought tears to her eyes.

'When I bed you,' he went on, speaking as lightly as if they were discussing the weather, 'you will do as you're told – unless you want that pretty little nipple slicing right off.'

She gasped in shock at this crude threat and fear skittered through her to sit in a quivering mass in her belly. He would do it, too. She knew that now, for he had abandoned all pretence of being a gentleman and was showing himself in his true colours – a beast, not a man.

This was why Mrs Elkin and her maid were so afraid of him? What had he done to them?

Matthew, she prayed. Oh, Matthew, please come and find me!

'Ah.' Elkin's voice was soft and throaty now. 'That frightens you, doesn't it? *Admit it!*' He shook her hard.

She nodded, not knowing what to say to placate him, but heaven help her, desperate to do so.

'If you value that soft, pretty body of yours, you had better realise that I always mean exactly what I threaten. Stop trying to fight me and learn to please me. Ah. The wench has gone inside again.' He sat up to scan the horizon again then jerked her to her feet without warning, hurting her and forcing her to start walking again.

When she opened her mouth to ask where they were going, he shook her hard. 'I told you to keep quiet, you stupid bitch. Can you not understand the King's English?'

After that she could only stumble along beside him, horrified that she had so stupidly got herself into this trouble and terrified that no one was going to rescue her from it before Elkin carried out his threat to bed her. She was absolutely certain she couldn't pretend docility if he tried, couldn't let him touch her intimately without instinctively struggling.

And then what would he do?

What had happened to her mother? Had Elkin killed her when he took the wedding ring? And Bessie, poor Bessie? What had he done to her?

–

Frank made good time on the road, pushing his horse to its limits to reach Newgarth. When he dismounted at the Hall, it stood where he left it, exhausted and trembling. 'See to it!' he yelled at the stable lad, striding off towards the house without waiting for an answer.

It being past noon, he had hoped to find his master at home, but wasn't in luck.

'The family's gone to visit the Finchcombes at the Priory,' the housekeeper told him. 'Very set up about getting the invitation, the master was, but the fellow as brought it told me his master was inviting everyone in the neighbourhood, to put on a show for their fine London visitors.' All the servants knew that some of the old county families would have little to do with the Lawrences, who were newly rich, and most of them secretly relished seeing their master fail to get what he wanted.

Frank stood there biting his lip. Should he leave this till his master came home? No, definitely not. 'I've not broken my fast bar a slice of bread at dawn,' he said abruptly. 'Can you get me something to eat while I change my clothes? I think I'd better ride over to the Priory and speak to Mr Lawrence. I've urgent news for him.'

'Certainly. What would you like?' She knew it paid to stay on the good side of Frank, who was close to the master and could be even nastier if not treated well. Like master like man, they said, and she lived with proof of that, heaven help her.

'Get me anything you have. But plenty of it.'

She walked away, wondering at that. Fond of his food, Frank was. If he didn't care what he ate, it meant something really serious had happened. She hoped it wouldn't put the master in a bad mood. They'd all suffer for days if it did.

An hour later Frank set off again, his stomach comfortably full and his appearance that of a rich man's servant, clad in black broadcloth and wearing a neat scratch wig that always made his head itch but which his master insisted on when they called at the houses of the old gentry. He'd written a note to his master telling him he had vital information about his niece that must be acted on immediately. After all, they couldn't have Elkin getting hold of Miss Deborah's money, could they?

Frank went to knock on the back door of the Finch-combes' commodious new residence and ask for the note to be taken to his master, as a matter of urgency.

Within minutes the footman was back, looking down his nose at Frank but beckoning him into the house. He was shown into a small, plainly furnished parlour, and a minute later his master joined him.

'What's happened!' Walter asked immediately the door shut behind the footman.

When Frank had finished his tale his employer growled under his breath. 'It's a damned nuisance, but you did the right thing coming straight to me. I'm not having anyone else benefiting from that stupid girl's good fortune.'

'Elkin is dangerous,' Frank cautioned. 'As nasty a villain as I've ever encountered, and his man's the same. We shouldn't face him without loaded pistols pointed at his heart and even so, we should be careful.'

Walter was surprised. 'He's that bad?'

'I think so. From something I overheard, I'd guess he's been playing highwayman for a while – and to some purpose. The bullion robbery last year, I suspect, from something that man of his said one day when they thought I was out of hearing. Two guards and the driver were shot dead in cold blood, if you remember, sir. No one left to identify the thieves.'

Walter gaped at him.

Frank nodded again to emphasise his point. It might rankle that Seth had taken him for a fool, but it didn't rankle enough to make him careless again.

'We'll definitely take holster pistols and plenty of gunpowder and bullets, then.' A smile twisted Walter's narrow, bloodless lips briefly. 'After all, it's my *duty* to rescue my niece from such a villain, is it not?' After chewing his lip for a moment, he asked, 'Is her husband involved in any of the crimes?'

'No. Definitely not.'

'Could we implicate him in something?'

'I doubt it. He's got a lot of friends in the village who'd swear he was with them. He's no gentleman, that one, hobnobs with innkeepers and all sorts of low folk.'

'He'll have to be killed in the fighting, then. She's no use to me if she's not widowed. Remember that, Frank, if you want your share of the profit.'

'Yes, sir.' As if he needed telling! But he'd take care that it appeared to be done in self-defence. He wasn't risking being hanged, not for anyone.

'Well, tell them to bring my carriage to the door, then go home and make the necessary arrangements then, while I find my wife and take leave of my host. We'll leave for Marymoor as soon as I've had time to change out of these clothes.'

'If we pay for fresh mounts at the post inns, we'll make better time.'

Walter frowned. 'That'll cause a lot of extra expense.'

'Nonetheless, we can't afford to waste time. What if Elkin killed Pascoe and married your niece out of hand?'

'You're right.'

Frank went out through the kitchen. He only hoped they'd get to Marymoor in time. He suspected that Elkin would act quickly once he decided to move, and he had a lot of respect for the man's astuteness.

But he also had a lot of respect for his own master's cunning. If Elkin thought he had bested Walter Lawrence, he was mistaken.

–

Jem had made sure Seth overheard him talking about the stock his master was supposed to be buying at a farm on the other side of the village. He hoped Seth and Elkin would follow him and show their hand, though Elkin had, it seemed, gone out walking.

Riding at a moderate pace, as if enjoying the morning, Matthew listened for signs of pursuit, scanning the horizon covertly. He heard nothing, saw nothing. Was all this in vain? A couple of times he felt for the butt of the holster pistol which he had concealed beneath his coat and made sure the coat itself wouldn't impede him drawing and cocking it. He had taken immense pains to keep his powder dry and to load the pistol with care.

Suddenly he caught sight of a horseman on the slopes to his left, standing behind some scrubby trees overlooking the lane. Most people wouldn't have been noticed the solitary figure, but Matthew knew the shape of the horizons round here as well as he knew his own hand. He laughed softly. He had a couple of men posted at the farm already, so the pursuer would see him making his way there on his own, but he would be warned if any pursuer came close. He might be setting himself up as bait, but he had no intention of losing his life in the process.

Nothing happened on the way there, so he went inside, drank a glass of ale with Ben Horshley, whose farm it was, then they walked out together to the nearest field where Matthew studied the animals as if intending to buy. He felt more vulnerable here, his senses stretched to their limits, because this was where they were most likely to attack him. But Jem was even now keeping watch from an upper window at the farm and another man was in place behind the barn.

When the shot rang out, it came from much closer than he had expected and on the other side from the pursuer he had noticed. As a searing pain ripped along the side his body, he cursed and glanced quickly down. The bullet had passed along his side, ripping holes in his clothes and leaving a deep groove that was pouring blood. Taking a quick decision, he clutched Ben. 'Pretend I'm mortally wounded.'

As he sagged against his friend, he heard a second shot ring out and another bullet whistled past close to him. He jerked, as if hit again, and pulled Ben down to the ground, hoping the assailant didn't have another loaded pistol to hand.

Voices called out from the direction of the farm.

'Keep yourself low,' he muttered to Ben, letting his body sprawl motionless.

He was furious with himself for having underestimated Elkin, who had also set a trap within a trap. Whoever it was must have been up and in place during the night to get so close without being seen, because a watch had been kept at the farm since dawn.

'You're bleeding like a stuck pig,' Ben whispered. 'We need to carry you back to the farm and tend your wounds.'

'Well, don't move me until you've checked that the intruder's gone.' Matthew stayed where he lay, ignoring the pain in his side, his mind was already working on his plans. He'd have to let Jem drive him home in a wagon to keep up the pretence that he was dead. That'd take longer and there was no way of letting Deborah know in advance that he was all right.

–

Elkin took Deborah to where a horse was waiting beside a wall. 'You'll ride pillion,' he said curtly.

She waited until he'd mounted, then stood on a chunk of stone and allowed him to pull her up behind him, hating to be so close to him, but not daring to refuse.

'Hold tight. We don't want you falling and injuring yourself, do we?' With a laugh he urged the horse into a trot.

'Where are you taking me?' she asked.

'Why, to your mother. Where else?'

'And where is that?'

'You ask too many questions, Deborah. I prefer my women to speak only when spoken to, and in a more polite tone than you're using.'

Remembering his threat, she swallowed a hasty retort and said nothing, but she took care to memorise the route. They were heading south, skirting the village, moving towards the Rochdale road, she thought.

'If we meet anyone, you are to say nothing,' he said. 'Not one single word, not even a glance. Remember there is not only your own safety at stake, but your mother's. You understand me?'

'Yes.' She prayed as she had never prayed before that they would meet someone she knew.

'Hell's hounds!' Elkin muttered suddenly.

Deborah looked up to see John Thompson from the inn riding along towards them on an elderly nag. He looked rather sleepy, with a relaxed, amiable expression on his face.

'Look the other way,' Elkin muttered, half-turning to watch her. 'If you try to signal to him in any way, I'll make sure your mother pays for it, believe me.'

So she did as he ordered, hoping desperately that John would understand that something was wrong. He had given no sign of even noticing her for as they passed him, she heard him offer a simple, 'Good morning, sir,' to Elkin.

A tear escaped her control and rolled down her cheek, leaving a line of coolness as it evaporated. Out of sheer pride she didn't allow any other tears to escape. She had to stay alert. Perhaps they'd pass someone else she knew, someone who would take notice of her.

But they didn't.

After half an hour, Elkin guided his horse off up a narrow track and soon they were completely hidden by the stone walls that separated the fields from the road. No chance of anyone seeing her now. Despair filled Deborah. Elkin was winning every trick, it seemed.

The lane led to a tumble-down cottage which stood on its own with no other habitation in sight, no stock or crops in the nearby fields. The place looked deserted, except that there were plenty of hoof marks in the dusty ground in front of it, some leading to an equally ramshackle shed at the side.

Elkin reined in the horse and said curtly, 'Get off.'

She slid down as best she could, taking a couple of steps away as Elkin dismounted, then waiting for him to tell her what to do next.

A rough-looking young man came out of the shed towards them.

'Take the horse and see to its needs,' Elkin ordered. 'I'll be leaving again within the half hour.'

Relief surged through her. If he was leaving so soon and had servants here, there would not be time for him to rape her, surely? The mere thought of him having his way with her filled her with sick dread because she knew she wasn't strong enough to fight him off. She realised he was glaring at her.

'What are you standing there gaping like an idiot for? There's no help to be had near here.' He grasped her shoulder and drew her towards the cottage.

She didn't even try to shake off his loathsome touch, but walked with her head held high and her expression as calm as she could manage. There would be bruises the next day where his fingertips were digging in, she was sure.

Inside the cottage it was very dark, because the shutters were closed across the one small window. As Elkin had banged the door shut, Deborah blinked her eyes rapidly and tried to make out their surroundings.

'Deborah!'

It was her mother's voice. She took an involuntary step in that direction, but Elkin's hard, bony fingers were there again, digging into the soft flesh of her shoulder and preventing her from moving.

She couldn't hold back the word, 'Mother?' and then, 'Bessie' as she saw two figures sitting on a high-backed wooden settle near the hearth, where a low fire was burning. She was surprised they hadn't come running across to her, but as her eyes grew more accustomed to the dim light, she saw that their ankles were tied to the legs of the settle, though their arms were free.

'Did I not promise to bring you to your mother?' Elkin mocked. 'I'll even ensure that you're sitting where you can see them, though I'm afraid we'll have to tie you up rather carefully. We can't have you roaming the moors and getting lost, can we?'

An old woman, whom Deborah hadn't noticed before, came forward from the shadows to one side. Her clothes were ragged, her sparse grey hair was lank and greasy, but her eyes were shrewd. 'Want me to tie her up for you, Master?'

'Yes, Mag. And make sure you do a good job of it. Hands as well as feet for this one, because she's young enough to give you trouble.'

'Don't worry, sir. I know how to keep young women in order as well as old ones.' She cackled with laughter and grasped Deborah by the elbow, pulling her across to a crude but solid wooden chair. She shoved Deborah down, then tied her hands behind her, fastening the rope to the slats of the chair back. Then, kneeling slowly and painfully, she tied Deborah's feet to the front legs of the chair.

'There! You won't be comfortable, but you're safely stowed.' Heaving herself upright she grinned at the young woman, then turned back to look at her master inquiringly.

'Thank you, Mag.' He strolled across and leaned over Deborah, lifting her chin with one finger.

She felt so helpless it was all she could do not to whimper.

Keeping his eyes on hers, he trailed his fingers across her breasts, laughing as she shuddered involuntarily. 'Tonight, Deborah, you will be widowed and in my bed. By tomorrow at the latest you'll be my wife. And if you have any thoughts of resisting me, look across the room and think whether you want to see your mother die.' He pulled out a pistol, walked over to Isabel Jannvier and cocked it, before holding it to her temple.

Isabel whimpered and shrank away from him.

Deborah saw a bruise on her mother's forehead and wondered if Elkin had done that.

Bessie wasn't even looking at them, but was staring down at her hands, which were clasped tightly together in her lap.

Elkin came back to slap Deborah's face, hard enough to sting and make her jerk away. 'You're completely in my power now. All of you. And it's very easy to shoot someone, Deborah. Remember that.'

As he walked outside, she sagged against the ropes and took a long, shuddering breath. When she looked up, she could see tears on her mother's cheeks.

Would he really manage to kill Matthew? If so, she would find a way to kill him, if she had to wait years to do it. That she vowed.

It was all she could do, make vows, because when she spoke to her mother the old woman told her to shut up or she'd gag her.

–

Elkin smiled as he rode back to Marymoor. At last things were going his way and it wouldn't be long before he had what he desired. He went into the village and made great play of calling for a glass of ale at the inn, claiming great thirst and engaging the landlord in conversation the fellow clearly didn't want.

When I take over here, Elkin thought, that one's going.

'Tenant of Marymoor, are you?' he asked casually.

'Lord love you, no, sir,' John said affably. 'Us Thompsons have owned this inn for over a hundred years, ever since the Great Queen's time.'

'Have you, now. You must be very proud of that.' Elkin smiled at him, but he had in no way changed his mind about getting rid of Thompson and anyone else who didn't treat him with the respect due to the local landowner.

A lad suddenly appeared in the doorway. 'Dad, come quickly! Mr Pascoe's been hurt.'

John rushed outside and Elkin followed, to stand in the doorway and watch the cart with its blanket-covered burden drive past. He wished he could see Pascoe's face, just to be sure he was dead, but there was plenty of blood on the blanket. The fellow must have bled like a stuck pig. He didn't smile, though he wanted to, just watched solemnly as the cart drove past, then went back to his place.

'Are you not going back to Marymoor House?' a voice asked, sounding disapproving.

'No. I've arranged to meet poor Deborah and I fear it must fall to me to break the sad news to her.'

'Oh. And where would that be?'

'At a mutual friend's house. I am to escort her back home.' As he stared down into his pot of ale, the landlord hovered beside him for a moment, then went away. Elkin sighed happily and allowed himself one smile at the amber fluid before he took a good pull of it.

The second part of his plan had gone well. He had even been here at absolutely the perfect moment for proving he hadn't been involved in the shooting.

He sat for perhaps five minutes longer, then called for his horse.

John came out from the back. 'It'll be a moment or two, sir. The ostler's just stepped out. Would you like another drink while you're waiting?'

'No. What I'd like is more efficient service. Do you really have only the one ostler?'

'It's a small village, sir. There's not a lot of folk come here on horseback.'

Elkin sat tapping his fingers, letting his impatience show. When John reappeared to say the horse was ready, he tossed a coin on the table so that it fell off the edge and walked out.

The ostler brought his horse round and hesitated palpably to accept a coin in thanks.

I'll remember him, too, Elkin decided angrily as he mounted and rode off.

When he'd left, John picked up the coin, regarded it distastefully and set it aside. He'd put it into the church collection. He wanted nothing from that man.

Then he went to join his wife, feeling immeasurably sad. How had Matthew Pascoe let himself be ambushed and killed? If he hadn't seen the body being driven home himself, John wouldn't have believed it.

13

The cart jolted along the narrow lane with Matthew lying very still in the back of it, his body and face covered by a blanket. It was stifling under the heavy folds and he could see nothing, which added considerably to his worries. But this pretence gave them a chance at least of flushing Elkin out into the open and stopping him from harming Deborah and destroying the life Matthew hoped to have with her.

Next to him sat Jem, not talking much, but seeming to understand Matthew's need to know where they were. He addressed the occasional loud remark about what they were passing to Ben, who was driving.

It seemed to take a very long time to get back to Marymoor House and by the time the cart drew to a halt, Matthew's face was covered in sweat. 'Don't uncover me till I'm in my bedroom,' he said in a low voice as hands began to move him. His order was unnecessary, he realised a minute later. You didn't have to tell Jem things like that.

'Shh!'

It was infuriating not to know what was happening. Matthew lay there, hearing the pounding of footsteps as people ran towards the cart, followed by brief explanations and cries of shock. He heard the sound of a woman sobbing nearby and strained his ears. Was it Deborah? Who else would sob for him?

And all the time he could only lie there!

After listening for a while, he decided it wasn't his wife weeping but Merry. That thought brought him no comfort. Where was Deborah? She *should* have been there. Had she collapsed at the sight of his supposedly dead body being brought back on the cart? That idea made his heart lurch, as did the thought of her lying on the hard ground in a faint? Oh, hell, he hadn't meant it to happen like this! Pray that it worked. Pray that they fooled Elkin and uncovered his machinations.

Suddenly he heard Jem's voice saying sharply, 'Keep back, there. Me and Ben will carry the master up to his bedchamber. George lad, you come and help us with the doors.'

'I can lay him out for you. He'll make a lovely corpse.'

Mrs Simley's voice, Matthew thought grimly, and she didn't sound at all upset.

'No, thank you. We'll send for Mrs Gurrey from the village. She lays out all the folk born round here.'

'*He* wasn't born round here,' Mrs Simley protested.

'He was *made* by the master of this very house, though,' Jem's voice was rough with anger, 'so he belongs round here same as the rest of the Jannviers, doesn't he?'

'He used to belong round here. Belongs in the church-yard now.' Mrs Simley's voice took on a coaxing tone. 'Show us his face, then. I like to see how they look when they're dead. Never can tell how it'll affect 'em. Some of 'em look surprised, some angry, but some look at peace. I bet he looks angry.'

Jem's voice was rough. 'If you think I'm putting my poor master up on show for you lot to gawp at, you can think again. Get back, you damned ghoul!'

236

Hands lifted Matthew up and he tried to stay limp and motionless, though it was hard.

Then a new voice interrupted. Seth. Matthew recognised it at once.

'What's happened?'

The people carrying him started moving and behind them, fading into the distance, came Mrs Simley's voice. 'Someone's shot Mr Pascoe and killed him. They don't know who did it, neither. What is the world coming to?'

The voices faded away into the distance. Matthew heard his two guardians breathing heavily as they carried him slowly up the stairs. Well, he was no light weight. His nose was itching. He was going to sneeze. He fought desperately against it.

A door opened and Jem's voice said, 'Thank you, George lad. Just stand outside the door, will you, and don't let anyone in except the mistress?'

'Yes, Jem.'

Then the door shut and Matthew was deposited on a bed. He couldn't hold back the sneeze any longer and it erupted from him.

As the blanket was lifted from his face, Jem looked down at him anxiously. 'You all right, lad?' he whispered.

Matthew kept his own voice low, asking the question nearest his heart first, 'Where's Deborah?'

'I don't know. Haven't seen her.'

'She'd have heard the fuss and come running if she'd been in the house. Fetch young George in and find out where she's gone.'

Jem looked at Ben. 'Will you keep watch outside the door while George comes in? We don't want anyone taking us by surprise. But keep your pistol handy. And don't trust anybody.' He turned to Matthew. 'Better lie still till the lad's come inside or he'll screech in shock at the sight of you.'

George came in and Jem clapped his hand across the young groom's mouth and hissed, 'The master's not dead, just pretending.'

George stilled, staring at the bed open-mouthed, then beamed. 'Eh, I'm glad you're all right, sir.'

'Keep your voice down, you fool! Do you want to tell the world? And he's *not* all right,' Jem said grimly. 'He's been shot in the side.'

'Where's my wife, George?' Matthew asked.

'She's not been seen since breakfast, sir. Went out walking with Mr Elkin across the moors and didn't come back.'

'*What?* Did he force her?'

'No, sir. She went willingly. I saw her myself. Well, it seemed that way.' He frowned as he tried to picture the scene. 'They were walking briskly, soon out of sight.'

'Damnation! What was she thinking of? I warned her not to go with him.'

Matthew tried to sit up, but Jem put one hand on his shoulder and pushed him down again, frowning. 'You're still bleeding.'

'It's only a flesh wound, for all it bled so freely. The bullet just grazed me. Get it tied up quickly. I've got to go after Deborah. She's not *safe* with that scoundrel.'

'And how do we get you out of the house again?' Jem asked sarcastically.

Matthew stared at him in frustration. 'I may just have to come back from the dead. Deborah's safety comes before everything else, even exposing Elkin.'

George looked down at himself and back at his master. 'If we could get the Simleys out of the way, sir, you could mebbe put my clothes on and slip out?'

Matthew nodded. 'Good idea.'

'You're not going anywhere till I've looked at that wound,' Jem said firmly. 'Fetch us up some hot water, George lad, and send Simley down to the village to fetch Mrs Gurrey, then go and bring some of your clothes. Mrs Gurrey will keep her mouth shut about what's going on. She was born a Thompson.'

Merry brought the water upstairs, her eyes reddened. After studying her thoughtfully, Jem beckoned her inside, clapping one hand over her mouth to stop her shrieking at the sight of her master, alive if not well.

'Eh, sir, I'm that glad you're all right!' she gasped when Jem removed his hand.

'He's not all right, girl. He's hurt. And we need your help. Can you find us something to bind up his wound? And after that we need to get Mrs Simley out of the way while the master slips out again to look for the mistress. She went off with Mr Elkin this morning, George says.'

'She'd never have gone off willingly then,' Merry said quietly. 'I've seen her flinch from him.'

'How's his mother?'

'Better, but staying in her room.' She looked across at the bed. 'Shall I wash your wound for you, sir? I know what to do.'

He nodded.

'I'll just go and fetch an old sheet to rip up for bandages.'

Outside the door they heard her exclaim in shock.

Jem opened the door a crack to see Seth drag her round the corner. He exchanged a quick glance with Ben, shaking his head to tell his friend to stay where he was, and crept after the maid, ready to intervene if necessary, but hoping it wouldn't be. Nothing was going as they'd hoped. Well, he'd told Matthew he was being too rash in setting this trap and now look what had come of it!

At the corner he listened carefully.

'Have you seen the master?' Seth asked.

Merry put one hand to her face and sobbed. 'Yes, poor soul.'

'He's dead?'

More sobbing. 'To think of that poor lady, widowed so soon after they were wed. It doesn't bear thinking of.'

'Ah, you fool, she'll soon find another husband. She only married that one to get hold of the house.'

Jem saw him shove Merry aside and heard him clumping down the back stairs.

Merry came back round the corner, her lips tightly compressed. 'I didn't tell him anything,' she whispered. 'But I'd be grateful if you'd wait for me here. I don't want that brute snatching hold of me again. He might get ideas. I'll just get that sheet and some basilicum ointment and then come back with you.'

'Good lass!' Jem stayed with her then accompanied her back inside the bedroom. Merry washed Matthew's wound, clucking softly as she worked and apologising when her patient winced. When she'd finished she bandaged the wound over a pad of cloth, making several layers to protect it.

Jem went over to the window and saw Seth stride across to the stables to emerge a few minutes later riding one of his master's horses. 'Wonder where that Seth's going? And where Elkin's got to?'

George came across to join him. 'Shall I follow him?' he asked eagerly.

From the bed Matthew said quietly, 'No. Definitely not. We don't want to risk warning them if they've got Deborah captive. We'll go and search that bit of road where you lost sight of the old ladies, George. It's my guess Elkin's got them prisoner somewhere nearby and that's why Deborah went with him.' He'd been thinking about that while Merry bandaged him, and it was the only explanation that made sense. His wife wouldn't go with Elkin for any other reason, he was sure. He put on George's clothes, wincing as he moved his body.

'You need a hat to hide your face,' George said and raced out, returning a minute later with the shapeless felt hat he wore when taking messages around the district. 'There. You can pull this right down over your eyes and tuck your hair up under it. Your hair's darker than mine.'

Jem watched Matthew do this and whistled in surprise. 'It's a good disguise. From a distance you'd easily pass as George.' He turned to the grinning youth. 'You've been growing taller again, my lad.'

Matthew settled the hat more firmly in place. 'Right then, Seth's left the house, but we still need to distract Mrs Simley and check where Simley is.'

Merry cleared her throat and when she had their attention, said with a blush at her own forwardness, 'I could go and break something in the parlour, if you don't mind losing an ornament, sir. That'll bring the old devil running. She loves shouting at me. Probably slap me across the face again.'

His gaze softened for a minute. 'Thank you. And if she does slap you, we'll make it up to you later, lass. Wait till

Jem gives you the nod to do it, though. Oh, and break that porcelain horse, if you can. I've always disliked it.'

She tittered and left.

They waited a couple of minutes then made their way towards the back stairs, with Jem leading and George making up the rearguard.

Ben stayed on watch outside the empty bedchamber, arms folded, prepared to deny anyone entry, be it King George himself.

Jem left the others at the top of the servants' stairs while he went to find Merry and tell her to break the ornament now. He returned, nodding to show his mission had been successful, then stood at the top of the stairs, head tilted in a listening position.

There was the sound of a crash, then a shriek from the front of the house, followed by loud sobbing. Mrs Simley erupted from the kitchen below them.

'What's wrong?' Jem called from the top of the stairs.

She paused to scowl up at him. 'Sounds like that dratted girl has broken something else, and as long as I'm working here, she'll not get away with it.'

When she had gone through to the front of the house, Jem ran lightly downstairs, checked the kitchen and found it empty, so returned to beckon to the others. He and Matthew made their way swiftly out towards the stables. George would follow a few minutes later, quite openly.

–

Deborah looked across the cottage at her mother and Bessie, thinking how tired and bedraggled they both looked. She wished she could ask how they'd got here, but Mag had said no talking or they'd gag her, so she didn't dare try. If there was a chance to shout for help later, she wanted to be free to do so. Her mother had that vacant look on her face again and it upset her.

As Mag turned her back to add a piece of wood to the small fire, however, Isabel's expression changed briefly into alertness and she blew a kiss at her daughter, then lapsed back into the absent look.

Deborah's heart lifted, but she tried not to let it show. 'Could I have a drink of water?' she asked, wondering if the old woman ever left the room. Not that she could have done anything even so. Her bonds were too tight.

Mag shuffled across the room and slopped some water from a bucket into a horn beaker, then came back to hold it to Deborah's lips.

Deborah drank thirstily. 'Thank you. It's good.'

'Best water there is, out here. Don't get folk soiling the streams like they do in towns.' Mag went to sit by the fire, subsiding with a sigh and holding her gnarled hands out to the warmth.

Deborah tried to think how to escape. There must be a way, surely? But though she racked her brain she could think of nothing. An hour passed, maybe more, and her thoughts grew darker and more unhappy, for she was terrified of what would happen when Elkin returned.

Eventually a man came in. 'Want owt doin', gran?' he asked.

Mag looked across the room. 'They'll need to relieve themselves, I reckon.'

'Oh, yes!' Isabel said at once. 'Please.'

Mag went across and untied Isabel's legs. 'You take this one out to the privy, lad. I doubt she'll manage to escape from there. She can't hardly walk, let alone run.'

Isabel went out with the man, moving slowly and painfully, which was not like her normal gait. When she returned a little later Mag tied up her ankles again.

Bessie followed her out, rubbing her back as if it ached and walking as if her feet hurt.

When she came back Deborah said, 'Me, too, please.'

Mag scowled and looked from the two older women to the younger one. 'Take good care of that one, lad. Master will kill us both if she escapes.'

Deborah went outside and used the primitive privy at the end of the garden while her guard stood outside. She scanned the horizon as she walked to and from it, but the place was as bleak and desolate as it had appeared when they arrived. There was no other house in sight, just the moors with the dull green grass rippling across them at the wind's whim.

Elkin had chosen his spot well. No one could possibly know they were here.

She remembered the innkeeper passing her and Elkin, and wondered if he'd recognised her? John had given no sign of it, but if he had, he would at least know who she was with. Surely Matthew would realise that she hadn't gone willingly? Surely he would trust her?

But there still remained the question of how her husband would find her? She doubted he'd be able to. Which meant that Elkin might be able to carry out his threat to ravish her. Even the thought of that made her shiver.

Elkin had also threatened to kill Matthew before he returned.

Surely he'd not be able to do that? Matthew was a clever man, with many friends in the district. And he had Jem, too.

No, she had to believe that her husband would outwit Elkin — even if he didn't rescue her in time. And had to believe, too, that he wouldn't blame her for what might happen. Another shudder racked her body.

—

Frank watched Walter Lawrence ride along with his usual grim determination. His master wasn't a good horseman, but a carriage would make slow time on such roads and there was money at stake. Frank rode in front of him, warning his employer of obstacles and trying to find the best way round the badly rutted parts of the road.

He always kept his amusement at his employer's poor seat to himself. At least Walter Lawrence stayed on a horse once he got up there. Perhaps no horse would dare to toss such a choleric gentleman off its back, for fear of a whipping.

They changed horses twice. The first time Mr Lawrence was known at the inn and there was no problem about getting new horses. The second time they had to endure a catechism about their destination and identities from the innkeeper before he'd trust them, and even then they had to leave five guineas as earnest of their good intentions, four of the guineas to be returned to them when they brought the horses back.

'The impertinence of it!' Mr Lawrence muttered as they rode off at a smart pace on their fresh mounts. 'Has the man no respect for his betters? What is the world coming to when rascals such as that question gentlemen going about their lawful business?'

Not so lawful, Frank thought, but profitable, he hoped.

After the third change of horses, his master was notice-ably silent and was starting to look tired, so when they came to a small inn, not the sort of place usually patronised by gentry, Frank suggested a glass of ale to revive them and perhaps some cold meat and bread. They were getting quite near to Marymoor from the information on the last milestone but it wouldn't do to arrive too tired to act.

'Good idea!' Walter said. 'I don't know why you didn't think of that at the last inn, which was much more suited to persons of my status than this one.'

Because if I'd let you carry on ranting at the innkeeper like that, Frank thought, he might have changed his mind about letting us have the horses. 'I'll go and inquire if they can cater for us, sir,' was all he said.

A lad came rushing from behind the inn to hold their horses and seemed to know his business. Frank went inside and came striding out almost immediately. 'There's a corner of the room at the rear where you can be private, sir, and the place is nearly empty. Shall I help you down?'

Inside the inn, Walter allowed Frank to relieve him of his hat and sank down on the settle with a groan of relief.

The landlord came bustling out with tankards of his best ale, followed shortly afterwards by his wife, who fussed over them and provided them with slices of tender roast lamb and pieces of crusty new bread.

Made mellow by the sight of food, Walter waved one hand in permission to Frank to eat with him and the two men fell to with hearty appetites.

–

Simley came into the stables just as Jem and George were saddling up the horses, while Matthew kept out of sight.

'Where do you think you're off to, then?' Simley asked in his usual surly tone of voice. 'You should stay here till the mistress comes back. No one's give you permission to take them horses out. I could have you cried for thieves!'

'Who by?' Jem asked scornfully. 'Anyone in the village knows we're honest.'

'Where are you going?'

Jem could see the man's eyes darting hither and thither as he tried to assess the situation, and was relieved they hadn't saddled the third horse yet, something they'd not have been able to explain away.

'Me and George are going about our business, which is no concern of yours.'

'Who's to look after the body until then?'

'Ben's doing that.'

'He's an outsider, don't belong at Marymoor. It's me as should be doing that.'

'You thank your Maker he *is* there. He's got a pistol and is a good shot. You won't get any rascals coming into the house shooting at you with Ben there.'

'Why should anyone do that?'

'Why did anyone shoot at the master? There's a madman on the loose, I reckon.'

Simley stared at him, then shuffled off, grumbling to himself.

George tiptoed across to the stable door, clicking his tongue in annoyance and returning to say, 'He's standing outside keeping watch on us. How are we going to get you out of here without him seeing you, sir?'

'Hit him over the head and knock him out. He won't see anything then.' Matthew was in a fret of anxiety about his wife and also in more pain than he would admit.

'I'll do it.' Jem walked outside, nearly bumping into Simley, who was standing staring suspiciously round the yard. 'You still here? Haven't you got work to do?'

'I'm waiting for Mr Elkin. He rode out earlier. He'll need someone to see to his horse when he gets back if you two aren't here.'

'Well, let me get past to the tack room. I need a new strap. There's a buckle come loose on one of 'em.' In the tack room, Jem picked up a piece of wood and went outside again, concealing it behind his back. To his relief, Simley was facing the other way. Quickly, before he lost the will to attack a defenceless old man, he hit the fellow over the head and watched him crumple to the ground. A check showed him to be unconscious so Jem rolled him out of the way, then went to tell Matthew and George the coast was clear.

The three of them rode out quickly through the back garden, skirting the village and aiming for the track over the moors. Matthew kept George's shapeless felt hat pulled down over his face, hoping they wouldn't meet anyone. You couldn't easily explain two Georges, yet he preferred to have a third man with them.

Once on the track they spurred the horses to a gallop.

'Show us the place where you lost sight of the old ladies,' Matthew said, wincing as he was jolted over some rough ground and trying not to let Jem see it. The wound might not be serious, but it was hurting.

The thought of Deborah in Elkin's clutches was hurting even more. He'd kill Elkin if he'd hurt her in any way, or if he'd… Matthew pushed that thought back sharply. He should probably kill Elkin anyway. None of them would ever be safe while he still lived.

Only Matthew didn't think he *could* kill someone in cold blood. Not unless the man had hurt Deborah.

–

Harriet Elkin heard the noise and sent Denise to find out what had happened.

When her maid returned, she was ashen-faced.

'What has he done now?' Harriet quavered.

No need to ask who the *he* was. 'Someone's killed Matthew Pascoe. Shot him.'

There was silence, then Harriet began to weep, burying her face in the pillow because she didn't want Anthony to hear and start shouting at her again. They both knew who must have done it.

Denise went to pat her mistress's shoulders, trying to comfort her, but couldn't help glancing over her shoulder from time to time.

At last Harriet was calm enough to sit up and have her face washed. 'Bring me my Bible and my eyeglass,' she said as Denise straightened the covers. 'I'm going to ask the Lord's help.'

When she had the well-worn volume in her hands, she opened it at random, as was her custom when seeking enlightenment, holding the magnifying glass so that she could make out the small print, then reading it aloud to her maid:

> '*What shall it profit a man, if he shall gain the whole world, and lose his own soul?*' St Mark, Chapter 9, Verse 36.

She moaned and clutched the book to her bosom.

Denise watched her wide-eyed, knowing how much importance her mistress set on this process.

Taking a deep breath Harriet opened the book again.

> '*Eschew evil and do good*' Psalm 34, Verse 14.

Tears were running down the old woman's cheeks now, but she closed the book and opened it a final time.

> '*All they that take the sword shall perish by the sword.*' St Mark, Chapter 26, Verse 52.

She sat in silence, with the maid standing beside her, head bowed. 'Anthony was such a charming little boy,' she said at last, her voice breaking on the words. 'How has he come to this? And why have I let him drag me into his sins?'

Denise made an inarticulate murmuring sound.

Silence lay heavily upon them for a long time, then Harriet threw back the bedcovers. 'I can't let him do this any longer. I'm nearing my end and I dare not face my Maker with a guilty conscience.'

Her voice was stronger than it had sounded for a long time, but when she tried to move, she stumbled and nearly fell so that Denise had to hold her up. 'I can't go myself.' Harriet sank back on the bed and raised one trembling hand to clutch her maid's arm. 'You must go for me.'

'Go where?'

'To the parson. He must hear me confess my sins and then surely a man of God will know how to stop my son from doing any more evil?' She shook Denise's arm. 'Go quickly! Take a horse from the stables and ride into the village. Tell Parson I'm dying. Tell him anything, only bring him to me.'

Denise found only an old mare in the stables and no one to saddle it for her. However she was the daughter of a farmer, so she did it herself, muttering in annoyance at how long it took because she was out of practice. All the time she worked she was terrified of Elkin or Seth catching her. At one stage she thought she heard a sound, but when she tiptoed over to the stable door to look out, she could see nothing.

Getting up on the horse with great difficulty from the mounting block, she rode slowly towards the village, turning off along the lane that she knew led to the parson's house just before Elkin came round the bend, heading in the other direction towards Marymoor House. She saw him and nearly screamed out loud, clapping one hand to her mouth to hold the noise in as she reined in to watch him ride past, his tall figure showing clearly over the top of the hedge.

He would have seen her had he glanced to the left, but he didn't. Her heart sank when she saw he had that triumphant look on his face, a look he only got when he was gaining something he wanted.

As he vanished from sight she sagged down in the saddle, putting one hand up to her meagre bosom as if to still her pounding heart. Then she took a deep breath and carried on. She would do this if he killed her for it, because she loved her mistress and because Anthony Elkin had got away with his evil deeds for too long.

Her mistress wasn't the only one afraid to face her Maker with this burden on her conscience.

–

Elkin rode into the stable area and waited for the groom to come running. But there was complete silence and no sign of anyone. Had Pascoe's death demoralised them all? With a shrug, he dismounted and tied his horse up to the nearest wall ring.

As he was turning towards the house he heard a groan and swung round again, his eyes searching the yard. The sound came again, from beyond the corner. He went round it cautiously, ready to defend himself if necessary, and nearly stumbled over a body. Simley. He bent to give the man a shake. 'Hoy, you rascal. What's happened to you?'

When Simley groaned and tried to sit up, Elkin kicked him in the ribs. 'Tell me what happened.'

The old man looked up into the face of the man he regarded as his master, but could do no more than raise his head. He tried hard to think, but his thoughts were still muddled and all he could come up with was, 'Someone hit me'.

'Who?'

'Jem. Or George. They were saddling horses. They got no right to do that with Mr Pascoe dead, and so I told them.'

'Where's Seth?'

'Rode out earlier.'

Elkin tried to stay patient because Simley wasn't noted for his intelligence. He hauled the man to his feet, ignoring his moans, and propped him against the nearest wall. 'When did Seth ride out?'

'Just afore Jem come down to the stables.'

'And when exactly was that?'

'I can't rightly say, sir. I don't know what time it is or how long I was knocked out for.' He closed his eyes for a moment, groaning.

'It can't have been long ago.' Elkin chewed one corner of his lip, torn between going inside to gloat over the body of his enemy and going back to the cottage to take possession of Deborah's lovely body. He smiled. He'd go back to her. Seth had orders to take the parson to the cottage once he was sure Pascoe was dead, so his servant must have checked the body.

He looked down at himself. No time to change his clothes and he definitely didn't want another encounter with his mother, who had wept all over him this morning and begged him to take her home. Best get back to the cottage and get the deed done. Marriage. And with it, at last, Marymoor.

He'd have Deborah too, for a time at least, and was looking forward to taming her. She would find him a very different proposition from Pascoe. He would enjoy schooling her.

14

Elkin rode slowly back towards the isolated cottage, feeling jubilant. It was all coming together, just as he and Seth had planned. If it were not for the difference in their station, he'd call Seth a friend, his only real friend. But there was a difference between master and man, a difference that could never be bridged, especially in the life he would soon be starting as a landowner. Thank goodness Seth understood that and didn't try to be over-familiar.

He didn't hurry, wanting to enjoy his feelings of triumph undiluted by a woman's tears and pleadings, for he had no doubt that Deborah Pascoe would weep and plead – they all did. But he had her mother captive and that would bring her sharply to heel. The old woman appeared to be nearly witless and once he was safely married, with Marymoor legally his, he'd shut the hag away in the nearest madhouse and forget about her.

As for that old maid of theirs, he'd turn her off as soon as he didn't need her to care for the old bitch. Who was she to look so disapprovingly at him? He'd slap her face if she did it again after he got back.

His smile faded as he thought about his own mother. She plagued his life with her weeping and drooping, but she *was* his mother and he had fond memories of her from his childhood, which was more than he could say for his father. If she and that maid of hers behaved themselves, he decided, he might even let them continue to live at Marymoor. They could stay in their own rooms, be no trouble to him, but having them there would look better in the eyes of the local gentry.

He continued on his way, arriving at the cottage half an hour later.

Mag's grandson came shambling out to take his horse.

'Has Seth returned with the parson?'

'No, sir.'

Elkin frowned. Seth should be here by now. But perhaps the parson was out at a death bed or some such thing. Parsons were always getting called out to minister to the lower orders, whether the fools deserved it or not. It might take Seth a little while to trace Mr Norwood but Elkin did not doubt that his man would manage that. And after all, what did an hour or two more matter now Pascoe was dead? Dismounting, he handed over the reins with a curt, 'See to my horse.' Then he walked briskly towards the cottage, his smile returning.

Time to tell Deborah she was a widow.

And that she was about to remarry.

–

Seth had indeed found the parson away from home visiting a sick parishioner. Hiding his impatience, he questioned the housekeeper as to where he could find Mr Norwood and tried to understand her tangled directions for reaching Rob Dunham's farm, which was, it seemed, at the very limits of the parish to the south.

His master wouldn't like the delay but there was little Seth could do about that. Doggedly he set off in the direction indicated.

Half an hour later he admitted to himself that he'd lost his way and banged on the door of the nearest cottage. 'How can I find Rob Dunham's farm?'

The woman stared at him dully. 'Don't know.' And shut the door.

Swelling with anger Seth went on to the next cottage, only to receive the same answer. 'Well, who *would* know where this Dunham fellow lives?' he demanded, setting his foot in the door to prevent the man shutting it.

'How should I know?' With a deft kick that took Seth by surprise, he got the protruding foot out of the way and slammed the door, dropping the wooden latch with a clacking sound.

Seth remounted and turned to stare back at the two cottages. He'd remember them when he came to live round here and would make their occupants sorry they'd refused to help him. Very sorry.

—

While Seth was searching for him, Mr Norwood was making his way serenely home on his old black gelding, glad to have left Rob Dunham on the mend. He arrived at the parsonage to find Mrs Elkin's maid, Denise, sitting waiting for him in the hall. When she saw him, she burst into tears and it took him a minute or two to calm her down and find out what she wanted.

'I've never seen my mistress like this, sir. You have to come and talk to her. She could die with her sins on her conscience.'

'She's worse?'

As Denise nodded vigorously, then broke into even louder sobs, he tried to calm her down, but she continued to weep and wail, so in the end he patted her shoulder, gave up the attempt to get any sense out of someone so distraught and said simply, 'I'll come.'

'Straight away, sir? *Please?* There's no time to be lost. If her son gets back and finds what she's doing, he'll kill her, kill us both. Now that Mr Pascoe is dead—'

'*What did you say?*'

She stared at him in shock. 'Didn't you know, sir? Someone shot Mr Pascoe this morning. That's what's upset my mistress so.' She lowered her voice and added, 'It was probably Mr Elkin or Seth. Jem brought the body back to Marymoor and—'

His mind reeling from the implications of all this, Parson interrupted to ask, 'What about Mrs Pascoe? How is she coping with her loss?'

'I don't know, sir. No one's seen her since this morning when she went out walking with Mr Elkin. I reckon he's got her prisoner somewhere.'

Mr Norwood stared at her open-mouthed, then bowed his head and thought rapidly. Somehow he didn't doubt that Elkin would do anything, including commit murder, to get his own way and he understood perfectly well that he would be putting himself in danger if he went to Marymoor and tried to intervene. That wouldn't prevent him from doing his duty.

However he did take the time to write a note to John Thompson, explaining what was happening and begging him to give the note to the nearest Justice of the Peace if anything untoward happened to him. He gave this to his housekeeper and asked her to take it into the village at once.

With a sigh he then remounted his weary horse and jogged off with Denise, who was still weeping, but silently now, at least. As he rode he prayed for the strength to do his duty and confront Elkin.

Could not help adding a prayer that he would survive that confrontation.

–

Seth found Rob Dunham's farm in the end by sheer chance, because he recognised a tree blasted by lightning standing in the middle of a field, something the parson's housekeeper had described. He took the lane that led off behind the tree and burst into the farm to find Mrs Dunham cooking a meal for her husband, who had, it seemed, made a miraculous recovery.

Realising it would do no good to set her back up he apologised for coming in without being asked, but explained that Mr Pascoe had been killed and the parson was wanted at Marymoor.

She exclaimed in shock and informed him between sobs that the parson had left quite a while back.

With a growl of anger at these delays, Seth left her to her daughter's ministrations and rode back to the parson's house. When no one answered his knock he went inside and checked, finding it empty, so came out again and sat down on the wall to await the return of the damned parson. He had no doubt that if he went to make inquiries in the village as to where Mr Norwood was, no one would know. People seemed suddenly to have clammed up, to be deliberately refusing to help him and his master. But when the parson came home, he'd get him out to the cottage to marry his master and Mrs Pascoe if he had to hold a pistol to his head.

Mr Elkin was not the only one who intended to benefit from today's doings.

About an hour later, the housekeeper returned to the parsonage and squeaked in shock at the sight of Seth sitting there. When she turned to flee, he went after her, shaking her hard to stop her screaming.

'What the hell's wrong with you, woman?'

'You frit me, sir. I didn't expect to see you sitting there.'

'Oh? And why should seeing me frighten you? I've only spoken to you once in my life, which was this very day, and you weren't frightened of me then.' When she didn't answer, he tightened his grasp on her arm. 'I'll have a straight answer out of you, or you'll be sorry. Where – is – Parson?'

She sobbed and protested, but when he twisted her arm behind her back, she screamed in pain and capitulated at once, telling him Parson had gone over to Marymoor House.

'Why?'

'I don't know. He doesn't tell me anything. He just goes out when someone sends for him.' She hung painfully in his grasp, praying he would believe this, sure that if he knew the full truth he'd hurt her even more.

When Seth threw her aside and left, she ran back to the village as fast as she could, to collapse into Patty Thompson's arms and sob out her story.

Since her husband John had gone out, Patty kept the housekeeper with her at the inn. It was a crying shame when a decent woman got hurt like that by a nasty brute. She'd seen the bruises for herself and if that Seth came into her inn again, she'd go for him with her frying pan, as she once had a beggar who tried to cause trouble. It was a nice solid frying pan, that.

–

Elkin found everything peaceful inside the cottage, with the two old women sitting where he had left them, feet tied to the settle, and Deborah slumped in the chair, bound hand and foot. She straightened up to glare at him as he walked in and he laughed aloud from the sheer pleasure of seeing her helpless like that.

Mag looked up from her stool near the fire and grinned at him. 'They're all here still, master.'

'Yes. You're doing well.' He tossed her a coin. 'Leave us alone for a bit, will you, Mag? But stay within call.'

She nodded and went outside.

The three women left behind were watching him as if he were a wild beast about to spring on them and devour them. Good. He wanted them afraid. He let the silence continue for a minute or two, then turned to Deborah, ignoring the other two.

'I'm happy to inform you that you've just become a widow.'

She gasped and her eyes widened in shock, but when her lips began to tremble she pressed them together and said nothing. He could see her eyes welling with tears, though, and that pleased him.

'I've sent for the parson and when he arrives you'll marry me,' he added casually.

'*What?* Never!'

He turned to study the two old women and then looked back at her. 'I think I have the power to compel you. But if you wish me to prove it, I shall.'

As she continued to stare at him, stubbornly silent, her mother said, 'Don't do it, Deborah. He's wicked and will make your life a misery. Even if he kills us, don't do it.'

In two strides he was at the old woman's side. He slapped her face as hard as he could then slapped it again for good measure. 'If you cannot keep your mouth shut, I'll cut your tongue out, old dame. And don't doubt that I'll do it.'

He let go of her, watched in satisfaction as she shivered and closed her mouth, then turned towards Deborah again. 'Do you wish me to prove that I can find ways to persuade you, or are you going to be sensible and spare your mother and her maid a great deal of pain?'

For a moment longer, she stared at him, then said coldly, 'If I must marry you to save them, I shall. But how shall you ever feel safe with me afterwards, knowing how much I hate you?'

It was his turn to gape for a moment, then he chuckled. 'Oh, I'll soon have you so tame you'll be begging to do as I ask, believe me.'

As she clamped her lips shut into a narrow, bloodless line, he began to pace up and down the room, wondering what had happened to Seth. It shouldn't have taken this long to fetch the parson. Still, with Pascoe dead, matters were not urgent. A few hours' delay would make no difference to the outcome.

–

Deborah watched him pace up and down as she tried to come to terms with the news that Matthew was dead. How had he died? She wasn't going to ask, wasn't sure if she could trust herself not to weep if she did so. Elkin had killed him, of course. And if so, whether she was hanged for it or not afterwards, one day she would find a way to kill him for that.

As for his threat to tame her, just let him try. He would never be able to reduce her to the abject, mindless obedience of his mother, though he might make her pretend to it. She let anger fill her up, concentrating on it because if she didn't she'd start weeping.

Strangely, when she tried to picture Matthew dead, she couldn't. She wondered why not, then remembered suddenly that he'd gone out that morning to set a trap for Elkin. She frowned. Had it all gone wrong? Or was the trap still set and about to be sprung? Was it possible – could Matthew still be alive? Oh, dear heaven, she hoped so. Would never complain about anything again if she could only have him back.

That thought gave her the courage to ask, 'How did my husband die?'

Elkin swung round, giving her his wolf's smile. 'He was shot by some passing villain.'

'You.'

'Why ever should you think that?'

She knew it was him, though whether the shot had killed Matthew... She let that thought comfort her. 'I won't marry you until I've seen his body.'

'You will, you know. You'll do exactly as I tell you.' Again he glanced at the two old women, his message clear.

She realised that if she went through some form of marriage and Matthew did prove to be alive, it would be meaningless. So it wouldn't matter – unless Elkin consummated it. She shuddered as she did every time at the thought of him touching her so intimately. She stared down at her lap, trying not to let her thoughts show.

Elkin said abruptly, 'Mr Norwood will confirm that your husband is dead when he arrives. The whole village must know by now.'

She still wouldn't believe it until she saw the body herself, Deborah decided. And clung to that thought as the minutes crawled slowly past to give herself courage.

'That was Elkin riding past the inn,' Frank said suddenly, nudging Mr Lawrence. 'I'm sure it was.' He got up and ran to the door, then dashed back to his master. 'I'm going to follow him, see where he goes, then I'll come back to you.' At his master's nod of agreement he ran out, calling for his horse.

He kept a good distance behind Elkin, not wanting to be noticed, let alone recognised. The land hereabouts was hilly and the rough road twisted about a good deal, so he lost sight of him from time to time. When he came to a straight stretch of road, he realised he'd completely lost his prey and there was no horseman ahead of him, as there should be.

Well, if Elkin had turned off somewhere, it'd not be too difficult to find him. Retracing his footsteps, Frank checked the ground at every turn off. It had rained a little in the night and the earth was still soft enough to show hoof prints. When he found a turning with fresh prints clearly showing, he stopped to study it. The track had been used a few times lately, but not much previously, from the amount of grass growing along it.

It would be unwise to ride the horse openly down the track, for he'd be too conspicuous and someone could easily shoot him. He went back along the main road and found a gate, taking his animal through and tying it up inside the field. Then he bent his body into a half-crouch and moved along behind the dry stone wall that bordered the field.

At the far end, he had to climb over the wall to get to the next field, which soon gave way to yet another. Small fields. It meant rolling over the tops of a lot of cursed walls, each time praying no one had seen him, but it paid off, because as he breasted a small slope he found himself overlooking a cottage, a tumbledown place with a small barn behind it in even worse condition.

'Ah,' he said in satisfaction as he saw Elkin's horse tied up outside the shed. A man Frank didn't recognise was giving it a drink of water from a wooden bucket whose rope handle was broken.

What was Elkin doing in a shabby little place like this? Nothing good, Frank was certain.

He crept down the hill beside the wall, getting closer than was, perhaps, wise, but there was a lot of money at stake and he had to find out more.

An old woman came out of the cottage and spoke loudly, in the tones of one half-deaf, 'Well, lad, the master's already killed Mr Pascoe and is going to wed Mrs Pascoe. I told you it was worth keeping in with him.'

The young fellow scowled at her. 'I don't like this, Gran.'

'Not yours to like. You just do as you're told.'

He didn't answer, stroking the horse's neck as if that were more important than what the old dame was saying.

'Are you listening to me?'

'Yes, Gran.'

'She don't want to wed him, o' course, but he has her mother in there, so she'll have to do as he says. He allus gets his own way in the end, Mr Anthony, don't he?' She cackled and went to dip herself a drink of water from the butt with one twisted hand. 'He'll look after us once he's settled in at Marymoor.' When her grandson didn't reply, she went to grasp his arm and shake it as she repeated, 'Now, mind you do everything he tells you.' She wiped her arm across her lips and turned back towards the cottage.

Crouched behind the wall Frank let out a long exhalation of surprise. Pascoe dead! As the knowledge sank in, he smiled. Well, that was one problem taken care of, anyway.

He began to make his way back to the road, his mind busy with the possibilities. Now Deborah was a widow, the way lay open for his master to take charge of her and therefore Marymoor House. Well, the way would be open if they disposed of Elkin. Pity they hadn't brought help with them, though. They'd have to deal not only with Elkin but Seth, and the pair of them together were formidable. And there was also the old woman's grandson, who would probably work with them, however reluctantly.

But he and his master had brought pistols and plenty of shot, and if they took things carefully, they might still be able to win the day. Mr Lawrence was always quick to see and seize an advantage and Frank knew himself to be a good shot.

He smiled as he crept back to the main road and retrieved his horse. Mr Lawrence wouldn't like clambering over walls and walking over rough ground, but it was the only safe way to approach the cottage.

–

Matthew, Jem and George rode along to the point where the latter had lost track of the two old women.

'This is the place, sir. The woman in that cottage said she definitely would have seen them if they'd passed. If Elkin did abduct them, he did it before this point.'

'Show us where you last met someone who had seen them, then.'

They rode on, noting the lanes that led off the road at regular intervals. There were far fewer lanes to the left and not far away they could see the rough-looking brownish grass of the moors sloping upwards. On the right the ground sloped downwards towards fields which looked more fertile than the higher terrain on the left and even had occasional clumps of trees. Jem shook his head at each turn-off, saying, 'I know the folk there. They'd never get mixed up in anything like this.'

After a while George stopped and pointed. 'This is where I spoke to a woman – she was weeding that very field. She was sure she'd seen the old ladies.'

'Right then.' Matthew turned his mount round. 'We'll just have to check every lane until we find where Elkin is hiding them.'

'With all due respect, sir,' Jem said quietly. 'I think we should check the tracks on the moor side of the road first. There are less people living up there, often only the odd field or two belonging to one of the farms lower down the slopes. I think there are one or two cottages up there, but I can't say I know exactly where they are. But Elkin wouldn't be keeping prisoners where everyone else could see them, would he?'

'No. That's good thinking.' Matthew's side was hurting, but his determination to find his wife hadn't faltered. And wound or no wound, he intended to batter Elkin senseless when he did find where the man was hiding his captives.

They went up two rough lanes, each of which soon petered out, then came back down them again in silence.

The third lane they came to looked more promising, for it was wider and bore the marks of recent traffic.

'Better watch our step from now on, sir,' Jem advised, pulling out his pistol and cocking it.

Matthew followed suit and George felt in his pocket for his slingshot and pebbles. A slingshot might not be a sophisticated weapon, but it had brought in many a meal for his family when he was younger, rabbits and such, because he had a good eye.

When they came to a bend in the lane, they all slowed by mutual accord and Jem pushed forward. 'Let me go first, sir.'

George looked from one to the other and screwed up his courage to ask, 'Wouldn't it be better if I did that? They don't know me as well as they know you two and I can pull my hat down.' He suited the action to the words with the disreputable felt headgear he usually kept for rabbiting.

Jem pursed his lips, then nodded. 'But you're not to take any risks, lad. If anyone sees you, pretend you're searching for Mr Horrocks to give him a message from Mr Norwood in Marymoor. Horrocks has a farm just down the road a piece.'

George nodded and rode forward, hat pulled down.

They heard a voice call out then George reply, 'I'm looking for Mr Horrocks. Does this lane lead to his farm?'

'No. You missed the turn-off,' a voice yelled back. 'Go back to the road and turn right. It's about a mile away, on your left as you ride towards Marymoor.'

'Thank you kindly.'

There was the sound of a horse clopping gently along and George reappeared, his face full of suppressed excitement. 'Mr Elkin's horse was there, sir. I only saw its head, poking round the side of the cottage, but I'd know that horse anywhere, because it's a nasty-tempered brute.'

'Ah,' said Matthew softly.

'Best ride back towards the road and hide the horses, then approach the place on foot,' Jem advised. 'They're obviously keeping a careful watch and if we give them warning that we're coming, they may hurt your wife.'

Matthew nodded, feeling frustrated and anxious. He felt reluctant to leave Deborah in Elkin's hands for longer than necessary, but Jem was right. They had to approach the cottage stealthily.

Without knowing it, they retraced Frank's footsteps, tying up their horses in a field which had a dip in the ground where they'd be hidden from the road, then striking out across the fields.

It was a matter of grim endurance for Matthew, whose side was getting more painful by the minute and who was having to force himself along. He was aware of Jem looking at him in some concern and said to his old friend, 'You can coddle me after we've rescued Deborah. Till then, as long as I can move, I shall keep going.'

They came to the piece of rising ground that hid the cottage and checked out the landscape.

'We can go round the cottage that way and approach it from the rear.' Jem pointed. 'If we crouch down behind the wall, we won't be seen till the last minute, and if we choose our time carefully, perhaps not even then.'

-

Inside the cottage Elkin was getting bored. The old women kept staring at him while Deborah avoided his eyes. Time was passing with infuriating slowness and he was eager to tie up all the loose ends that still remained and take possession of Marymoor.

He went across to Deborah and began fumbling with her bonds. 'I thought you might like a short walk, my dear.' He might even take her there and then on the rough moorland grass. The thought of that titillated him. It wouldn't matter how much she screamed out there. In fact, he'd enjoy making her scream. A good lesson in obedience never came amiss.

15

At Marymoor House the parson and Denise went straight inside. They both kept watch for Elkin, but to their relief there was no sign of him.

As they went up to Mrs Elkin's bedchamber, they passed Ben, still guarding the bedroom door.

The parson stopped to ask, 'Is Matthew Pascoe's body in there?' and when Ben nodded, he said quietly, 'I'll come in to pray for him after I've seen Mrs Elkin.' He was surprised to see a look of uncertainty on Ben's face, but as Denise was tugging him onwards, he couldn't stop to ask if anything was wrong.

Mrs Elkin started sobbing at the sight of them, saying, 'Thank you, thank you, oh, thank you!' over and over again.

Denise bolted the door while the parson went to sit beside her mistress. The maid then went to stand at the end of the bed with her hands clasped in front of her and her eyes lowered.

Harriet Elkin faltered out the tale of her own weakness over the past few years and Anthony's crimes, which included even highway robbery, something she was not supposed to know about.

'Are you sure?' Mr Norwood asked, horrified.

'Yes. Denise and I overhear many things.' She looked at her maid. 'She's been wonderful to me. If it weren't for her, I think I'd have taken my own life.'

He found it hard to believe that the son of a well-known local family could turn to evil like this, but spoke gently to the distraught woman and prayed with her, assuring her of the Lord's forgiveness if she truly repented.

It was some time before he took his leave, but when Denise tried to show him out of the house, he shook his head. 'I must go and pray by the body of my old friend now,' he said firmly, walking towards the door of the other bedroom.

'I'm sorry, Mr Norwood, but no one's allowed inside.' Ben put one arm across the door to bar the way.

The parson puffed indignantly and his cheeks took on a red tinge. 'I'm sorry, too, but I'm definitely going inside and if you want to stop me, you'll have to keep me out by force. Shall you dare do that to a man of the cloth?'

Ben hesitated for a moment, then looked round with a distinctly furtive air and drew the parson inside quickly, bolting the door behind them.

Mr Norwood looked towards the bed and gasped in shock, for it was empty and there was no sign of a body anywhere in the room. He stared round for a moment, then realised what this might mean and whispered, 'Is Matthew Pascoe still alive?'

Ben nodded.

'Where is he?'

'Gone after Elkin, who's captured his wife and her mother as well, they think.'

'May the good Lord watch over him – and over them too.' The parson studied the bed and frowned, remembering childish tricks of his own. 'Would it not be better to put something in the bed, to make it look as if there's a body lying there?'

'Good idea.' Ben went to the clothes press and pulled out a bundle of clothes, stuffing them haphazardly under the bedcovers.

Mr Norwood clicked his tongue in irritation. 'Not like that!' With a great deal more care he rearranged the bed, so that it did indeed look as though a body was lying there. The sound of a horse trotting up the drive made them both hurry to look out of the window.

'It's only Elkin's manservant,' Mr Norwood said.

'No "only" about it. He's a devil's spawn, that one.' Ben pulled out a pistol and cocked it as he turned to leave, gesturing to Mr Norwood to go out ahead of him.

Parson didn't move for a minute, then said slowly, 'If I go out just as he's coming up the stairs, I can hold the door open so that he catches just a glimpse of the bed and believes there's a body lying there.' He turned to check that everything looked realistic and nodded in satisfaction. 'Then you must lock the door quickly and stay on guard. I'd be grateful if you could keep an eye on Mrs Elkin and her maid, who are also in danger.'

'Elkin wouldn't hurt his own mother, surely?'

'I think that wicked fellow would stop at nothing.' As he left the bedroom, Mr Norwood told himself not to be afraid, but to place his trust in the Lord. However his heart was beating very rapidly in his plump breast and his steps faltered for a moment as he came face to face with Seth, who peered over his shoulder into the bedchamber.

As Mr Norwood moved on, Ben slammed the door shut, turning to face them, one hand on the butt of his pistol and a scowl on his face.

'You're needed, Parson,' Seth said. 'If you'll come downstairs, I'll tell you about it.' He ushered Mr Norwood into the library but didn't give him time to sit down. 'My master sent me to fetch you.'

'Mr Elkin?'

'Who else?'

'I can't think why *he* should need me. He doesn't even attend church on Sundays.'

'He needs you to marry him.'

Parson stilled. 'Then he can come and see me at the parsonage, as others do.'

Seth could not hold back a rumble of anger. 'He needs you now and I won't take no for an answer.' He pulled out a pistol and prodded the parson's chest with it. 'You'll come with me or take the consequences, Parson.'

When Mr Norwood saw how cold was the man's expression, he felt more flutters of fear inside his belly. 'Would you shoot a clergyman?' he stammered, aghast.

'I'd do anything necessary to serve my master's needs.' Seth lowered the pistol slightly. 'But it needn't come to that, if you're sensible. Anyway, I didn't think a parson *could* refuse to do such a service.'

'Whom does your master wish to marry?'

'Why, Mrs Pascoe, of course. The poor lady is terrified and needs his protection against the villains who killed her husband.'

Mr Norwood stood gaping at him, then realised why the Lord had called him into this business. To try to protect Deborah Pascoe. If he was with her, Elkin would find it much more difficult to do her harm. 'I shall come with you, then, but shall do nothing unless I am convinced this marriage is what Mrs Pascoe really wants.'

Seth grinned. 'Oh, it's what she wants all right, as she'll be the first to tell you.' If she wanted her mother to remain safe and sound, and she seemed fond of the old hag, the stupid bitch would do exactly as his master told her.

Mr Norwood and Seth rode straight to the lonely cottage, travelling mostly in silence because the parson would not even attempt to converse with such a villain and Seth didn't give a hang about small talk. It worried Mr Norwood that they were heading towards the most isolated part of the parish and although he was still stubbornly sure that the Lord had brought him there, he acknowledged to himself that he was growing more afraid with each mile that passed.

At the cottage Seth dismounted easily, handed his horse's reins to Mag's lad, then turned back to the Parson, who had made no attempt to dismount. 'Let me help you down, sir.'

'I hadn't realised there was a habitation out here. Whose cottage is this?'

'It belongs to Mr Elkin. His old nurse lives here. Come, let me help you down.' This time Seth's tone was more peremptory.

With a sigh Mr Norwood allowed himself to be assisted to the ground. As he looked towards the cottage, the door opened and Elkin came out, pushing Deborah in front of him.

When she saw the parson, she tried to run towards him, but Elkin grabbed her hair and yanked her back by it.

Horrified, Mr Norwood rushed forward but was dragged back by Seth before he reached Elkin. He flapped ineffectually at the strong hands holding him, shouting, 'Let her go at once, sir! How dare you manhandle a lady like that?'

'She's very upset by her husband's death and is not acting rationally, but she'll keep nice and quiet now, won't you, Deborah dear? Because she knows I'm here to look after her.' He tightened his grasp on the back of her hair till it hurt.

Remembering the two old women sitting helpless inside the cottage, she dared do nothing but murmur agreement.

Elkin let go of her hair and took her by the arm instead. 'Now, Parson, we need you to marry us at once so that I can take care of Deborah – and her poor, mad mother.'

'My mother isn't mad!' But the fingers dug into her arm so painfully that Deborah didn't try to say anything else.

'I'm afraid you will have to face the fact that she is beyond caring for herself, my dear.'

Since her back was to Elkin and Seth was standing to one side, Deborah risked one quick, pleading grimace at Mr Norwood, but didn't protest again.

The parson realised at once that his worst fears had been correct and the lady was being coerced into this marriage. How was Elkin doing it? 'I'm afraid I cannot marry you today,' he said, trying to sound authoritative. 'Firstly it would not be seemly on the very day of Matthew Pascoe's death and secondly you don't have a marriage licence.'

Elkin's voice became harsh and he didn't attempt to hide his anger. 'You can easily sell me a common licence and that'll make it perfectly legal.'

'The licences are at home at the parsonage and nothing can be done without one.'

'Bits of paper!' Elkin waved one hand in a dismissive gesture. 'We can see to all that afterwards, but you will marry us here and now.'

Mr Norwood took in a deep breath to steady himself. 'I refuse.'

'Bring the parson inside, Seth. He needs a little persuading.' Without waiting to see it done, Elkin dragged Deborah back towards the door.

Mr Norwood found himself being propelled into the cottage in a very rough manner by Seth, and squeaked in dismay and outrage.

Elkin flung Deborah down on a chair and snapped, 'Stay there!' then turned towards the cleric. 'And now, Mr Norwood...'

'I meant what I said,' the parson told him, but to his chagrin, his voice came out fluting with nervousness.

Elkin pulled out a dagger. 'Will you say the same thing as I cut pieces off the old ladies's bodies, I wonder?' he inquired in the same tone another man might have commented upon the weather.

The parson goggled at him. 'Are you mad?'

'No, just very determined to win the right to protect my cousin Deborah.' He waited a moment and when the parson continued to stare in shock, smiled and pricked Isabel's ear lightly with the point of the dagger, causing it to ooze a drop of blood. He stepped backwards with a flourish of his arm.

Mrs Jannvier said nothing, but neither did she plead with him.

Deborah bit her lips to hold back a sob.

'You couldn't – you wouldn't!' Mr Norwood stuttered.

'Let me prove that to you.'

Elkin moved towards the settle again but Mr Norwood pushed him away, taking him by surprise as he flung himself in front of Isabel and Bessie, arms outstretched. 'You shall not touch them!'

'Get the old fool out of my way,' Elkin said and Seth dragged the struggling parson backwards.

Elkin stared at him in silence, then looked back at the old women. 'Unless you do as I say and marry us at once, I shall cut the mother's right ear off – or shall it be the left one first? Or perhaps both?'

'But I *cannot* marry you!' Mr Norwood gasped. 'It isn't possible.'

Then Deborah guessed suddenly that Matthew was indeed still alive and a great tide of joy flooded through her, for all her present danger. She kept her eyes on the ground, trying not to let this show, but the news gave her courage and a tiny thread of hope began to unfurl inside her.

Elkin was frowning at the parson. 'Why is it not possible?' When he got no answer, he moved towards him, looking like some feral creature hunting its prey. '*Why – not?*'

Mr Norwood tried to back away but Seth pushed him forward towards his master.

Since no one was gazing at her, Deborah seized the opportunity to look round desperately for something to use as a weapon, but could see nothing other than pieces of firewood. And anyway, what could one woman and an elderly cleric do against those two well-armed brutes?

'Stay away from me!' shouted Mr Norwood.

At that moment there was a shout from outside and the sound of scuffling.

'What the devil's that?' Shoving the parson so roughly out of the way that the old man fell over, Elkin followed Seth out of the door.

Immediately they were gone, Isabel said in a low, urgent voice, 'Get up at once, Mr Norwood, and find something to cut us free. We don't have much time if we are to act.' She indicated the rope fastening her legs to the settle.

He gulped, stared wildly round and saw a knife on the shelf near the window which contained some bread and other foodstuffs. Pushing himself to his feet he grabbed the knife and went back to saw at the ropes.

As he released the two old ladies, Deborah gave her mother a quick hug and then did the same to Bessie, after which she took the knife from him and slid it into her pocket. 'My husband's still alive, isn't he?' she asked in a low voice.

He nodded. 'He is, I believe, looking for you.'

She closed her eyes for a few seconds in sheer relief, then ordered, 'Find something to defend yourselves with, everyone!' She picked up a piece of knotted wood from the pile near the fire, hefting it in her hand. 'Maybe we can hold them off for a while.'

Bessie found an old iron ladle and held it behind her while Isabel picked up another piece of wood and did the same.

Mr Norwood was still looking for something to use as the door opened and Elkin came back inside. He lunged across the room without looking at the others, grabbing Deborah by the hair and dragging her across to the door. It happened so quickly she couldn't take out the knife because he was bumping her painfully across the floor.

Outside he hauled her to her feet and roared, 'Stop where you are or I'll kill your wife, Pascoe!'

Through the tears of pain brought on by the rough treatment Deborah saw Seth struggling with Jem and her husband, and the young groom, George, lying on the floor clutching one leg, which was bleeding profusely. Matthew froze as he realised the danger she was in and Seth took the opportunity to break free and range himself beside his master.

She knew if she tried to take out the knife now, she would not stand a chance of using it, so bided her time, hardly daring to breathe. Let her captor's guard slip for one minute and she would use it.

'Make sure that damned parson stays inside and doesn't try to intervene,' Elkin muttered to his henchman, 'and bring out the other pistol.' Seth moved slowly backwards and Elkin continued to stare across at Matthew, his hatred a livid light in his eyes. 'You may have escaped death this morning, Pascoe, but now it's a choice of you or your wife. If you don't do as I tell you, she'll die and then I'll kill you anyway. If you obey my orders, she at least will live.'

Deborah began to inch her hand towards the pocket hanging beneath her skirt.

'Keep still, you!' Elkin shouted.

He shook her so hard she could not help crying out, for it felt as if he was tearing her hair out by the roots, but even so she managed to grasp the handle of the knife with one hand. Then he pressed his own dagger against her neck and she stopped moving at all.

'So white and soft, her throat,' he taunted Matthew. 'My dagger will slice through it so easily. Do you want to see it spurting out her life blood?'

Matthew felt despair settle like a great heavy boulder in his belly. Was he to lose everything and leave Deborah in that vile man's clutches? Everything seemed to be happening very slowly. He could count every breath Deborah took, see the slight break in the skin of her throat where Elkin has pressed the point of his dagger in and drawn blood. To one side Jem was staring round desperately, not daring to move but seeking some way of stopping Elkin from killing his friend.

'Better tell your man to keep still,' Elkin said in a conversational voice, then raised it to shout, 'Seth! What's keeping you?' He heard the cottage door open behind him, saw the expression of surprise on Jem's face and half-turned as Isabel came out, a piece of wood in her raised hand. As she hit out at him with it, she was so close to his face he had to throw up one hand to defend himself and let the dagger slip from Deborah's throat.

She seized the opportunity to pull out her own knife at the same time as Matthew lunged forward.

In the mêlée that ensued, Deborah couldn't tell exactly what was happening. A heavy body crashed into her and knocked her flying. Seth and Elkin were struggling desperately against Matthew and Jem, and they seemed so evenly matched she was terrified for her husband.

The old woman came stumbling out of the shed and shrieked for her grandson to come and help the master, but there was no movement from behind her.

Deborah circled the struggling men, determined to end Elkin's life if that was what it took to save her husband's life, but at that moment two more men came from behind the shed to join in the fray. She cried out in shock as she saw her uncle Walter and his man Frank and stayed her hand.

They attacked Elkin and Seth, but both men continued to struggle so furiously that it seemed impossible to hold them down. Her uncle was flung off by Elkin and yelled out, 'Get some rope, Deborah, damn you. Have you no sense?' as he moved forward again to try to help Matthew hold Elkin.

It was Bessie who got to the struggling men first and struck out with her iron ladle, surprising Seth by a sharp blow on the temple. He blinked and hesitated for long enough for Isabel to hit him hard with the piece of wood. As Bessie raised the ladle again he fell backwards to measure his length in the dirt. The two old women rushed to stand over him, ready to thump him again. But he didn't stir.

Elkin was still cursing and fighting like a madman, but there were enough of them now to hold him. As they dragged him to his feet Deborah saw Frank look questioningly at his master and Walter Lawrence give him a quick nod. Frank took out his pistol, holding it hidden from Matthew as he looked for an opportunity to use it.

Deborah realised suddenly what he was doing and screamed, 'Watch out, Matthew!'

Her husband jerked backwards but there was no way he could avoid being an easy target.

Before anyone could move a piece of stone flew through the air and hit Frank on the temple, making him jerk his hand as the pistol went off. George let out a shout of triumph at hitting his target with his sling, but the shot rang out immediately afterwards and Matthew fell to his knees.

Deborah couldn't see what had happened and for one moment of sheer, blind terror, she thought Frank had killed her husband. 'No!' she screamed, running forward.

But the shot had hit Elkin instead and it was he who was dragging Matthew down. A red stain appeared in the centre of Elkin's chest and he let go of his opponent to hit the ground with an inarticulate, groaning sound.

As Matthew righted himself, Mr Norwood came forward to place himself in front of him and say sternly to Frank. 'Put that pistol away. You cannot kill all of us.'

As Frank lowered the pistol, Deborah went to stand between her husband and her uncle.

Mr Norwood knelt beside the twitching figure.

'Get away – from me – damned preacher!' Elkin looked beyond the parson to Deborah, such a malevolent expression on his face that she flinched, even knowing he couldn't now hurt her. And then his body jerked one last time and his eyes rolled up.

'He's dead,' the parson said quietly, closing the staring eyes.

'Won't you introduce us to your husband?' Walter Lawrence said, his voice as smooth as if this were a mere social gathering, as if his manservant had not just tried to murder his niece's husband.

Deborah glared at him. 'So that you will know the man Frank just tried to kill?'

'It was Elkin I was trying to shoot,' Frank said quickly, 'though I meant only to wing him. He had a madman's strength and was a danger to us all.'

'I know what I saw and what I believe,' she told her uncle. 'And I want nothing more to do with you. Not now or at any time in the future.'

Matthew put his arm round her. 'You had best leave before we hand you over to the law,' he said to Walter. 'There are several witnesses to your action and only the fact that you're related to my wife stops me from reporting what you tried to do to the magistrate.'

As Isabel came forward to join them, Deborah asked urgently, 'Are you all right, mother? They didn't hurt you?'

'I'm better than I have been for a while.' She turned to her brother. 'I never wish to see you again, either, Walter. Your sins must be on your own conscience.'

'What sins? Fine gratitude this is,' he bluffed, 'when I came all this way to help you. Why, Frank just saved your lives.'

'You came to see what you could steal for yourself,' Isabel told him roundly. 'But this time Deborah has a better protector than I could ever be.'

Matthew smiled gently at her. 'I can ask for nothing better than to look after my wife and her family, Mrs Jannvier.' His smile faded as he turned back towards Walter Lawrence. 'If anything untoward ever happens to me from now on, be sure my friends will know where to look first for answers.'

Walter cast a malevolent glance in his direction, then said loudly, 'There was *no* attempt to kill you.'

But everyone except Jem and the young groom had turned away from him, and those two were watching him steadily, George with another piece of stone looped at the ready in his sling, Jem with a loaded pistol in his hand.

He and Frank walked away towards where the lane began.

Mr Norwood let out a shaky sigh, then tried to pull himself together. 'We'll need to take the body into town and inform the magistrate of what has happened.' He looked down and shuddered at the wickedness still graven on Elkin's still features.

Mag's grandson, who had been hovering near the barn, came forward. 'There's a cart round the back, but no horse to draw it – unless we use his.'

'This lad could have warned your uncle's man that I was about to fire my slingshot,' George said. 'I saw him watching me. And I think he only betrayed our presence to Seth out of shock at the sight of us.'

The lad pointed to the body. 'Gran was his nurse and thought the world of him, but I allus hated him.' He looked at his grandmother, who was crouched over Elkin, her face streaming with tears as she stroked his cheek. 'Are you going to hand her over to the constable?'

They looked down at her.

'No,' Matthew said softly. 'No, you look after her, lad, and if you need money come and see me. For now, take what's in Elkin's pockets. I want nothing from him.'

'I'll do that, sir, and thank you kindly for it.' He looked round. 'I'll need someone to help me get the cart out and harness his horse to it.'

'And someone should tie up this villain,' said Mr Norwood, pointing to Seth, who was just starting to stir. 'We don't want him causing more trouble.'

Matthew saw that Lawrence was still watching them from the end of the lane and raised his voice. 'Have you two not yet started for home?'

As they began to walk away Deborah called out 'We'll send a dray to Newgarth within the week to collect our furniture and possessions.'

Her uncle turned briefly to snap, 'They've already been sold or thrown away.'

Was the man really so greedy and unprincipled that he would even steal the contents of his sister's cottage? Matthew wondered. 'Then they'd better be found again,' he called, 'for if we don't get them back, we'll accuse you of theft. I'm sure the goods are of enough value to hang you.'

'And even if you escape hanging,' Isabel added, 'your rich neighbours will never speak to you again if you're brought to trial.'

Walter scowled at her. 'I dare say the things may still be in one of my barns. And I'm well rid of *you*.' He walked away from them, shouting over his shoulder, 'Come on, Frank. Let's find our horses and return to civilised parts.'

Frank followed him, not looking back.

Isabel watched them till they were out of sight, then heaved a sigh of relief. She turned to her daughter and smiled. 'Do you have room for me at Marymoor, darling?'

'Oh, yes.' Deborah couldn't say anything else, because her heart was too full. She felt like clinging to Matthew and weeping all over him now that the danger had passed.

He seemed to guess how she was feeling and gave her a quick hug. 'Let me take you home, love. Will you ride pillion with me?'

She turned to him and nodded, her face so full of love that Bessie nudged her mother and beamed.

Seth brought Matthew's horse. 'We can settle everything here and bring the parson back to the village. Take your wife home, lad.'

Matthew mounted wincing at the pain from his wound, then Seth helped Deborah up behind him. They rode down the lane at a gentle pace, neither saying anything, just glad to be close. As they reached the road, he reined in the horse and turned his head to look at her. 'What are you smiling at?'

Her voice was soft, her smile radiant. 'I was thinking how happy I am. In spite of what's just happened, I've never been happier in my whole life.'

'I feel the same.' He urged the horse on and they travelled in silence for some time, then he said suddenly, 'I think we'll probably have to provide for Elkin's mother as well.'

'That poor woman! Of course we shall. Though I doubt she's long for this world.' She hesitated, then asked in her turn, 'Shall you mind my mother living with us, Matthew? And Bessie, who will make an excellent house-keeper?'

'I shall mind nothing as long as I have you, Deborah.' His voice faltered for a moment, then he reined in again, determined to say it and keep on saying it so that she should never doubt his feelings. 'I've grown to love you dearly.'

'And I you.'

'When I knew Elkin had captured you, I wanted to kill him. I made a bad hash of it, though. I'm a farmer, not a killer.'

'I'm glad it wasn't you who killed him. I don't want to be married to a man who can take a life as easily as Elkin could.'

'Ralph gave me the best present anyone ever has in my whole life,' he said, his eyes steady on hers.

'Marymoor?'

'No. Much better than that. The mistress of Marymoor – a valiant lass whom I love to desperation.'

She felt tears of joy well in her eyes. 'Oh, Matthew.'

As the horse whickered its annoyance at these stops and starts, he let it move forward again. He could feel her head resting against his back and her arms circling him with loving warmth. Neither of them even noticed when they arrived at Marymoor and only the horse stamping impatiently and neighing plaintively brought them to their senses.

It also brought Simley out of the barn to scowl at them.

Matthew slid off the horse. He'd forgotten the Simleys were still there. 'Elkin is dead. You and your wife have one hour to leave Marymoor.'

The man gaped then rushed back to the house without a word.

'Stay with me while I unsaddle my horse, my little love.' Matthew was reluctant to let her out of his sight.

Deborah nodded and sat down on a pile of hay, saying little as he worked, but smiling from time to time as they exchanged glances. She felt exhausted now, but the happiness was still there, running gently through her veins and warming her.

Jem had to clear his throat twice to gain their attention. 'We've arrived.'

They walked outside and saw Isabel clinging to Bessie's arm, looking exhausted.

'We'll see to the horses, Matt lad,' Jem said quietly. 'You take your wife and her mother inside.'

'We'll go in the front way,' Matthew said, as he led them away from the stables.

'But the kitchen door is closer,' Deborah protested pulling away to stare at him in puzzlement.

'Yes, but today you are more truly mistress here than ever before and it's not fitting that you go in like a servant. Not this time.'

At the front door he stopped and lifted her into his arms, carrying her across the threshold and kissing her before he set her down.

Bessie and Isabel nudged at one another.

'He's a fine man,' Bessie whispered.

'And he loves her.' Isabel sighed happily.

Then the two re-appeared in the doorway, Matthew's arm round Deborah's shoulders. 'Welcome to your new home, ladies. Bessie, Deborah assures me that you'll make a fine housekeeper. Will you work for us?'

'Of course I will.' She dropped him a quick curtsey to acknowledge his new status as her master.

'And Mrs Jannvier, you can be sure that my wife's mother is always welcome in my home.'

'I'm sure we're all going to be happy here,' Isabel said. But it was her daughter she was smiling at, not the house. And her new son-in-law.

It was left to Bessie to study their surroundings with added interest and she was instantly drawn out of her lethargy by the sight of such shoddy housekeeping. 'Well, it certainly looks like I'm needed here and I for one shall not be happy till this place is set in order.' She went to run a finger across the dusty oak panelling and make a loud tutting noise. 'Did you ever see the like?'

The very normality of her reaction to the house made the world seem right again and Matthew chuckled. 'There's a maid Merry who should be in the kitchen,' he told Bessie, pointing to the door at the rear of the hall. 'She's a willing worker, but the other two are leaving straight away. Ask Merry to bring up some warm water to our bedchamber, will you, please?'

He winced as he turned incautiously and Deborah saw the blood on his shirt. 'You're hurt!'

'It's nothing more than a graze.'

'Come upstairs and I'll change the bandages. Will you be all right, mother?'

'I'll be better than I have in years,' Isabel assured her, following Bessie towards the kitchen door.

Deborah accompanied her husband slowly up the stairs, her heart overflowing with joy. She was home at last. As she looked round, tears welled in her eyes and she vowed in her heart to make Marymoor a happy home for them all.

She had a husband she loved and who loved her, her mother and Bessie were safe – she needed nothing else in the world. Well, just one thing – she smiled – Matthew's children. And she was sure he would be very willing to help her achieve that ambition.

'What are you smiling at?' he asked, watching her from their bedchamber door.

She smiled back at him and reached up to kiss his cheek quickly. 'I'll tell you tonight.'